◆ ◆ ◆

"When the Huntswomen go to Feed, they are taking the earth's power within them and delivering it to the sea." I sigh and start to protest, but Yanori continues. She's on a path now and can't be swayed. This will end in something profound, I am sure, so I close my lips and continue cleaning. She doesn't do this as often as she should and now her pink tail is half green. She says it is because she cannot see the algae, but I believe that to be a lie. I think some part of her likes it there. Yanori often gets lonely. "But it has to be a back and forth trade. Something from the sea must be given to the earth, do you understand?" I nod, but I'm not sure I do. She can't see me, but she senses the motion in the disturbance of the water and continues. "When we have a queen that sits the throne, that realizes this, then we will be great again." She looks down at me with her cloudy eyes, her pale hair twisting around her face like kelp. "Muoru will wake up and the sea dragons will come back." I nod again and release her, but this time, I know I don't believe her.

The creatures of myth are dead and dead things don't come back to life.

◆ ◆ ◆

Books by C.M. Stunich

<u>The Seven Wicked Series</u>
First
Second
Third
Fourth
Fifth
Sixth
Seventh

<u>Houses Novels</u>
The House of Gray and Graves
The House of Hands and Hearts and Hair
The House of Sticks and Bones

<u>Indigo Lewis Novels</u>
Indigo & Iris
Indigo & The Colonel
Indigo & Lynx

<u>The Huntswomen Trilogy</u>
The Feed
The Hunt
The Throne

She Lies Twisted

Hell Inc.

The Feed

C.M. Stunich

SARIAN ROYAL

The Feed
Copyright © C.M. Stunich

All rights reserved. Printed in the United States of America. No part of this book may be used or reproduced in any manner whatsoever without written permission except in the case of brief quotations embodied in critical articles or reviews.
For information address Sarian Royal Indie Publishing, 1863 Pioneer Pkwy. E Ste. 203, Springfield, OR 97477-3907.
www.sarianroyal.com

ISBN-10: 193862324x (pbk.)
ISBN-13: 978-1-938623-24-0 (pbk.)

Cover art and design © Amanda Carroll and Sarian Royal
Optimus Princeps font © Manfred Klein
Celtic Garamond font © Levente Halmos
Stock images © Shutterstock.com

The characters and events portrayed in this book are fictitious. Any similarity to real persons, living or dead, businesses, or locales is coincidental and is not intended by the author.

*to Amanda for saying we should
"take mermaids back"*

this one's for you.

The Feed

Prologue

They came out of the quiet sea in small numbers and wicked intentions. Their eyes glowed dark and their lips twisted darker; they crawled from the sea foam in a primordial mass that writhed and spasmed. Like lizards they slithered through the sand and came for the men. The women watched them come and were disgusted, but the men, the men loved them as if they were goddesses born from the ocean's gelid waters.

They were paramours and cannibals both, consuming, taking, destroying. They broke spirits and souls; families crashed to the floor like glass and were never again whole.

They came to steal seed, life, came to bleed flesh.

They came to feed.

Chapter One

I live in a world that doesn't understand me.

I've been raised with a life already planned and a destiny chosen. But what if I want to make my own destiny? What if I want something different than everyone else? What does that make me?

These questions have no answer as far as I know. But then, it's not as if I can ask them to anyone. If I even uttered a breath of dissent, my mother would come down on me like a hurricane, sweep me in the air and throw me against the rocks at the edge of the sea. I would never recover.

I take a lungful of air into my chest and dive, swirling below eddies and fish that sparkle like diamonds. I shouldn't be out here, I know, not before my birthday, but I had to look.

What I saw did not boost my confidence.

The humans were not as I had been told. They were not the pale, spineless creatures of myth with sharpened spears and nets of iron and steel. I saw children with chubby legs and appendages on their feet that *wiggled*. I smile. So strange but beautiful. I liked them.

My hair billows around my face as I pause, wiping it away with turquoise nails.

Yuri and Ira are coming.

Their muscular tails flash like silver, winding them between rocks and through crevices that would take me the better part of an hour. I'm in trouble. I'm not supposed to here. If my mother finds out ...

"Natalie?" Yuri is asking a question. He asks a lot of them. Yuri is the type of person who would span both land and sea if he were able. He loves to learn. "What are you doing?"

Ira is already scowling. I can't stand his face, can hardly call him a friend.

"She's spying," he says; a leer is apparent now. I turn away and kick my legs. Water billows around his horrible sneer and makes him sneeze. Bubbles flutter around my feet and tickle. "She can't control the bloodlust any longer, and her skin burns for the touch of a human man." I ignore him and wait for the waves to subside. Yuri is looking at me curiously.

"I wanted to see if the texts were true." Yuri is nodding; his eyes are sparkling from the sunlight streaming down from above. It's weird to see him in this light. I'm used to the cool whispers from the caverns and the *sispa*, the glowing shells that line the walls of the city.

"Were they?" he asks, his face upturned to the light like the kelp that clings to the rocks around us.

"Why are you asking?" Ira throws back at him, raising his brows and brushing hair from his face. It's so dark, so crimson, it looks like blood. It makes me sick. "We should go and look for ourselves."

And then his tail is knocking me back and sending me tumbling. I throw my arms out to the side, still myself.

I'm treading water, but my heart is pounding.

"Yuri?" I ask, wanting him to stop Ira. Ira is a male. He isn't allowed to watch the humans. It's expressly forbidden. If I am caught, I will receive a light punishment. My status as heir keeps me afloat when others would sink; Ira would be killed.

In Yuri's eyes I see the desire for truth. He wants to know for himself.

"Don't," I say. Yuri looks away and doesn't move. His feelings for me will keep him below the waves which means I will have to go after Ira. The fool is already bobbing at the surface, tail flickering, scales coruscating like the metal coins I collect.

I turn, weightless, nothing but air and scales under the water. It is so different from land, so much freer. I kick my feet, my legs bunching, pushing water behind me as my arms help me navigate whorls and currents. I'm only half-*merighean* so I'm not as efficient, but I'm certainly stronger. I grasp the edge of a rock and use it like a ladder, the sea pushing my bottom as my shoulders drag me upwards.

When my head breaks the surface, I gasp. There are people coming this way in a boat. It growls through the water with speed, the device that powers it rumbling and gobbling water, spewing foam. The wakes it creates are bobbing Ira and I like buoys.

"Down below the surface," I say, but his eyes are open so wide, peeled back from his face and already starting to dry out. He wasn't made for this world. "I said now." I put authority in my voice. This rouses him briefly. He

The Feed

knows that in this moment, I am not his friend. I am his future queen.

Ira ducks beneath the water and is gone in a flash of silver and crimson. He wheels through crevices and past rocks like an eel, twisting and whirling through the currents as fear takes over him. He wanted to see, but he wasn't ready. None of them are.

I stay a moment longer and breathe air into my lungs. I can absorb oxygen through the slits in my neck, but real air is so much sweeter. Then I dive, before the boat and the people inside it see me. That would not do. Not yet. Not until the Feed.

When I get back to where Yuri is waiting, Ira is already gone.

"He was spooked," Yuri says and brushes blonde from his face. It's getting tangled in some kelp so I reach forward and help him unknot it. It isn't fair that the males have to wear their hair free and long just because the women like it. I touch his cheeks with my nails.

"You two should not have come here," I breathe and little bubbles drift between us like stars. I can feel my body aching for something foreign, something that I have never experienced. Unlike the other Huntswomen, I have restrained myself.

"I saw you leaving, and I knew," he says. His face is melancholy, and I know why. The Feed is coming too soon for either of us. But he wants me after. I know that. I just don't know if I want him. "I tried to come alone, but Ira followed. I'm sorry." Yuri shakes his head, and my hand floats away from him.

"It's okay," I say, trying to assure us both but not about Ira, about what's coming. Yuri nods but he doesn't believe me. I don't blame him. I don't believe myself either.

◆ ◆ ◆

When we get back to the city, Yuri disappears in search of Ira and I find myself surrounded by a group of my fellow Huntswomen.

"Where were you?" they whisper, their breath tickling my face with tiny bubbles. I shrug and they shiver as one, like a school of angelfish, bright and colorful. Mindless. They're giggling now, kicking their feet and doing pinwheels, trying to entice some of the males that are swimming nearby, their tails slapping the water in invitation. I ignore them all and allow myself to sink to the ocean floor. There's a gasp as I do this though I do it everyday. The *merighean* don't like it when I walk with my legs. It reminds them that we're not the same, that we're different and we'll always be different. That the Huntswomen are to be feared. After their initial fear passes, however, they poke fun at me and say that I look like a crab. They make scuttling motions with their fingers that I ignore as I step inside the antechamber to my mother's palace.

The walls are open to the sea, as they are in most of our structures; the rib bones of an ancient sea dragon surround me on all sides, curving up through the dark waters like the branches of trees that I've spotted on the mainland. *We used to be great,* my mother always says when she gazes up at them. *We had cities throughout the world, civilizations that could've ground the humans to dust, but our passiveness was our downfall and so we must remain strong.*

I take a deep breath and start forward. If she sees me walking, I'll be punished, but I do it anyway because I like the feeling of solidness beneath my feet. The earth grounds me in a way the sea never can; it's so tumultuous. I sigh and bubbles burst from my mouth, spiral up towards the faded light of the sun. It seems so far away though I was there only hours ago. It's a different world above the sea, to be certain.

"Is everything alright?" my sister asks from behind me. I know it's her because she swims crooked, making odd gurgling noises that no one else does. Half of her tail fin is missing, taken by a shark in her earlier days. I turn around and smile at her. She's the only one besides Yuri who treats me like a person and not a Huntswoman. She is also blind so I answer her quickly so that she's able to hear my smile. Not many treat Yanori with the respect she deserves.

"I'm nervous about the Feed," I blurt before thinking to check around us for eavesdroppers.

"We are alone," she replies in that confident way that I admire so much. I rely too much on sight, she often tells me. "But we won't be for long. Let's go." Her tail flickers to the left, trying to compensate for what's missing. I bend down, push through the strong currents of the water and use the power in my thighs to launch myself after her.

We swim up and through the ancient bones, picked clean long ago, decorated now with the colorful shells of sea snails and the crusty lumps of barnacles.

Yanori guides me expertly through the city and sometimes she forgets that even with her disability that she is faster and more slippery than I am. There are times where I'm forced to grab the edges of houses, use bits of kelp and rock to propel myself forward, to follow after her. She takes me to an underground cave that's so dark she has to double back and steal a *sispa* from the outer wall of the farthest house so that I can see.

"There," she says as we swim to the bottom of the cave. It is more like a burrow, I realize. A vestige of something from the past. This is a place where the giant worm, Muoru, had once lived. It's been a long time since we've had such creatures in our ranks. I touch the smooth walls reverently. Even sea creatures do not dare to come here. Only the *merighean* would be so foolish as to disturb such an ancient site. My sister is so brave and foolhardy; she would've made an excellent Huntswoman. I sigh. But she is not. That is my job. I was born to my mother and a human man after her foray on land. Yanori is my *merighean* father's child, just a mer, with no legs to carry her ashore. "Now you can tell me what it is that's bothering you."

"I saw some humans today," I tell her, confident that she won't betray me. She never has before. She doesn't even gasp at this, just floats there with her arms out, brushing the sides of the burrow.

"You can feel the power here, can't you?" she asks, surprising me. Yanori does this a lot; she starts off on something that doesn't seem related and ties it back to the conversation. I love her for it. She teaches me more than any instructor. "It's so old, so powerful, so perfect. In here, we are one with the sea and the earth; they're interchangeable, Natalie. Only once we realize that, will we be whole again."

I float down to the bottom of the cave which is sandy and warmed by the underground vents that heat the city and spew boiling water and bits of hardened rock into the sea around us. Yanori doesn't mind me doing things like this. She often tells me to embrace my differences as she does hers. I reach forward and take her tail in my hands. She allows this and leans her back against the wall so I can pick algae from her scales.

"When the Huntswomen go to Feed, they are taking the earth's power within them and delivering it to the sea." I sigh and start to protest, but Yanori continues. She's on a path now and can't be swayed. This will end in something profound, I am sure, so I close my lips and continue cleaning. She doesn't do this as often as she should and now her pink tail is half green. She says it is because she cannot see the algae, but I believe that to be a lie. I think some part of her likes it there. Yanori often gets lonely. "But it has to be a back and forth trade. Something from the sea must be given to the earth, do you understand?" I nod, but I'm not sure I do. She can't see me, but she senses the motion in the disturbance of the water and continues.

"When we have a queen that sits the throne, that realizes this, then we will be great again." She looks down at me with her cloudy eyes, her pale hair twisting around her face like kelp. "Muoru will wake up and the sea dragons will come back." I nod again and release her, but this time, I know I don't believe her.

The creatures of myth are dead and dead things don't come back to life.

Chapter Two

"I can't be expected to chase after you every time I require your assistance, Natalie," the queen says and in her voice is venom. The mer that's doing her hair is pulling too hard and she hates that. We're floating in her bedroom, an open balcony of stone that faces the city. Curtains drift in the currents of water and obscure my view. Even now, they're being cleaned; schools of fish are being chased from the folds and away. Some are netted and will be used as part of tonight's feast. I swallow my words and wait. There isn't anything I can say now that will appease her. I will only be drowning myself.

The Feed

My father, not my biological one since he is, of course, dead, but the one who has been by my side since the moment of my birth, is resting his arms along the back of my mother's bed. She is the only one that has one. It is a sturdy iron thing, rusted by the sea, but well maintained by the servants here. She found it in a shipwreck and had it dragged here for her pleasure. The rest of us sleep upright, leaning against the walls of our homes or perhaps, if you're a Huntswoman, you might sleep curled on the floor. I know that I am not the only one who considers this uncomfortable. We all long for beds. Some of us even use hammocks though the fabric that we make them from is hard to find.

"Natalie was studying hard," my father says, coming to my aide as he's done a hundred times. If it weren't for him, my mother would pierce me with the needle she keeps at her side and let me anguish in belly rumbling pain for hours. I've only had it happen twice before, but I will never forget those hours of agony. When I am queen, I will do away with the Spindled Blade and find myself a new royal weapon. My mother scowls and shoos her servants away. Her hair is this massive thing now, like a nest of coral. There are so many creatures in there, some dead, some alive, that it looks like she is a part of the rocks that surround the city and protect us from human invasion.

She turns to face me and reaches for a shell on her dressing table. Inside of it are pearls which she crushes with her massive strength and smears along her naked skin. She is particular about getting it between the scales on her hands and along the sides of her face. When she is done, she sparkles like the stars that reflect on the water at night. I have only seen them thrice, but I will never forget. She hands the shell to me.

"Make yourself presentable," she says as she picks at my hair. She hates it, I know. I am the only Huntswoman with black hair. It's a human color, a horrible remnant of the Feed she's said before. Everyone else has hair that sparkles like jewels, like rubies or emeralds. I nod and use the pearls as she has, making sure that I cover the webbed parts between my fingers and toes. My mother sniffs at me and gestures at my father to follow her out. He kisses me softly on the forehead as he passes, yellow tail reflecting back the soft lights of the *sispa* in my mother's bedroom.

I turn to the mirror and touch my hands to my face. My eyes stare out at me, green as the algae on my sister's tail.

"What am I going to do?" I whisper. The Feed is days away and I'm so uncomfortable with the idea of it that it makes me sicker than my mother's Spindled Blade. There's nobody there to answer, so I gather a few clips from the dressing table and pin my hair up as best I can. Most of it floats around my face as it always does, but at least she'll see the effort.

I leave her room in a hurry, careful not to bump into any servants on my way to my room. I don't want anyone to know I'm in there. I need time to think. Since I first saw the humans, I haven't had much of a chance to do so.

I open the wooden door with a sigh and step into darkness. My room is the only one in the whole of the city

The Feed

that's completely enclosed. The only opening to the sea is the tiny window that I've boarded up with shutters. Granted, I do open them on occasion, but for the most part, they remain closed. I grab a *sispa* from the wall and it separates with a pop. I blow into the shell and the snail inside flickers and flares to life, a warning against enemies. It's highly poisonous, but it doesn't matter, the *merighean* know how to handle them. The spiral design on this one is quite pretty: a swirl of purple and pink over a translucent cream. I stick it to the door and sit down on the sand that covers the rock beneath my feet.

I rest my head in my hands and let the water flow through the gills at my throat. The air in my lungs has long been spent and they sit uncomfortably tight in my chest. Like flattened sacks, I can almost feel the edges touching. There are nights where I wake up screaming, where I dream I'm drowning. After fifteen years, I still am not used to it. And in three days, it will be my sixteenth birthday. This is the day of the Feed.

I open my mouth and swish the seawater around my teeth.

There's a fish in here. How it got in, I don't know. It happens sometimes. I reach out and poke it with my nail. It shivers, green and yellow scales sparkling as it thrashes; the venom from my nails is coursing through its veins, killing it. I wait for it to die, for it to float motionless in front of my face. In just over a week, I will be doing this to a human man, killing him with my touch while he begs for more. I will take his child back into the sea and marry a mer, take over my mother's throne and watch it happen all over again with my child.

Again, strange thoughts overtake me, fight against all that I've been taught.

I don't want to do this. I want to make different choices, decide different things. My life is already laid out before me like a map. There are no detours, no hidden caves, no whirlpools that descend into the unknown. There's nothing but a path to follow. One that I didn't choose.

◆ ◆ ◆

The banquet that night is wild and happy. The Huntswomen are whipped to a near frenzy by my mother's words, their own thoughts, the feelings in their bodies that convince them to couple with the *merighean* men. And though my own body aches for it, tries to tell me I should, I hold back, clamp down on the strange tingling between my legs with force. I don't want my first time to be on the Feed, but I am guessing it will have to be as I can't bring myself to do it.

There is a table here in the center of the throne room, suspended by chains from the rock walls around us. The food is laid out before us in shells, bowls carved from fine stone, items salvaged from shipwrecks. My brethren swim around me, twist under the table and snatch food on their way up. Nobody sits still here except me. I make myself so conspicuous with my lack of movement that my mother calls me on it.

"Natalie," she says and her voice swells with false pride. I know that she's only cloaking her anger, only faking it. She hates me, always has. I swallow a bit of crab and look up at her. Her eyes flicker once, the only sign of her distaste for me. She has to pretend. After all, I'm the princess, the future queen, her only heir and prodigy. I am so important that my birthday has become the birthday for all the children born from the Feed in which I was conceived. When I turn sixteen, so do they. So then they begin this journey that they all thirst for, but that chokes me with every beat of my heart. "Come here." I know better than to argue. Nobody has stopped moving, but they are all looking.

I swim to my mother's arms and float next to her chair, next to the throne she's carved from pearls, from the tears of the Huntswomen who have failed. She's the only one of us permitted to sit.

"Tell us where you will go," she says, gesturing with her arm at the map that's carved into the wall at her left. I swim over to it and try to remember the lessons I've been taught. This map is old though and things have changed. The one I was shown in class had bridges and roads on it. This only has mountains and villages that no longer exist.

I'm supposed to have my route mapped out by now though it's ludicrous to expect a Huntswoman who has never been on land before to decide where she's going to go, to decide what type of man she will take. None of us, save me, has ever seen a human man. I only saw my first ones today. When my back is turned, I scowl. The girls will be quite surprised to see what awaits them on their week on land. The human men look nothing like the *merighean*. The *merighean* men have colorful hair, long and beautiful and silky. All the human men I've seen, even in the old texts, have short hair. The mers have eyes that sparkle like shells and skin that's as smooth as the carved coral bowls that my mother uses. The human men I saw today had hairy chests and legs and muddy brown eyes. I sigh and start to point at an area on the left. There was once a lake here. There might not be one now, but this is where I will go.

"I will climb from the sea using the rocks of Muoru," I say and have to smile a bit at my sister's naughtiness. She took me there for a reason. I feel a little surge through my body of excitement. There is something right about this. I don't know what it is, but I'll have to worry about that later. Everyone is listening to me now. The other Huntswomen are absorbing what I'm saying. They won't follow me, not outright, but I would be surprised to learn if a single one of them didn't come out of the sea the same way. "I will walk this path," I continue, touching my pointed nail to the wall. I feel suddenly sorry for that fish I killed. It was a pointless death; I couldn't even eat him. I swallow seawater in a silent apology. "I will go along the edge of these trees and I will submerge myself in this lake." Fresh water is supposed to soothe the skin and make the eyes glow. I read it in an old tome that's been preserved in the library. There aren't many books here, under the sea, and I've taken them all in. "I will circle the lake until I find a suitable mate." I tap a random spot on the map and use the wall to spin myself around in the water. I ride the current down to the table and start to eat again, hoping to deflect some of the attention I've drawn to myself.

"Wonderful," the queen says and on her purple lips is the promise of pain. If I fail this, I will be punished severely. I purse my own, identical lips and look up at her. Would she kill me as she's done to so many others? I don't know. All I know is that I better come back from the Feed with a child in my belly and flesh in my throat.

◆ ◆ ◆

All children born to the Huntswomen after the Feed are girls, all half-merighean, sirens of the sea. The magic of Neptune promises that this will be so.

I read this sentence four times before I realize that I'm getting nowhere. Rereading the same books again and again will give me no answers. *I want to run away,* I think as I put the book back on the wall of the cave. There is an air pocket here, one that seems to shrink everyday, where we keep these books. They'll have to be moved soon if there is going to be anything to preserve. Even the one I was just reading has left bits of paper on my fingers. It's falling apart. I sigh and dive deep, kick my legs in powerful sweeping strokes until I get to the exit, propelling myself forward and directly into Yuri.

I push away from him and untangle our hair.

"Ira?" I ask. Yuri's already nodding.

"He was shaken, but that's all. He hasn't said a word." I breathe a sigh of relief, glad to have my lungs swollen with air, if only for a short while. "Learn anything new?" he asks me, silver tail swishing softly, keeping him afloat with much less effort than it's taking me.

"Nothing," I say, unable to hide my disappointment. The little bit of rightness I felt last night has faded, leaving me feeling sicker than ever. Yuri nods his head like he understands, and maybe he does, a little. But not fully, not completely.

"Go exploring?" he asks me though he can tell I'm going to refuse. My body feels sapped of energy and I've barely moved today. I shake my head and run my hands down the pale, blue skin on my arms.

"I'm not up to it," I say, thinking of the Trials tonight, the tests that are supposed to make sure we're prepared for the Feed. I think about failing them, but again, my mother's angry face swims into mind. She might kill me or she might not. But if she does, then all of this whining about choice will be for naught. If I am dead, I will have no choices. I will go the watery hell of Imenea, Neptune's daughter, Goddess of the Failed Huntswoman. "I need to study," I say and Yuri grabs my arm as I try to swim away.

"Natalie," he begins and in his voice is the fear of failure. "I … " His words trail off, lost in the swish of the sea around us. I know what he wants, and if I were a typical Huntswoman, if I were in my right mind, I'd leap at the chance. He wants to couple with me, love me, marry me when I come back after the Feed. I know he's the most logical choice. In fact, there is no other. I don't want to marry anybody, but if it has to be someone, it can only be him. I nod and his face lights up.

I press my purple lips against his pink ones, just a light touch, just a small promise.

"Not right now," I say as his hand brushes the bare skin of my breast and trails down my belly. My body is aching but not for him. For a human. I feel it now in my ancient blood. There's that lust that Ira was teasing me about, that heat for sex and pain. It's in me whether I want it there or not.

I kick my legs and leave him in a swirl of sea foam.

Chapter Three

I waste away the rest of the day in my room. I spend most of it in the dark. The pretty *sispa* I had last night has disappeared and I don't care to look for another. I haven't eaten in hours and my tummy is grumbling angrily, but I ignore it in search of other physical release. I lay in the sand and revel in the heat at my back, touch my hand between my legs and stay there until I'm partially satisfied. Still, the magic of the Feed is seeping into me, just like my teachers and my mother always promised.

"Neptune will find a way," she'd said, violet lips in a grin. "To make even the most stubborn of us fulfill our destiny."

When the time for the Trials comes, I slink out my room and drift to the throne room. My mother's had it cleared out for us. Even her throne is gone, placed in a ballroom on the other side of the palace so that she can continue with the daily business of being the ruler of the last *merighean* city still standing.

The other girls are whispering, gathered together on the opposite side of the room in a glittering mass. They've woven ribbons into their hair and made cups for their breasts. I remain naked, as most of the *merighean* do. Clothes are useless here and will only hinder them in the tests to come. *I hope you get caught in the nets,* I think meanly as I watch the instructors prepare an obstacle course for us. Immediately, I feel sorry for thinking this. We each must pass at least four of the five tests, or my mother's judgment will fall upon us.

I stand alone in the corner until they drift over to me, faces happy, willing to put aside our differences for the time being. They think I'm strange, but they always try.

"What are you looking for in a man, Natalie?" one of them asks. I'm supposed to know all of the Huntswomen's names as they'll serve as my palace guard come crowning, but I don't. I spend most of my time hanging out with

Yanori or Yuri and Ira. I barely speak to them.

"Love," I say and instantly regret it. They all laugh and touch their hair, their breasts. They think I'm joking because all they can think about is sex. I can't say that I never think about it, but I'm more cautious than them. I stand there while they gossip around me and think about my statement. Yes, that's it. Or at least, that's part of it. I want love. And choice. And freedom. And I know that if I were able to pass as human, that I'd run away and leave the sea forever, much as that would break my heart. There's something that isn't right about all of this that I can't put my finger on.

"Natalie." My head snaps up and I see Coreia, my mother's right hand, watching me with dark eyes. I'm the heir, so I'll have to go first. "Choose the order of the tests." I nod and point at the obstacle course first. It's designed to test us against whatever the humans might try to use against us: nets, cars, guns, knives, women. Women are the scariest part of all of this. Human women hate the *merighean*, or at least the Huntswomen. It's a hatred that's buried in their DNA. Even the ones that don't believe in us will try to kill us if they see us.

I point at the oldest Huntswoman in the village, Tejean, next. Her skin is so wrinkled that it floats around her frame just a little, like a second shadow. She will verbally test us on the knowledge of the Feed, the history, the rules, what's expected of us.

Geography is next. I want that one in the middle since it's the easiest. All we have to do is name parts of the land and the sea, show that we know how to get where we're going and that we know how to get back. That will be a good rest for the fourth Trial. Here we'll need to prove our fighting skills, show our prowess with weapons and with ourselves. This is where we'll need to demonstrate that we can defend the city against intruders and convince our instructors that we have the gall to kill the men we'll sleep with.

I don't even point at the fifth Trial. It is the worst, so I've saved it for last. This one is all about the coupling. I swallow and step forward, ready to dodge nets, swirl around bits of metal that are supposed to be cars. I don't say how useless I think this test is, that I think we should be practicing on land and not in the water. This is one of the reasons that the failure rate for Huntswomen is nearly fifty percent, why our numbers dwindle with each passing year. How can we be expected to survive land when we've never even seen it?

I pass this test with flying colors; we all do. The helpers, younger Huntswomen whose eyes glitter with excitement, poke at us with spears, try to ensnare us with nets, and hurl projectiles that are caught and slowed by the water, making it almost impossible for us to fail. Nobody struggles through this and there's a great celebration when we all pass, a chorus of howls and a wash of bubbles that swirl up and pass through the opening in the ceiling.

"To a glorious reign," Tejean howls as we move to her station. Helpers fan bits of woven kelp behind me, making a screen of bubbles and noise that will block my words from the next girl in line.

"State your purpose," she says flatly, eyes narrowed.

The Feed

Her excitement has been put aside for the moment and now, she's very astute, a leftover relic from my great grandmother's days.

"To take seed, life, to bleed flesh, to return the power of the land to the ocean, to restore the rights of those in the water and equalize us to those that walk on the earth unknowing." It's not a very creative answer, pulled straight from the old texts, but Tejean nods anyway.

"State your intent."

"Leave the sea for one week's time. Find a male, mate, take his child, and ... " Here I falter a bit. I know what I'm supposed to say, but it hurts somehow. "Kill him, taste him, return his essence to the sea." Tejean grunts and crosses her arms under her breasts which float like massive buoys.

"State your punishment."

"Punishment for failure is death. Failure to find a mate, to eat him, to come back barren, to die. A failed Huntswoman is a daughter of Imenea, destined to revel in her failure forever." Tejean nods, shoos me away.

With the map, I do what I did last night, plot out my route and name off major roads, neighborhoods, bodies of water that can be used to rest. I trace the shape of our city in the sea and the paths of the riptides. I show them where the rocks of Muoru are and how I'll use them to get up the cliff. Once they're satisfied, I move away to stretch. I watch as the other girls come out of Tejean's test with smug grins. But it's never those tests that anyone fails: it's the next three. There will be a lot of girls begging at my mother's feet come the end of this.

It's usually common practice to let them try again and again until they get it right. There are few enough of us as it is, but I don't trust the queen. This is her daughter's year and she's bound to be in a foul mood. I stand straight and look up.

A rainbow of colors is swirling around the roof. It's all hair. There are boys up there, watching us in giddy flurries of silver tails and bright eyes. They're all wishing that we'd pick them, elevate their status by marrying them, taking them to our beds. Huntswomen, after all, are rumored to be the best lovers in the sea. I wonder briefly if Yuri is up there and turn my attention to Coreia.

She's standing in a ring drawn with glittering pearl dust. This time, her feet are actually on the ground. I appreciate that, at least, though I still wish we were sparring on land. I step over to the helpers and try to smile. These girls are younger than the rest, twelve maybe, thirteen. They're all staring at me with adoration and respect, *want*. There's a need there to be a part of this, to be a part of a tradition that stretches the five hundred years of our recorded history. Still, something about it all sits badly with me. I must find out what it is and I have only one more day to do so.

I select a spear from the choices in front of me and check the wood to make sure that it's still firm and not rotting. The head looks okay, nice and sharp, carved from bits of stone that the gatherers collect in the fields of sand that surround the palace. I run my finger along the tip and watch as drops of blood blossom and float away. Perfect.

I take a fighting stance at the edge of the ring and wait

The Feed

for the signal. A handful of shells are tossed between us and Coreia crushes them instantly beneath her booted feet. I've chosen to stay barefoot, to feel the sand beneath my feet and the water against the scaled skin on my calves. She's also wearing a metal plate over her breasts and a small belt with knives, poisoned needles, and sharp rocks. Some of the girls will don armor for the Feed. I will not. I will remain nude. Everyone will think it's because I'm brave, but I will know the truth. It's because I'm a coward, because some part of me hopes that I won't have to do this. If I wear the armor, it will all become so real. I just can't do that yet.

I step back, use the current of foamy water that passes between us like a smoke screen, and come up behind Coreia. I take the head of my spear and nick the skin on her arm. I don't know how far we're supposed to take this test, but I'm going to make sure that I, at least, don't fail. If I know that I can defend myself, I'll feel better, more in control, more self sufficient.

I'm lost in my thoughts and miss a feint from Coreia who's recovered fast. Her violet hair fans out behind her as she barrels into me with her shoulder, knocking me back where I tumble through the water and nearly get ejected from the circle. I know if that happens, I fail. So I kick my legs and arms out to still myself, pushing against the water as I propel myself forward. Coreia ducks low and tries to come up beneath me. I close my legs tight and come down hard, my feet smashing into the sand where she'd been crouching.

"Good, Natalie, very good," she says as she moves

back and reaches into her belt. She pulls free a handful of poisoned needles and tosses them at me. They're tinted with aqua poison that will give me a headache and make my belly roil, but they won't kill me. I avoid them expertly and use the liquidity of the water to spin through the space between us. My spear comes out and smashes into Coreia's breastplate, knocking her back several feet. She manages to stay inside the circle though and uses one of the knives at her hip to charge me again. I can hear cheers on either side of the ring, but I ignore them, focusing only on this moment, on this one single task.

When she nears me, I put out my foot and trip her. She doesn't expect this; we are water dwellers after all and the idea of tripping anything is foreign to us, but I've seen the otters do it on the rocky island that's situated just north of here. Coreia flails and steps a single foot outside the circle, effectively ending this portion of the trial.

When she turns to face me, there's a smile on her red lips. To win this trial, all we must do is show a sense of ingenuity and bravery, a willingness to fight. The circle is just an extra element added to make things interesting. Nobody expected any of us to knock a teacher out of it. The cheers, both around and above me, are wild. I hear, "Long live the queen!" shouted from the windows. It seems the whole city's shown up to watch. I flush and turn away, depositing my spear back with the helpers who gush and reach out, run their pretty fingers along the pale blueness of my skin.

"Excellent job, Your Majesty," Coreia says respectfully, bowing at me as I move aside and feel my gut twist in a painful knot. The fifth Trial awaits me now. I think briefly about skipping it. I have beaten the four previous tests, thus passing the Trials as a whole. I glance over my shoulder and watch the next Huntswoman move into position.

"Right this way, Natalie," Aremia says. She's the most beautiful Huntswoman, at least, I think so. She has hair like spun gold that twists around her slender neck when she moves. Her skin is a soft yellow that shimmers under the lights of the *sispa* and her eyes are orange, like the octopi that are migrating through here this time of year. She's a sensual woman with a warm gaze and lips that always seem to smile, regardless of the situation. Of course they would choose her for this test. I sigh and follow Aremia through the curtained doorway into a small room where extra *sispa* are kept. Their cages have been cleared away to make room for us both to sit, a rare treat amongst the Huntswomen. I appreciate this as I sit across from her, shooing blue and silver fish out of the way.

Her smile gets brighter and she reaches across the space between us, taking my hands between hers. She's careful not to nick either of us with our nails. We won't die from the poison, but it will make us so sick that we'd wish we were dead.

"Tell me, Natalie, how many men have you been with?" She pauses. "Or women, although you may not find those exploits as useful on your journey." I bite the edge of my lip like I'm counting. My number is easy to get to though; my number is zero. If I answer her truthfully, then I will surely fail.

"Just one man," I say instead, thinking of Yuri's handsome face and his kind eyes that sparkle like pink pearls. Aremia is nodding gently, an understanding smile on her face. My answer was a good one; it makes me seem innocent but not ignorant. Perfect. I smile back, knowing my mother will be extracting these answers from my instructor one way or another. What I say now will determine my fate in so many ways it's scary.

"If you'll remember from your anatomy studies, human men are a bit different than *merighean* men." She looks me straight in the face; she's waiting for me to supply some sort of information that will let her know I understand. This is why the other girls, despite their propensity for the act, are going to fail. Aremia is a subtle teacher but an effective one.

"Indeed," I reply, pretending we're just here to make pleasant conversation and not determine the fate of an entire generation of Huntswomen and their daughters. "Human men lack the skill to control their reproductive organs to the degree that *merighean* men can. Therefore it's our duty to spend as much time with them as possible." I meet her gaze and lift my chin, tilting my head to the side like my mother does when she's considering a proposal.

"They're not frugal with their seed, but it still must be coaxed. Do you believe you've learned enough methods to reach your end goal?" I nod my head briskly, refusing to let her see the trepidation in my eyes. I could very well be the first virgin Huntswoman to enter the Feed. This could be a fatal mistake on my part. Suddenly, I'm overwhelmed with emotion. All of my fear and my hesitation might very well cost me my life and then where will I be? Wallowing in Imenea's slimy arms for eternity. I keep my face neutral during all of this, careful not to give anything away. All I want is to make it out of that room with a passing score.

"Ma'am," I begin, careful to keep my voice level and polite, aristocratic. I am the heir after all and although my instructors pretend otherwise, I know that in part, they are all just the slightest bit frightened of me. *If she is anything like her mother,* I hear them whisper when they think I'm not listening. I don't want to, but I believe that if I try, I can bully my way out of the rest of this test. I need as much time to analyze my situation as possible. If there is a way out of all of this then I will find it. "My hands are the hands of a queen and my will is the will of a Huntswoman, there is nothing I cannot do and nothing that I do not excel in. If I may be excused, I would very much like to practice my skills before I leave. My lover awaits." I twist my purple lips into a naughty smile, one that mimics my mother's at her worst. Aremia blinks at me softly, orange eyes flickering back the twinkling lights of the *sispa*.

"Be careful out there Natalie," she says in response and I remember the stares and the accusations she faced after her Feed, when her belly remained flat much longer than the other girls. There's a fear in her face that's just for me. *She knows I'm lying,* I worry as Aremia sits up and blows bubbles from her mouth in a sigh. "You've passed, congratulations and enjoy your journey. May Neptune carry you on his loving shoulders." I nod and stand up quickly, pushing a school of fish out of my way as I step from the room and nod at the next Huntswoman in line. She grins at me and a cheer explodes from the hall. Everyone is watching: the Huntswomen, the instructors, the men. They're all calling my name, whistling, swishing their tails in excitement.

I turn away quickly and follow the winding halls of coral and stone to my room, afraid that my shame and my fear will show on my face and disappoint them all.

My mother is waiting outside my door when I arrive. I pause and bow my body forward as I float in the gentle current, unsure of her current mood. She has just come from court and is dressed in her most luxurious jewelry. Bits of pink and white shells mixed with pearl and gold waft in the water around her solid form. If things at court went well then she will be in a good mood. If not ... I look up from my crouch surreptitiously, trying to see if the Spindled Blade is at her belt. It is not.

"How did it go?" she asks in her nicest voice. I incline my chin and answer her respectfully.

"I passed all five Trials, Great Mother." Her laughter bubbles around us and scares away a lurking shark. I've seen her kill them with her bare hands, bathe in their blood and consume their raw flesh. I shiver involuntarily.

"Don't fail me, pretty daughter," she says, reaching down and touching the bottom of my chin. I raise my head and meet her sharp gaze. "If you do, I will see that you suffer greatly." My mother scrapes the side of my face with her nails, using just enough pressure that I'm

The Feed

afraid she's going to puncture my skin and poison me. But she doesn't. Aleria is more careful than that. "Sweet dreams." She presses a kiss to my lips and leaves me alone in the nearly dark hall with only a crab for company.

I let myself drift to the floor, burying my feet in the sand for stability. Tomorrow night, when the moon is high and the waves are dark, I will lead my fellow Huntswomen to the shore. Many of them will die; many more human men will be killed. I touch my hand to my belly and wish I could breathe sweet oxygen into my lungs. The weight of the ocean seems to be sitting on my shoulders now and it's stifling. If I'm to come up with a solution, it will have to be soon. I'm running out of time.

There's only one person who can help me through this.

I enter my room quietly and shut the door before swimming to the shutters and opening them. Grabbing the edges of the window, I propel myself out and catch a current, one that swirls and twists through the upper spires of the castle and past the group of males that are still hanging around the opening to the throne room.

I think I spy Yuri in the throng, blonde hair wafting around his face, mixing with the blood red strands of Ira. I don't want any of them to hear me, to call attention to where I'm going, so I let the water carry me as far as it's able, making sure to keep my arms and legs very still. When the currents begin to peter out, I kick my legs once, using the rush of power to push me down and closer to the row of stone and coral houses that line the edge of the kelp forest.

Green stems stretch high above me, drifting gently in

the currents that rock the water back and forth like a new born babe. I would rather dive into those shadowy depths, navigate between the long thin leaves, then I would be certain not to get caught. But I would also certainly die. Not a single *merighean* that has probed more than a few meters into the forest has come back alive. Some say the giant sea snake, Amahna, still lives there and that she spirits wandering mers to her temple under the plates of the earth. It's considered another form of hell, usually reserved for sloths and deserters. Maybe if I ran away then I would go there instead of Imenea's. It would be better though not by much. Of course, I am certain that Amahna is dead, just like Muoru, just like the great sea dragon.

I no longer have the luxury of entertaining fantasies so I push this nonsense out of my head and use the walls of the houses to propel myself along the western wall of the city until I reach the place that Yanori calls home.

The massive bunch of coral is five times my height, white as the bones of the sea dragon with bits of kelp intertwined between its branches. My sister's had the palace guards carve out the center for her so that she might have her own little space in the middle, surrounded by the jagged arms of the reef. She used to live in the palace, but my mother did not like her there. After my second sister, Adora, was killed, she kicked her out completely. I think if it weren't for her loneliness, Yanori would've moved out here long ago. It had always seemed to me that she enjoyed it.

"I've been waiting for you," she says before I even get

the chance to announce myself. She's sitting in front of a mirror though for what reason, I can't ascertain. Barnacles have covered most of the surface and there's even a starfish wrapped around the edge of the frame. Yanori turns to face me, the pale pink of her hair obscuring her smile. "Talk to me."

I sigh in relief, bubbles escaping my lips and disappearing through the cracks in the coral reef. I drift down to the floor and curl up on my side, letting the warmth of the earth soothe me, bring me back to myself.

"I can't do it," I say to her, wanting an answer, knowing she won't give me one. She'll let me talk this out with her, give me a sliver of her infinite wisdom, but the choice is and will always be mine. Even if I don't see it that way.

"You did a good job," she says, tilting her head to the side. Her milky eyes scan the horizon like she's looking for something, but I know that in reality she's listening to the drift of the ocean, the waves, the currents. "You haven't been followed." She pauses and floats to a shelf she's hung from bits of rope. From it she takes a metal box and opens it, removing a small knife that glitters in the light from the nearby caverns. It's the only light source she has and it's dim enough that I have trouble identifying the other items she's holding. "Continue."

"Who am I to take these girls where they're not prepared to go? To claim the lives of people whose ancestors may or may not have had anything to do with the downfall of our other cities?" Yanori drifts back towards the ocean floor, curling her damaged tail gently to the side so that she can get as close to where I'm laying as possible.

"You're their future queen, the one person who can right the wrongs of our damaged people." I sit up and stare at her, wishing I could blow my frustration out in a bubble and let it drift away. But it isn't that easy; I'll have to work through my problems one at a time.

"You should've been queen," I say and she interrupts me. Yanori isn't one for idle chitchat and useless words.

"What options do you see for yourself, Natalie? If you lay them out before you, maybe it will be easier for you to make a choice." Yanori bends forward and lays the pile of items near my feet. I know better than to ask about them; if she wants me to know, she'll tell me.

"I suppose I don't have any options," I say with a sigh. I grab my hair on either side of my head and cross it together in front of my neck. The slight pain in my scalp helps me think. "I have to go. It's the only choice I can rightfully make." Yanori shakes her head and spins away so that she's looking at the mirror again.

"It may be the right choice, but it isn't the only one. What are your options?" She leans forward and gently begins to peel the starfish away from the mirror. It relaxes at her touch, like she's its oldest friend, and allows her to remove it quite easily. I've never had much luck with the stubborn things.

"I could run away, disappear into the depths of the sea and find one of the old cities. I might die trying to get there or I may die soon after. Maybe Mother would even send the Hunt after me. Then I'd go to Hell and wallow in the agony of my choice for eternity." Yanori is nodding, petting the back of the orange starfish gently.

The Feed

"I'd miss you quite a lot," she says sincerely. "Especially in the afterlife."

"I could talk to the other girls about this, try to convince them that this isn't right. I could talk to Coreia and Tejean and Aremia." I relax my grip on my hair and let my head hang. "But nobody will listen to me. They'll report me to the queen and she'll have me killed or caged up."

"Sometimes to change the minds of others, a test of courage must be passed. You'll have to earn their respect before you can change their lives. It's the way of the world, Natalie, in all things and not just this." Yanori floats to the doorway and lays the starfish on the sand. It begins to move across the ground, sliding over rocks in its search for mussels and clams.

"I could go ashore and try to live in the lake I saw on the map." Even as the words leave my mouth, I feel my chest tighten. That existence would be just that, an existence. Not a life. And I would miss the sea with every bit of my heart. Its absence would eat away at my soul and leave me barren and miserable. I could play with that fantasy all I want, but it isn't plausible, not really.

"What is it that you want, Natalie?" Yanori asks, spinning around so quickly that she tilts off balance for a moment before correcting herself. The bumpy flesh of her damaged tail scrapes the edge of the coral and I cringe. She doesn't seem to notice. It's an old wound after all.

"Freedom," I say suddenly, looking up and staring her in the face. She can't see the determination in my eyes, the desperation. I put everything I'm feeling into my voice.

C.M. Stunich

"Love." Yanori smiles like I've just passed a test.

"At your feet you'll find a knife, a necklace, and a crown. Take them." I reach down and pick up the knife first. It's only as long as my pinky finger but very sharp. As soon as I touch my flesh to the tip, blood wells out and floats before my eyes in a pink cloud. It's very pretty, a dark turquoise that mimics my nails, gleams my reflection back at me in perfect clarity. The hilt is bejeweled with pink pearls and bits of mottled green serpentine.

"What are these for?" I ask as I set the knife down and examine the necklace. It's finer than any of Mother's and I'm surprised that Yanori has it. The queen is very particular when it comes to jewelry. I have seen her take quite a number of pieces from her Huntswomen, spiriting them away to her own collection. Yanori's necklace is the most beautiful of them all. The entire necklace is made of silver, crusted black with the deposits of the sea. When I hold it up, tiny rectangles float around the chain, waving in the water like bits of kelp. Each has a symbol carved into it that's impossible to read. I imagine though that if I were to clean it off, the markings would be quite stunning. Each is lined with more bits of serpentine and flecks of gold.

"Protection, understanding and power," she says in that cryptic way that's always been hers. I touch the crown next, admiring the swirling curves of the metal and the bits of abalone shell that fill in the gaps between the blackened silver. It's a lovely piece, most likely something that belonged to one of the old queens with their elaborate headdresses that my mother can only attempt to imitate.

The Feed

The *merighean* are certainly a much poorer people than we once were.

"I can't take this," I say, holding it out to her. "It's forbidden." Only Aleria may wear a crown. It's one of her strictest rules. Yanori ignores my hand. She pretends it's because she can't see it, but I know it's really because she has a plan in mind, some great scheme that won't make sense to me for quite some time. She floats back to the shelf and removes a square of cloth, held down by an orange and pink rock. When she hands it to me, I see that it's a satchel made from burlap. There are letters on it in a faded red ink that's no longer legible.

"Put them in there and take them with you," she says and I can tell she means more than just back to the palace. She's telling me to take them on the Feed; she's telling me to go.

"But I can't," I say as she reaches forward and takes my face between her hands.

"But you can and you will, Natalie. It's your destiny and the only hope for the survival of the *merighean*. There has to be a balance between the earth and sea and you're the only one that can find it. Restore us, sister, give us back our glory." Yanori drops her hands and takes the items from me, putting them in the bag and cinching it with a bit of twine that's sewn into the top.

"I may not be able to kill him," I say, thinking of the man that's unknowingly waiting above for me, who will drop everything to be by my side, who will give his life for just one week in my arms.

"There are answers everywhere you look. Some are

obvious, others require a bit of searching," Yanori begins and I'm afraid she's about to go off on a tangent. Much as I enjoy her words, I need to come to a decision and I need to do it now.

"I've never been with a man, Yanori. I wasn't ready. I'm still not ready. I don't know what to do."

"Do what you have to do, Natalie. Your path will reveal itself in time." Yanori kisses my forehead and turns away, returning back to the mirror and curling her tail beneath her like she's preparing for a very long wait. "Forge your own destiny, then your freedom, and your love, will come to you."

I take the satchel in my hands and stand up, wanting to ask her more questions but knowing she won't answer them. She's given me all the information that she intends to.

I bunch my legs beneath me and swim up and out of the coral reef. As I swim, I make my decision.

I will join the Feed.

Chapter Four

Yuri is waiting for me outside my room. I had expected

this, knew he would come to me one last time before the Feed.

"Is Yanori doing well?" he asks, displaying a wealth of intelligence and foresight that has made him so popular amongst the other *merighean*. I nod and swim past him, through the open window and into brightness. The *sispa* I had admired previously is back, cream shell glowing from its position above my chest of coins. Next to it is its mate, a male *sispa*, with its dark brown shell speckled in taupe spots. Their dual glows are what has lit my room so beautifully.

I set the satchel down on the floor and spin to face Yuri. His arms are resting on the inside of my windowsill, head cradled on his hands. His blonde hair is flowing around his face like kelp, blocking my view of the city. There will be great parties tonight, feasts, treasure hunts and I'll be expected to take part in them. I let myself drift to the floor and cross my legs beneath me. Yuri is waiting for an invitation to come in, but I'm afraid that if I extend it to him that I'll be offering something else as well. I have decided to go to the Feed, but I have not yet decided on that.

"Does anybody else know that I went to her?" I ask, thinking mostly of Ira. He is Yuri's best friend and quite nosy. If my mother finds out that I visited my sister, she will suspect something, and if Yanori is right, if somehow I do have a way to change things, I'll have to do it under her nose.

"Not that I know of," he says watching me with careful eyes. I nod and put my face in my hands. It's okay if Yuri sees me like this. He knows how I feel about the Feed.

"What did she say?" he asks as his body sags. He's stopped moving his tail and is now just floating, using his arms to keep him in place. I shake my head and open my hands, looking up at him with every bit of fear that I feel inside me.

"Nothing and everything," I say. Yuri's good friends with Yanori, too, so he understands this. "You know how it is," I say with a sigh. The bubbles that fall from my lips bump a fish that's nearly identical to the one I killed. Its green and yellow scales flash as it swims away, thinking itself safe next to the *sispa*. I'm still feeling guilty about its brethren and so I stand up and shoo it away before the female recognizes that there's prey nearby. "She's so much smarter than everyone else that sometimes it's hard to understand her." I put my hands on my hips and pace. Yuri is watching me carefully, absorbing my movements. He's seen them often enough, but I think he still finds them strange. I pause and turn to look at him. "I think she told me to go," I say, shaking my head. He nods slowly, like he's been thinking about this, too.

"I think she's right," he says and in his voice, I hear his love for me. He loves me, but I don't love him. *How did I get in this position?* I wonder. Love. It's one of my few desires in life and it's sitting right before my eyes. *Why am I this way? Why am I so different?* "But I wish you didn't have to." I look at Yuri looking at me and I make another important decision. I don't know if it's right, but it makes the most sense. If I am to go on the Feed, then I must be prepared. I cannot be like those girls who think a block of metal will teach them to avoid a car. I'm smarter than that.

"Come in," I say and Yuri rushes to obey, silver tail flashing as he moves through the porthole much easier than I can. "And close the shutters."

◆ ◆ ◆

In the morning, I avoid Yuri by leaving my room before he's awake. I can't think about what I did with him last night. It makes my chest tight but not in a good way. Yuri was a good lover and very patient, but now that the morning of the Feed has come, I realize that I've made the wrong decision. Yanori had told me to forge my own destiny, but I have gone and joined the school. I'm so angry with myself that I swim straight into my mother's muscular back.

"Your Majesty," I blurt, using the walls of the hallway to push myself back. Aleria turns around, her turquoise hair brushing the ceiling and shedding a few, tiny white shells as she narrows her eyes on me and purses her violet lips.

"Natalie," she says, annoyed that I've bumped into her, but so obviously in one of her better moods that I don't bother to bow. My father is swimming ahead of her, his yellow tail flicking up bits of sand as he waits patiently near the entrance to her room. Her belt is just a simple braid of kelp; the Spindled Blade is nowhere to be seen. "I was just about to send a servant to your room. Come, I have something to show you." I follow after her, anxiety twisting my gut into knots. I swim crookedly, much sorer than I had expected and once again grow angry with myself. Now I will have to swim the sixty miles or so to the rocks of Muoru with a body that's aching fiercely.

My mother shoos the servants from her room with a wave of her hands and kisses my father gently on the lips, banishing him as well. Once the two of us are alone together she swims to a wardrobe on the far side of the room. It takes her a few tries to get the swollen wood to open, but she manages it with a grunt and a rush of seawater. Inside is a bag which my mother withdraws and brings over to me. It's so heavy that she lets it drag across the sand on the floor, depositing it near my feet.

"Open it," she says, moving over to her dressing table. I try not to sigh and let myself drift down until I'm crouching next to the bag. I can only guess that what I'm going to find in it will be much less pleasant than the gifts my sister gave me. I untie the knot at the top and slide the decaying fabric away so that I'm staring at a pile of rusty chain mail. Aleria turns to face me, her cheeks covered in the bright sparkles of pearl dust. "I wore that armor during the Feed," she says and I know without a doubt that I'll be expected to wear it, too. I try to smile and pretend that I'm excited. The rest of the girls will be when they see me in it. I sift through the pieces and find that it's a full body suit. It's harder to keep my smile now. *How am I expected to swim with this?* I wonder as I lift the chest

The Feed

piece. It hangs heavy in the water, making me even more concerned for my climb up the cliffs.

I've spent a lot of time with the otters on their rocky island. One of the things that always manages to shock me is how heavy I feel when I'm on land. It often takes me an hour or more to even find my feet. If I am wearing this heavy metal on my skin, it is very likely that I will not make the climb up Muoru. "Thank you," I say instead, retying the bag and hoping that she'll let me leave now. I was up late with Yuri last night and so I slept late. There are precious few hours until the Feed and I want every second to myself.

"You are quite welcome," she says and I can see that she's done with me. She feels that she's done her part in preparing me for what's to come. I vow to myself that I will only wear the armor for as long as it takes me to lose the other girls. Once I am alone, I will take it off and bury it somewhere where I might find it again later, after the Feed. The thing that frightens me most is what kind of person I will be when I dig it back up.

◆ ◆ ◆

I go to the anemone gardens and am disappointed to find the other Huntswomen there. I had wanted some peace and quiet for myself surrounded by the waving arms and bright colors of the little polyps. They are laid out in delicate spirals and outlined with white sand that is carried here from the edges of the shore. There are gazebos carved in coral and covered in the bodies of black mussels that cling to the columns in clumps. Some of the girls are sitting on the edges of the railing, eating them, while others chase each other, playing with spears and chattering so much that above them, the sea is a white wash of bubbles and foam. I spin away before they see me and make my way to Yanori's house.

She isn't home.

I sit in her hammock and wait. Sometime later, Yuri surprises me by swimming through the opening in the coral, silver tail flashing brightly. His blonde hair is in knots, caught around his neck and stuck to his lips. He pushes it away and pauses in front of me, seemingly shy. I wait for him to speak, unsure if I'll be able to get any words out.

"I've been looking for you," is all he says. I fight the urge to say something mean. Yuri has done nothing wrong. It was my decision and I made it. I must own it.

"You've found me," I say, trying to smile. My lips feel tight though. I am anxious and my body is burning hotter than ever before. Coupling with Yuri did not make that go away; it has only made it worse. And now, I feel a strange hunger in my belly. I can see why the other Huntswomen are eating the mussels; they're starving just as I am, but no sea creature will fill this hunger. The taste for human flesh has been put into us by Neptune and it's rising quickly.

I reach out and begin to unknot his hair, not knowing what else to say.

The Feed

"The city's as alive as I've ever seen it," he says and his eyes sparkle bright, the eyes of an observer; Yuri misses nothing. "They've decorated the dragon's bones with bits of kelp and shells, and your mother has even authorized a dolphin hunt for the Final Feast." I purse my lips and hope I don't look too much like Aleria. The Final Feast. The last time any of us will partake of the sea and the sea alone. When we come back, we will be different, with a bit of the land in our bellies and our wombs. Nothing will be the same again. We'll be invited into the dark room at the back of my mother's palace, the one where only accomplished Huntswomen may go. There we will plot and plan, continue the queen's desperate attempts at reclaiming the sea and the power that was once ours.

"Yuri," I begin as he lowers himself to the floor and rests his head in my lap. "Promise me something." He nods and the movement of his face against my belly stirs up that heat for sex and pain that has frightened me since before I can remember. "Promise me that when I come back, if I've forgotten who I am, that you will remind me."

"I will," he says, but I'm not sure if he really understands what I mean. He's kissing my belly and working his way down. I know he believes that we are a couple now, that when I come back, I will marry him. I stop Yuri with a finger under the chin and raise his eyes to mine.

"I am serious," I say, wanting this vow to be something that he takes to heart. I'm so afraid now that I feel my mind will burst from the strain, spiral down into the trenches that line the southern part of the city. Yuri leans back and takes my hands in his. In pale eyes lies a question. He wants to know what I'm thinking, what I'm planning. Somehow he knows that I'm different. I think it's what attracts him to me.

"You're too strong for that," he tells me. "But if it does happen, then I will be here." Yuri kisses my knuckles gently. "I would not want to lose you, Natalie. You are special. You are the cure for this kingdom." I pull my hand away from him and look him straight in the face.

"You've been spending too much time with Yanori," I say as I rise from the hammock and swim to the opening of my sister's home. I want so desperately to find her, but why? So she can tell me the same things she told me last night? The decision was mine; it has been made. I have to hold strong to that. "I need to be alone," I tell Yuri as he swims up behind me and slides his arms around my waist. His hair tickles my back as he nods and releases me, planting one last kiss to the back of my neck.

"I love you," Yuri tells me as I kick off from the ground and spiral away into the sea. I pretend not to hear him for I haven't any answer that will satisfy us both.

◆ ◆ ◆

I waste the last hours of my day sitting in the library. I've heard tales from the old ones, like Tejean, about massive structures carved from the bones of whales. *Bone dry, completely and utterly bone dry,* they'll say. *We had more books in there than we had people in the city.*

I'm sitting on the edge of rock that serves as a seat, one single seat, and before me is a bookcase carved from stone that holds exactly thirty-one tomes. Thirty-one tomes that are falling apart, flaking away in my hands as I run my fingers across their spines. There are three that are almost completely unreadable. Nobody touches these. They sit in the right corner of the bottom row, guarding their secrets from curious eyes.

I reach out and touch one, dig my fingers into the damp pages and pull. The book falls apart as it moves, shedding bits of paper across the pool of water between us. I drop it and it floats for just a second before beginning to sink. I recover it quickly and scan the pages as fast as I'm able, trying desperately to glean some new bit of information. I'm hungry for it, for knowledge. I'm as parched for that as I am for human flesh. I shiver and am about to give up on the book when I flip the page and find a bit of ink that hasn't run, that's still legible enough that I can make out some of the images.

There are symbols there, sharp lines and swirling curves that make up tiny pictures. On the right side of the page is a key, explaining what each means. This however has faded with time and I can make out nothing. I run my fingers across the pictures, feeling that they're vaguely familiar. I cannot, however, come up with the reference in my mind.

"Where have I seen you before?" I ask, my voice echoing in the silence. I'm running out of time and must head back soon, before my mother sends her Huntswomen after me. But in the air, thrumming in my rapidly drying skin, is a bit of excitement, of rightness. It's of the same variety that I felt when outlining my path up the rocks of Muoru. A bit of my fear fades and I tuck what's left of the book back on the shelf. I will study it when I come back. Right now, I have a task ahead of me the likes of which I have never accomplished.

I dive into the water feeling refreshed and reenergized. I don't know what has just happened, but I feel better somehow, stronger. The fear is still there, but it has lessened, leaving me ready for what's to come.

The Final Feast is set up outside the palace, under the ribcage of the sea dragon. I am sad to see that the Huntswomen have managed to catch some dolphins. Their bodies lay open on the table, held down by nets that the other girls are sticking their fingers through, grabbing bits of flesh, shoving them into their mouths in a frenzy. I feel a strong urge to join them, this clenching in my belly that's aching for blood. I close my eyes briefly and regain control of myself.

"Ah, Natalie," my mother calls from her throne. She's sitting at the head of the table in an ostentatious dress that makes it impossible to swim. Her servants have to carry her around when she's wearing it. She inclines her head at me and beckons to me with sharpened nails. I swim around the other girls, my eyes searching for Yuri and Yanori. They're floating outside the antechamber, watching through the massive rib bones with the rest of the citizens. Yanori can't possibly know that I'm looking at her, but she winks anyway; Yuri just smiles, sadly but

The Feed

gently.

I swim to my mother's side, allow her to pet my hair.

"You're late," she says quietly, just loud enough that I can hear, but nobody else can. I nod my head slowly, trying carefully to keep my face stoic. I can't let her see any of my thoughts, not a single one. "No matter," she says, a wicked smile on her purple lips. Her gaze is locked onto the feeding frenzy that's happening at the table. "There's plenty to go around. Now, go and join your Huntswomen before I decide to punish you for your tardiness."

I move away from her without acknowledging her words. I don't want to eat the dolphins. They're such intelligent creatures; I swim with them from time to time. I think there's something about their carefree attitude that's to be learned from, not eaten. Instead, I grab a bowl of mussels and begin to crack their shells.

"Now that we're all here," Aleria begins, holding her chin high and letting her gaze scan the crowd. The whole city is here to watch. Nobody would dare miss the Feed during the heir's year. "We can celebrate the glorious reunion of earth and sea. What has been taken from us will be rightfully returned." The crowd cheers at this; the Huntswomen crow. I remain silent. "Our ranks will swell and our power will grow. From the Feed, we will gain the seeds that will sow our brilliant future." More cheers. The queen is looking straight at me now. I look up and catch her dark gaze. "They came out of the quiet sea in small numbers and wicked intentions." She's only reciting the words from tradition, but somehow, she has aimed them at me. I stop treading water, catch the edge of the table with my hands and watch her carefully. "They came to steal seed, life, came to bleed flesh." She suspects me, suspects what I haven't even quite fully understood in myself. In me, she sees a rebel and rebels must be crushed. I look away and in her next words, I hear a quiet promise, a promise of pain. *If you fail me, you will die.* "They came to feed."

The crowd explodes in a frenzy; the Huntswomen, tired of sitting still for so long, grab their spears and swim around the crowd, kick out with their legs, and perform tricks. Like trained fish, they swim in a school that's loyal to one thing and one thing only: their hunger.

Chapter Five

I don my mother's armor, hiding Yanori's necklace beneath the rusting folds. Around my waist, I tie a bit of rope with a small sheath for the knife. I have made the decision that this is the only weapon I will carry with me ashore. Most of the other girls will be outfitted with poison darts, spears, swords as long as their arms, but I know they won't be able to wield these effectively on land. They will be more of a hindrance than a help. I move my chest of coins and stash the crown in the sand, making sure to bury it as deep as the rock beneath allows. I then move the chest back and clear the ground of any evidence. If my mother finds it there, trouble will await me upon my return. She is already suspicious enough, will already be examining every inch of my soul for failure.

When I am as ready as I'll ever be, I leave my room and walk the twisting halls of the palace until I get to the throne room. My body is still sore from last night and swimming in the heavy iron chains is hard enough. I wait until the last minute before kicking up from the ground. I struggle for a moment, my legs and arms fighting to compensate for the extra weight. After a few strokes of my arms, I find an easy pace and emerge to a frenzied crowd of cheers.

"Long live the Huntswomen!" they shout. "Long live the queen!" I try to smile at them. They are, after all, innocents caught in a circle of tradition that they barely understand. The other Huntswomen are waiting for me in various states of dress with ribbons in their hair and sparkles in their eyes. They are so excited, they are having trouble holding the formation we must swim out in. Once we are out of sight of the city, the race is on and all order is lost. I will let them get ahead of me, disappear into the murky depths of the ocean, and then I will remove my armor. I'd rather climb the cliffs alone anyway. If I see a girl fall, if I see one die, then I will never forgive myself.

My mother is still wearing her ridiculous dress,

standing on the head of the dragon, its empty eyes gazing out across the dark waters. I swim straight to her, allow her eyes to take in my form with false pride. If she sees the necklace between the links of chain, she shows no sign of it.

"You are just like me," she says with a sigh as bubbles escape her dark lips. "I took only a small knife with me. So brave," she coos and although I know her praise is forced, I smile. I must leave her on good terms. Whatever I decide to do in the next week will be something that she doesn't like. My eyes search the servants behind her for my father. He is drifting between them with a sad smile on his face. Little tears come from his eyes and join the salty waters of the sea.

I reach my arms out to him like I did when I was a little girl. He waits for approval from my mother before swimming forward and embracing me in his strong arms.

"Be careful," he says, slipping a bit of *kimtazi* into my belt. It's just a bit of filleted fish wrapped in seaweed, but my father seasons it with something special so that it tastes like nothing else. It's the only *kimtazi* that I will eat. "Stay safe and come back to me." He kisses my cheek so gently that for a moment, I am afraid that I, too, will cry. I control my emotions by using my mother's steely features to ground myself.

"It is time," she says as my father pulls away and disappears into the crowd. I turn around and face my people. In their eyes, I see hope for the future. *I must give that to them*, I vow as my eyes search desperately for my friends. But there's too many people shouting and spinning. The water is frothing and bubbling, blocking my view of large swathes of the crowd. I will have to find the strength in myself. My mother steps up next to me and holds up her hand, effectively silencing everyone. They are all waiting for me now. I touch my fingers to my gills and wish I could take a calming breath.

Dropping my hands, I raise my chin and utter the only words that will come to mind, planted there by Yanori and growing stronger by the moment.

"To the restoration of balance." I suck in a mouthful of seawater and blow it out in a geyser, like a whale. I kick off from the skull of the sea dragon and it takes every bit of my strength to fool my onlookers into thinking that the armor, and my soreness, is not affecting me. I spin in the water and angle myself up, aiming to avoid the kelp forest.

My Huntswomen follow in the shape of an arrow, with me at the point, like a flock of birds I once saw when I was playing with the otters. There are fifty of them on either side, a colorful collection of killers, armed with venomous nails and teeth that are just a bit sharper than those of the *merighean,* just a bit better equipped to tear flesh.

They swim quietly at first, caught up in the rush of tradition and the excitement of starting the journey that they have been raised with the sole purpose of completing. After awhile though, chatter starts, bickering. Some of them are teaming up, forming groups or pairs. They think it will give them an advantage, and it might, it is hard to say. We know so little of what's to come that it's almost impossible to prepare any further.

Once the city is out of sight, the girls rush past me,

shouting goodbyes and bits of advice, wishing me luck, praying they'll have the same. I let them go, slowing my pace enough that even the most hesitant of them are forced to leave me behind in their wake.

When they have all gone, I sink closer to the ocean floor looking for a place to hide the armor. It must be somewhere distinct; the ocean is vast and if I'm not careful, I will have to go back without it. My mother would be quite angry to see me swim naked into the city. After awhile though, I realize how unlikely it is that I will be following this same path back. If I'm off by even a few meters then I won't find it anyway. I drop quickly to the sand, landing in a painful crouch that makes my thighs burn with the effort of slowing myself.

I peel the chain mail off and toss it near a cluster of rocks. Fish swim away and back, curious about this change in their environment. I think about eating one of them to regain my strength but decide to go for the *kimtazi* instead. I haven't been out more than an hour but already I'm hungry. The metal has sapped more of my energy than I'd even suspected. Or maybe it's just the Feed, filling me with magic, making me crave something I don't want. I chew my father's salty gift quickly, poking at the fish that swim to my mouth, trying to steal a crumb or two.

When I'm finished, I swim to one of the underwater rocks that line this area, using the crags as handholds as I pull myself to the top, letting the buoyancy of the salty water do most of the work. When I hit the peak, I bounce off, rocketing into the water in a spin. I feel so much lighter now, almost weightless. I close my eyes and revel

The Feed

in the feeling of cold liquid against my skin, forgetting for just a moment where I'm going or why I'm going there.

◆ ◆ ◆

Sometime later, I find one of the Huntswomen dead. She's floating, belly splayed open, in the water just south of the rocks of Muoru. I'm so tired now that I've been stopping to rest, sitting on the ocean floor and trying to convince my aching muscles to carry me just a bit further. I have done long distance swimming before with Yuri and Ira on our treks for treasure. But this is different. It's much further than I've ever gone and there's a time limit that I can't push from my head. Every so often, I go to the surface to check the time. The moon has been chasing me across the sky, teasing me with its pale light. If I don't get to the shore before the sun, then I'll have to wait until tomorrow. I will not emerge from the sea during the day. To do so is to play with death's hand.

Still, even this type of caution won't protect me from what has killed this girl. She has the bite wounds characteristic of a large shark. I'm not sure what kind; it was most likely killed and eaten by the other girls. I search around for its corpse but find nothing. I touch the Huntswoman's face reverently. Sharks are not normally a problem for the Huntswomen, but are an occasional cause of death for the softer *merighean*. I can only guess that this girl was caught off guard, lost in a fog of fatigue or excitement, either of which can be deadly given the right circumstances. I shoo away some of the crabs and fish that have already started to eat from her and give her forehead a light kiss.

"May Neptune carry you on his loving shoulders," I say although I know that she's more likely to spend eternity in Imenea's pale arms. I swim away quickly, afraid that the cloud of crimson blood that's blossomed around her will draw more of the spiteful creatures.

I don't encounter another person until I hit the shore.

The water here is much rougher than that of our home, and colder. Some of the Huntswomen are circling the rocks looking for a way up. Others are debating the wisdom of my choice.

"I don't know about you," one of them says, eyeing me suspiciously as I swim into her sight. I had planned on waiting for them to leave, but after spending almost an hour behind a row of sand dunes, I can see that they are going to take too long. If I wait, I will not make it up the cliffs before daybreak. "But I'm going to the beach. There's a smooth stretch of sand just west of here. It won't take long to get there." Some of the other girls nod, but I'm already shaking my head. I hadn't planned on helping them, but I just can't stand to watch them fail.

"There might be humans there," I say as the ocean grabs us all and pushes us against the rocks. I hold out my hands and take the impact gently. Some of the girls grunt as they smash shoulders, calves, backs into the rocky crags. "It's too risky."

The Feed

"Maybe there will be men," one of them says, her yellow eyes glowing with excitement. "Then we won't have to travel across the land."

"Don't forget about the women," I say as I swim above their heads, breaking the surface of the water briefly to examine the rocks. If I choose the wrong path, I could die. The rocks of Muoru tower above the water like a row of spikes, each one a different height, a different length from the shore. I'm going to have to swim between them and get a little bit closer. None of the ones that are close to us connect with the shore. It's going to be extremely dangerous though. The water there is furious and white, frothing and licking at the sides of the cliffs in bursts of pale foam. I could easily be crushed and killed. I dive again and find several of the girls have already gone.

"They went for the beach," one of them says to me. Her hair is as purple as my lips and her eyes are a pale lavender, very soft and sweet looking. I feel scared for her. Her skin is pale and she's trembling with fear, holding onto the rocks for dear life as the ocean swells around us.

"What is your name?" I ask, wishing that I knew, wishing I knew the name of the dead girl as well. That was my job and I have failed at that.

"Kiara," she says and then grunts as we're all slammed together violently. I look around me and count eight girls. Eight girls waiting to see what I'll do here. I hold their fate in my hands.

"To get to the shore," I say to them, having to raise my voice to a shout to be heard above the waves. "We'll need to get closer." I cling tightly to the cliff and move around it so that I can point at the thin channel of water that runs between the rocks.

"There's a nest of smaller rocks not far from here," one of the girls says. "We wouldn't have to climb." I'm shaking my head again.

"No," I say, looking her straight in the eyes, willing her not to go. "The small rocks are the most dangerous. They're much sharper and harder to spot." She nibbles her lip and looks away. "Look," I say, suddenly so conscious of my role as heir that it hurts. "I will guide you as best I can if you wish to follow me. I can't make any promises about your safety, but in my heart I believe this is the best course of action." They all stare back at me, looking much less fierce than the Huntswomen I saw earlier, mouths bloody with bits of flesh. I turn away from them and start forward, making sure to keep at least six feet of water between my head and the surface. It's much rougher up there than it is down here.

The going is slow and tough, so much so that I can't even look back at the other girls. I don't swim so much as propel, using the rocks around me to move forward until I'm at a spot that slopes gently upwards, ending in a series of shelves that will work as foot and hand holds. I swim to the surface again, struggling as I'm thrown back and forth like the little hermit crabs that the children keep as pets.

When my head is fully above water, I take a mouthful of sweet air, using it as fuel to haul myself up and out. That heavy feeling hits me hard, making me stumble. I fall back and crash into the sea, my head scraping the edge of another rock. I am lucky; a few inches back and I would've died or passed out, been crushed against the rocks and killed. I right myself quickly, hugging the wall of stone as I let the sense of vertigo pass. The only girl who is behind me is Kiara. I look at her frightened face and form a single question.

"Where?"

Her body rises with a swell and I'm forced to let go with one hand to grab one of hers, pulling her down beside me.

"They went to the beach, too," she says and in her eyes, I can see her questioning herself, questioning me. I vow to make sure she gets to land safely. If I can't save this one life then I'll never be able to change the lives of thousands.

"See that slope?" I ask, using my chin to point. "That's where we're headed. I'll go first. You stay here until you see my hand." Kiara nods and swallows a mouthful of seawater. I let go of the rock and kick off of it with my legs, hitting the sloping cliff in less time than it takes another wave to form. I grab the dips in the rock with my nails and pull myself out on my belly. My skin scrapes painfully along the crags, but this time, when the heavy feeling hits me, I don't fall. I lie there for a moment, waiting for my organs to settle, for my body to get used to gravity. I don't have the luxury of time, so I scoot forward and pull myself up into a sitting position, dipping my hand in the water and trying to see beyond the spray of sea foam that's crashing into my face.

Several moments pass and I feel nothing. Just as I'm

sure that Kiara is dead and that I'm going to have to go into the water to confirm it, I feel slippery fingers wrap around my hand. I pull her up as best I can, refusing to let go until she's got her chest on land.

Kiara gasps, hissing painfully as her stomach scrapes the rocks and leaves a trail of slippery red on the dark stone.

"I cannot breathe," she whispers and I stare down at her in sympathy. It is very likely that she has never been on land before, maybe never even broken the surface of the water with her head.

"It will pass," I promise, cringing as a wave crashes over the both of us, threatening to knock me back into the water. "Take deep breaths into your lungs and remember that the earth will only pull you down, not left or right. You are always fighting against down." Kiara is gasping now, her gills are fluttering gently, looking for oxygen. I bend down and help pull her up so that she's sitting on her knees. "Open your mouth and suck the air into your throat. Imagine your chest expanding with each breath. Then you can blow it out again. Can you try that for me?" She nods her head and, satisfied that she will not suffocate, I stand up and turn my attention to the cliff. We can climb on our hands and knees for quite a while. The hard part will not come until we are away from the waves, of which I am grateful. The ocean seems so angry here, so desperate to grab us and pull us back. I know we need to get away from it quickly.

"Are you ready, Kiara?" I ask, turning back to examine her. She doesn't look so good, but she nods anyway. "Just

The Feed

follow my lead," I say, glancing up at the moon. We have a good bit of light for our climb but not much time. I start forward in a standing position, falling to my knees only when the going becomes too slippery to keep my feet under me. There is seaweed and algae everywhere along with barnacles and bird droppings. I try to ignore it all, focusing only on putting one hand in front of the other, keeping my knees moving through the pain. When we reach the top, we will be bloody and torn. My plan to head for the lake becomes solidly cemented in my mind. The fresh water will help soothe our wounds. It is the only course of action that makes sense to me. Hopefully, I can convince Kiara to come along.

When I reach the part of the cliff that will require us to climb, I turn back and find Kiara is right on my heels. She is panting and crying, but her mouth is set in a stubborn line that tells me that despite her soft facade, she is exactly what Huntswomen are made of. Kiara is a very strong woman.

"We will have to climb here," I say and she nods, surprising me with her words.

"I spent all day scaling the palace walls for practice." She pauses. "Though this looks a bit harder." I nod. She is right, it is harder, but I will see to it that her effort has not been wasted. I look up at the cliff carefully, planning where I'll put each hand and foot, mentally climbing my way to the top.

"Remember," I shout above the whistling wind and the screaming waves. "The earth will pull you down, always down." I'm saying this for Kiara's benefit as well as my own. I have never before tried to do anything like this out of the water.

I reach up and grab the first bit of rock. The strain in my arms is so intense that I cry out, wishing I could stop, just throw myself back into the sea and go home. *You have made your decision, Natalie, you must stay strong.* I lift my leg up next, rise a few inches. The ache from my first coupling still hurts, but I use it instead as strength, trying to forget that I'm hanging from the edge of a cliff, just seconds from falling and crashing to my death. I imagine Yuri's handsome face and the way his arms held me so gently. His skin was so warm and soft and his touch so gentle yet strong. Even though I still consider it a mistake, it was not an unpleasant experience. It fuels me, keeps my muscles tight and my fingers tighter. *Climb, Natalie, climb.* I raise my arm and grasp the next bit of rock, pulling my foot along after.

The effort this is taking me is so intense that I can't look back and check for Kiara. I have to trust in her strength and in my own. If I fall, I will surely kill her as well, drag her down to the rocks with me.

When I reach the top, I have a moment of weakness. My legs give out and I'm left hanging from just my arms. In the sea, the ocean would lift me up, push me over the edge and beyond. On land, I must struggle to find a foot hold. It's either that or use the strength of my arms alone to pull myself over. I know that I don't have that in me, so I flail for awhile, startling when a hand wraps around my foot and guides it to an outcropping of rock. My Huntswoman has just saved my life.

The Feed

I use the strength in my leg for one last push and manage to rise up and over the cliff edge, rolling to my side in some scraggly plants. I don't rest though; I crawl to the edge and find Kiara struggling with the last few feet. I wait for her, my hand hanging over the wall, just in case she falls. When she reaches the top, I grab her shoulders and pull her up next to me where we both collapse in panting, bloody heaps.

I don't take as long as I want to rest, knowing that I have several hard choices ahead of me. At any moment, a human could come upon us and, depending on their gender, many decisions would have to be made. I still don't know if I'm going to be able to kill a man, much less eat him, or a woman either for that matter. Even if she tries to kill me.

"Are you still heading to the lake?" Kiara asks me, sitting up. Her decorative breast cups are gone, scraped away by the rocks. She is now as naked as me but with no weapons at her side. I finger my sister's necklace for strength and nod.

"It will soothe our wounds and make our eyes glow," I say, hoping that the texts are true. Even if they are not, it will be nice to get in the water. Even as we're sitting here, I can feel the dry sand and dirt getting between my scales. It's itchy and rather uncomfortable. I can't imagine spending a whole week out of water. If I am to find a man, it will have to be near the lake so that I can refresh myself.

Kiara is looking up at the trees with wonder in her eyes.

"It's like a kelp forest," she says, mouth agape. "But yet so different." I smile at her wonderment, hoping that at the very least, I can use the Feed to fuel my curiosity about the world.

"Come with me," I say, holding out a hand for her. She tears her eyes away from the trees and takes it, standing up on shaky legs. We hold onto each other for a moment, getting our feet steady. Already she is shaking her head.

"I think I'm going to go that way," she tells me, pointing in the opposite direction. There is a road there that I can see through slits in the trees. It's a thin stripe of gray cutting through the green and brown. Right now, it's empty, barren of cars and people, but come morning, that could change.

"Are you sure?" I ask, looking her right in the eyes. We've formed a bond over our short time together and I would hate to see her go, but it is her Feed, her decision. She nods and leans forward, pressing a kiss to my cheek.

"Thank you, Your Majesty," she says, taking a step back. "For all of your help, but I feel in my heart that this is the right decision." She quotes my words back to me and I smile. I reach down, untie my belt and hand it to her. She looks at the knife and back up at me.

"Take it," I say and without waiting for her response, I drape it around her neck. "Take it and you can return it to me when we get back to the city." I know that Yanori wants me to have that knife, that there's something special about it, but I'm willing to take a gamble. Kiara has shown me a lot of strength. She has also trusted me. These two things make me want to bet on her. *You will come home, I can feel it,* I think silently as I turn away and disappear into the darkness of the forest. She doesn't stop me and soon I hear her own footsteps fading away, drowned by the sound of the sea against the rocks.

◆ ◆ ◆

I follow the edge of the forest, making sure to stay under the cover of the dark branches. Thin leaves, like the spikes on a puffer fish, litter the ground and make my feet ache. When I stop and sit on a fallen log, I find that they are stuck in a number of cuts and scrapes on my soles. My belly is torn, too, bleeding from a number of wounds inflicted by the rocks. My hands didn't fare much better and I soon find that although I've experienced the pressure of gravity, I wasn't quite prepared for it. My whole body aches. Muscles that I didn't know I had are burning, begging for the soft cushion of the water. I spy a tiny, furred animal on a branch and after determining that it is not a threat, feel very sorry for it. Being on land for an extended period of time is much worse than I had expected. The sea cradles my body in her arms, holds it up and caresses my skin with her soft fingers. The land tugs it down, threatens to break it against its crusted surface. It dries my skin out and makes my scales flake off in coruscating piles that I mourn at with each and every step.

When I reach the edge of the lake, I'm overtaken by a wild frenzy. I run forward, crossing the grassy space between the trees and the water in an instant. If a human is nearby, they will not have had the chance to look too closely at me. Just as the sun peaks above the sky, I submerge myself in murky darkness, swim to the deepest part of the water and fall into a deep slumber.

Chapter Six

There is not a lot of activity on this lake during the day, so I sleep peacefully, curled in a tiny ball between two rocks. When I awake, there are small, silver fish sucking on my skin with gentle mouths. I shoo them away and sit up, stretching my arms above my head. I have slept so long that already, it is night again. It is very dark here with no *sispa* to light the depths. The moon provides only enough illumination that I can easily find my way to the surface. I would like a chance to further explore the lake bottom, but it will have to wait until morning.

I skim the top of the water with my head but don't come up for air, not yet. I'm still getting used to the feeling of the fresh water. It tastes good, but it doesn't hold me up like the sea does. I have to swim a lot harder to compensate for it. I practice a couple of spins and sharp turns, making sure that I'll be ready in case a human tries to chase me. The boats that rumble move very fast, maybe even faster than me. I'll need to know the geography of this lake, places to hide, spots where I can get out and run if needed. At least I'm not too far from the ocean. If worst comes to worst, then I can run back and be there within two hours.

I circle the lake for awhile, trying to judge its size. It isn't very big, almost like a puddle when compared with the vastness of the sea. When I'm satisfied that I've learned as much as I can in the darkness, I raise my eyes above the water and catch glimpses of light, little squares that sparkle in a circle around me. Windows. Those are windows and the square boxes are human houses. My heart thumps painfully in my chest, my belly growls, and my body heats with a need that I cannot deny. The Feed is fully upon me now and it won't be satisfied until I lie with a human man, until I eat him. *They are there, in those houses. You need only choose one and he will be yours.*

I duck below the water and swim away, sink back to the darkness of the lake bottom and sit in the sand until the silver fish come back. I wait until my heart slows down, until Neptune's magic subsides enough that I feel like I'm in complete control. Everything I do from now on must be carefully calculated and understood. Every decision I make must be mine and mine alone. If I do something in a frenzy, in the heat of the moment, then I will never forgive myself for it. The fish become comfortable with me, sucking and tasting my bare flesh. They stay away from the scales on my arms and legs, focusing instead on my soft belly skin and my breasts. I reach up slowly, careful not to alarm them by creating a current in the water. When I'm close enough, I snatch one; the rest scatter. I eat the loser, giving a prayer of thanks to the waters. I feel better with flesh in my mouth, more able to fight my bloodlust.

I rise to the surface again and spot a pair of humans. They're far enough away that I'm having trouble making out what they look like, but one of them is a woman. I can hear her laugh from here. She sounds strange, garbled, and I think maybe that she is intoxicated by something. At home, my mother sometimes collects pink and purple mushroom anemones that the servants crush up and feed her and her Huntswomen. It makes them laugh loudly and swim crooked; they sometimes mate with one another or chase fish they can never catch. I don't know what humans use for recreation, but as I get closer, I am almost certain this woman has had some of it. She stumbles, bright in her pink and white dress, and falls into a dark figure that I cannot make out, not yet. I swim closer.

They are walking down a wooden platform that skirts the water, turns into a small set of stairs and leads to a wooden platform with chairs and a tiny table. I wait for them to climb the stairs and pause at the door to the house. I don't intend to do anything with these people; even if the dark figure is a man, he is with a woman and if she lays her eyes on me, she will know what to do. She will try to kill me.

The Feed

Everything changes when I hear him laugh.

My body reacts instantly. *There,* it says. *There is a man. Go for him, take him, make him yours.* The Feed does not care which man I pick, what he looks like, if he's smart or kind or gentle. It will not matter in the long run. Half-*merighean*, sirens, almost always take after their mother. They are filled with the power of Neptune and bound to the sea by their blood. The land is just a little piece of their heart, a bit of magic that's stolen from the loins of a man. He is just a vessel, a catalyst for a greater purpose.

I'm swimming before I know what I'm doing, sluicing through the water like an otter, my arms held by my sides, legs kicking gently behind me. I'm silent, approaching my prey with rapid speed and singular intent. I'm nearly at the shore before I gain control of myself, kicking back, spinning into a somersault until I'm facing in the opposite direction. It takes me several moments to gain control of myself. When I do, I rise back to the surface, surprised by how close I am. The couple has gone inside and the lights are on. I hear clinking and they emerge with strange, clear glasses clutched in their hands. The man has a bottle clutched in his fingers. I can see them now; they are pale but not as pale as mine. On his knuckles are symbols that I cannot make out. I didn't know humans had markings on their skin. This intrigues me, so I wait, my eyes peeking above the water.

He laughs again and the dark sensuality of it draws me even closer. I want to breathe him in, take him, consume him. I swallow a mouthful of water to calm myself and settle down to wait. *Have I made my choice?* I wonder. *No, not yet. I'm just observing.*

"I can't fucking believe the nerve of that bitch," the woman says, flopping into one of the chairs. Her limbs are loose and rubbery, but the man's are not. He holds himself straight, his dark hair gleaming in the light from the window above him. They are speaking English. It takes me a moment to translate the words in my head. I have been trained to speak the language of the humans in this area. In the days of the ancients, when Muoru reigned over the sea, the Huntswomen were trained in twenty different languages, given the choice to travel to different countries. Now, we are reduced to one, just one. The people here primarily speak one language so the choice was easy. I understand all of the words except for the third and the last. Those are ones I have never heard before. The woman uses them a lot. "She stole three hundred dollars from my purse and another two hundred from that envelope I keep on the fridge for emergencies. It's like, fuck, can't I even leave shit in my own house? That bitch has a lot of nerve." She's also repeating herself a lot. There is no doubt in my mind now that she is intoxicated.

The man pours her a glass of amber liquid. It foams like the sea and sloshes over her breasts when she lifts it to her lips. Then he speaks and his voice is soft but confident; there's a strength there that I can identify with.

"You can never trust roommates," he says, and even though it is dark, I think I see a smile on his lips. There are markings along the side of his neck as well. They disappear under the shirt he is wearing and reappear on his

The Feed

right arm, snaking down to join the rush of color on his wrist. I want to get closer, try to make out what the symbols are, but I'm at the point where if I move forward anymore, I will have to stand. It will be too shallow to swim quietly.

"So you should fucking let me move in, Seth."

Seth.

His name is like a hiss. I mouth it quietly several times, letting water bubble lightly from my mouth.

"I can't talk about this right now, Jenna," he says, standing up and stepping off the wooden platform. I'm forced to move backward as he walks down the short stretch of grass and pauses at the edge of the water. He pulls something from his back pocket, a long, white stick. He lights this and blows smoke from his lips. I can't make out the color of his eyes; in the moonlight, they are shadowed and dark. I admire the curve of his cheekbones and the cut of his body. His legs are so strange to me that I stare at them for a long time. They are swathed in black fabric that tapers to a pair of foot coverings with laces.

"Not when you're drunk again," he whispers with a sigh. His words are not for Jenna to hear. They slide across the water of the lake like the wind.

"You are such a dick," she says, standing up and stumbling. A sharp noise, like a growl, breaks through the stillness of the air. I jerk back, making just the slightest splashing noise. Seth looks up and I see it the moment his eyes catch on mine.

Yes, the magic inside of me whispers. *Come to me.*

"There's a girl in the water!" he shouts, feeling a

compulsion to come to me but not knowing why. The growling continues, like a cough, that happens again and again. It sounds like an animal though I am not sure what kind. I have not been trained to identify most land creatures.

"So?" Jenna asks, leaning against the wall of the house. In her hand is a glowing square which she lifts to her ear.

"Are you okay?" he shouts, stumbling forward. The stick falls from his mouth and hits the water; its orange glow disappears as soon as it touches the lake, but Seth doesn't seem to notice. I drop my head below the surface and spin. I don't care about making noise. All I care about now is getting away from here. I kick my legs and feel them break the surface of the water. I splash into the depths of the lake, blowing the oxygen from my lungs in a rush of bubbles that break against my face as I dive. When I'm far enough away that I know Seth can't follow, I turn around and search for him. I heard him come in, swim after me for a short time. He can't look for long though. Humans are not good swimmers, I know. He'll have to give up and go back.

My heart is pounding furiously in my chest, chased by fear and an excitement that I didn't expect. It's the same feeling I had when I chose the rocks of Muoru, when I saw the images in that book. I look up at the surface, at the silvery light of the moon that's dancing there and I make another decision.

The man I will choose is Seth.

The Feed

◆ ◆ ◆

I don't wait as long as I should, too excited to sit still. I reason that I can most certainly swim faster than Seth or the bumbling Jenna. If I need to get away again, I can. I break the surface of the water carefully. That growling cough is still filling the night air. I ignore it, convinced that if whatever it is was after me, that I'd have seen it by now. I do a quick scan of the shore and find nothing.

Jenna and Seth are arguing on the wooden platform. He is wet from head to toe, black hair dripping into his face. His shirt is plastered against the smooth lines of his chest and belly. Jenna has that glowing square in her hand again.

"You're fucking delusional if you think I'm gonna stick around where I'm not wanted," she says and then, switching her tone to something more pleasant, continues with, "Yeah, Ang, is that you? Can you pick me up at Seth's? Yeah. Right now. Thanks." She drops the glowing square to her side and it disappears into a brown satchel that she's draped around her neck.

"That's not it at all, Jenna," Seth says, trying to put a hand on her shoulder. I wonder briefly if she is his mate. If so, then what I'm about to do could very well tear them apart forever. I still haven't yet decided what I'm going to do with Seth, if I'll sleep with him, if I'll kill him, eat him.

But my very presence will change him, that I do know. Jenna jerks away from him and turns around, putting her back to Seth's soggy form.

"When you're ready to rent a moving truck, call me. Until then, I don't want to see or hear from you ever a-fucking-gain." She pauses and casts a poisonous glance over her shoulder, blonde hair flying around her face like a *merighean* male. "And shut that damn dog up, would you?" Jenna stomps away, back the way they came and starts up another set of stairs that are built into the hillside. These lead up to a road with a metal railing. Seth watches her go and sit on the edge of that railing. He doesn't move until a car pulls up, lights bright against the darkness of the sky. Jenna gets into it and it screeches away, wheels burning against the gray of the road.

I am glad that she has left. Otherwise, what I'm about to do would be that much harder. I would've had to sneak up on Seth without her knowledge, draw him away into the trees. Now, it seems, he is the only one here, the only person on this quiet stretch of beach, and if her words were true, then she will not be back for awhile. It is of no matter anyway, once Seth sees me, fully connects with me, he will be able to think of nothing else.

I take a deep breath, let my lungs fill with air and start to swim forward.

Seth sighs and runs a hand through his hair. He peels off his shirt and tosses it over one of the chairs where it gets caught and hangs, dripping water onto the wooden platform. When he goes inside, I swim faster, wanting to catch up with him before he closes the door. Luckily for me, he comes back outside right away. Around his neck is a fluffy pink cloth with lots of tiny fibers. He uses this to rub at his hair. He's drying himself off, I realize.

Seth sits down in one of the chairs and grabs the glass of amber liquid. He stares at this for a long time before standing up and pouring it into the grass. Afterward, he goes back for the bottle and does the same thing. I pause again. Once I move forward, I will have to stand up, I will have to commit. Seth has seen my eyes, but he is not hooked. Once he is, he will follow me to the ends of the earth. I need to be careful.

After he pours the bottle out, he sits on the edge of the wooden platform next to it and starts to mumble to himself. I can't make out his words, but I take this opportunity to examine his chest. He is hairless here which surprises and pleases me. The men I saw on the beach, and in the old texts, had dark, curling hairs. Instead, Seth has more markings. They slide down his chest on either side, framing a central symbol that I still cannot make out. On his lower belly, more markings disappear into his pants. I find these so fascinating that I start to stand without realizing it.

Seth looks up at the sound and freezes.

Water slides from my skin and drips back into the lake. My hair is curling around my breasts, dark and soft, lit by the silver glow of the moon. Yanori's necklace clinks gently as I take my first step, rising from the water like a goddess from the sea.

Seth's mouth opens, closes. I feel the magic seep from my skin, flow across the water between us and slide over his body. He shivers and I know as I catch a glimmer in his eyes that he is now mine.

He can't sit still any longer; he rises to his feet and stumbles towards me, crashing through the water clumsily. The growling bark, that like of a seal, fills the air again. When Seth finally reaches me, I am standing knee-deep in the lake. His hands hover over my skin, warm and curious and his face flickers with confusion.

"I ..." He pauses and takes the cloth from his neck, wrapping it around my shoulders gently. His fingers accidentally brush my skin. I have to hold back a moan. The Feed is begging me to push him down, to take him now. "I knew I saw a girl," he says. "I thought you were drowning." I stare into his eyes, which are brown as I'd expected, but they're not muddy at all. In fact, they are quite pretty, like an otter's fur. I reach up, touch the soft skin on the side of his face. It takes me a moment to find my English words.

"I cannot drown," I say, pointing at the gills on the side of my neck. "Not easily." Seth continues to stare at me, enthralled by magic. I let my eyes slide down, land on the symbol in the center of his chest. What I see there chokes me, makes me stumble away from him, drop the cloth from my neck into the water where it floats between us briefly before sinking to the sand.

In the center of his chest is a drawing that I recognize from the ancient tomes. It is a simplified outline of the great worm, Muoru, with his sharp beak, curved body and the single fin that graces the top of his head.

"Where did you get this?" I ask him, pointing with a

single turquoise nail. When he steps forward, I drop my hand quickly. If Seth pierces himself with one of my nails, then he will die a horrible death. He pauses, touching a hand to his chest. It takes him a moment to work through his fascination with me and answer the question.

"I got it from my tattoo guy," he says, blinking his eyes furiously, like he's trying to wake up from a spell. But my magic cannot be overcome so easily. I don't understand his answer.

"Tattoo?" I ask, searching my mind for that English word. I don't know it. "What is a tattoo?" Seth moves towards me again and I let him. His fingers brush my arms and I can't help but sigh with pleasure.

"It's a mark," he says, pointing to his arms, his neck. "They take a needle and insert pigment into your skin to get the shape you want. This is my own design," he adds proudly, tilting his head sideways and gazing into my eyes. I look away.

"You drew this?" I ask and from the corner of my eye, I see him nod.

"I did." I nibble my lip but can't think what this may mean. Certainly there's some significance, but it will have to wait. I will probe Seth further when his mind clears a bit. As of right now, he's so deeply under my thrall that I come to another important decision. At least for now, I will not sleep with him. I cannot say what will happen during the rest of my week here, but I know that there is no way I can bring myself to couple with someone whose mind is somewhere else. "Your stomach," he says and his hand comes out again, brushes across the wounds of my belly. The water did not heal them as the texts have mentioned and though I cannot see my own eyes, I can only guess that they are not glowing. "God, uh," he pauses and struggles to find words again. "What's your name?" I smile at him, wrap my hand around one his, being very careful to keep my nails gentle on his skin.

"Natalie," I say. "My name is Natalie."

"Welcome, Natalie," he says and without realizing exactly what he's doing or why he's doing it, Seth takes my hand and leads me inside.

Chapter Seven

Seth's house is small but cozy and it's nothing like I've ever seen under the sea; my bedroom is the closest thing to it. Walls surround me on every side, above, and below. The only passages to the outside world are the front door and a back door where the barking sound is coming from. There are windows, but they are covered in glass. I touch them reverently as I walk around, admiring paintings and furniture carved from wood that glimmers in the soft, yellow lights that radiate from the ceiling.

The Feed

Seth dogs my every step, tripping over himself to keep up with me. This effect will diminish slightly over time if I do not touch him. During the Feed, the intent is for the Huntswomen to couple constantly, keeping their human enthralled so deeply that when the time for his death comes, he begs for it, just to have another moment in his lover's arms. I still don't know what I'm going to do with Seth, but if the symbol of Muoru on his chest is a sign, then I must be able to speak with him when he's more coherent.

"What is that noise?" I ask, pointing at the back door. It is loud and threatening and it's keeping me on edge. If I'm going to stay here then I must find out what it is. Seth thinks long and hard, rubbing at the side of his head. Finally, he answers me in a dreamy voice.

"That's my dog, Sarah," he says, trying to reach out and touch my neck. I duck away from him and move to the curtain that covers the upper portion of the door. A hairy face leaps up at me, wet nose smashing against the glass. My first thought is: *seal.* But then I see floppy ears covered in black fur. The creature is hopping now on strong back legs that propel it higher than Seth's head. When it opens its muzzle, out comes the growling cough noise I have been hearing. "Sarah," Seth says, sounding exasperated. He smiles apologetically at me and walks into the kitchen, opening a small window above a row of counters. Sarah pauses with her feet on the glass, blunt claws scratching at a spot near my face and tilts her head, muzzle tight and eyes keen. Then she barks again. "Sarah, shut up," Seth says, grabbing a bag from the counter and extracting something which he then tosses out the window. Sarah disappears with a speed that is frightening, loping across the wooden platform that lines the back of the house. Once she's got it in her mouth, she retreats to the fence that edges Seth's property and lies down, silent while she eats.

"Is she dangerous?" I ask as I drop the curtain and move away, into a room with cushioned furniture and electronic equipment that I am having trouble identifying. Each year, after the Feed, the Huntswomen bring back new knowledge of the world. The only trouble with this is, as busy as we are expected to be, there's never much to record. So I know what a car and a television and a refrigerator are, but I can't identify the other, smaller pieces that are stacked on the shelving units against the wall. They look like stereos, but I can't be sure. I decide not to ask Seth anymore questions until he answers my previous one.

"Sarah?" he says, still sounding faraway and confused. "Oh, God, no." He laughs and my skin shivers with delight. I continue my tour into Seth's bedroom, pausing next to his rumpled bed which sits on the floor amongst piles of discarded clothes. I can't wait to try it. "Hey," he says, coming up behind me and laying a hand on my shoulder. I move away from him before my body can react. Denying the Feed is not easy. "Can I take a look at those cuts for you? I've got a first aid in the bathroom." I nod and he moves away reluctantly.

I take this moment to compose myself.

I have done it. I have joined the Feed and survived. I

have found my mate. Why I have done it and what I am going to do now are still questions that plague me, but Yanori has told me to forge my own destiny. I must make decisions here that will accomplish that end, that will set the standards for our people. Do I follow tradition or break it?

◆ ◆ ◆

Seth tends my wounds gently, with a care and an attention to detail that surprises me.

"Are you a doctor?" I ask him and am surprised when he laughs.

"Just a paramedic," he says and there's a strain in his voice that I can't identify. He pauses and looks up at me; the clarity in his eyes fades a little as he tries to connect what he would normally do with what the magic is making him do. "What do you do, Natalie?" he asks. I sit there on the edge of his bed for a moment trying to come up with an answer that will satisfy. *What do I do?* I wonder. The answer is, quite sadly, nothing. Until the Feed, the Huntswomen do nothing but prepare for it.

"All of my life," I say, stopping his hand when it would wander too far down my belly. "I have been training to come here, to meet you, to kill you." Seth wrinkles his brow at me.

"Why?" he asks, tucking his medical supplies away

into a black case.

"To return a bit of the earth into the sea," I say slowly, but I don't mean any of it. Surely, this can't be right. Surely, somehow, between Neptune's reign and my mother's, the message has been lost. In my head, I can't justify the waste of life – that of the humans or the Huntswomen. For we are lost. We spend our entire lives waiting to come here and then waste the rest of it trying to regain what was lost so long ago that nobody but Tejean and her friends remember it. My head spins and makes my stomach clench tightly.

"I'm going to die?" Seth asks, falling back from his crouch so that he's sitting on the floor. This whole time, I'm watching him, trying to absorb his gestures so that I might be more comfortable here. Everything is different, the way I must hold my arms, the pressure in my legs, the tingle of the air against my skin. I shake my head.

"I don't know," I say. He rubs a hand over his face in an anxious gesture. I want to be honest with him though I can't say why. Maybe it's even crueler to do so? I choose not to mention the fact that I must also consider whether or not I will eat him. "Do not worry about it," I tell him, feeling sly but knowing that the magic will ensure that he takes my words as an order, not just as a turn of phrase. If he remembers this conversation when he is more coherent, I will deal with it then.

Seth shakes his head and although his face is not quite as droopy or as lovestruck as it was before, he calms down.

"Hey Natalie," he says as his eyes roam my body,

taking in my breasts, my belly, the soft hair between my legs. "I should probably get you a shirt or something to wear. You don't want all of the ointment to rub off yet." Seth stands up and moves to a dresser that's much finer than my mother's. The drawers slide easily, the wood still smooth and planed. Salt water hasn't ravaged it and swollen it beyond use. In some of the old texts, the authors make mention of furniture carved from stone, from coral, from bone. None of it exists in our city as I know it nor have I ever seen any in the abandoned city that lies closest to ours. The texts have lied about many things, about humans being pale, spineless creatures, about freshwater making the eyes glow. I would not have been surprised to find that this, too, is a lie.

Seth digs around in this drawer for awhile before extracting a small, white dress with thin straps and lace on the edges. It is very fine and simple, much more beautiful than anything I have seen before. There are few enough clothes at home to compare it to, but I am still very impressed.

"May I wear that?" I ask, feeling excited at the prospect. I've always wondered what it might be like to feel dry cloth slide across my skin. Already, I've run my hands across Seth's blankets, fantasized about their touch. Seth shakes his head.

"This is Jenna's," he says and the corner of his lip turns up a bit. "You don't want to wear this." Seth tosses it aside where it joins the piles of clothing already strewn across the floor.

"Is she your mate?" I ask, considering my choice of

words carefully. "Or your wife?"

Seth reaches into the drawer and extracts a navy blue shirt which he tosses to me. The fabric is soft and in the corner, there is a white star whose center holds a golden snake wrapped around a pole. *Lampica County EMT* it says. I put it on am strangely comforted by the swathes of warm fabric. Like the sea, it drapes my body and cups me.

"She was my girlfriend," Seth says with a sigh, extracting a shirt for himself and slipping it over the smooth lines of his chest. I am disappointed to see him dressed, but I know it's for the best. The less skin he is showing, the less tempted I will be. "But I think we just broke up."

"Good," I say, sighing softly. No bubbles escape my lips, just air that disappears with no indication that it has even gone. "This would be more difficult if you had a mate. It could even be deadly." Seth turns around and leans on his dresser, the muscles in his arms clenching slightly. He is such a colorful work of art; later, I will have to examine his body carefully and see if I can identify any more of his markings. The one of Muoru may just be a coincidence. I can't be certain until I check more carefully.

"How old are you?" Seth asks, surprising me. It's a strange question, one that I've never been asked before. Everyone in the city knows my age, my birthday.

"Yesterday, I turned sixteen," I say, pausing. "And you?" Seth cringes just a bit and stands up. He's nervous again though I can't say why. Seth paces to the window and picks up a glowing square like the one that Jenna had.

The Feed

It's attached to the wall with a black cord; he unplugs it and touches the screen with his finger. I repeat my question. "Seth, how old are you?" I don't know why I want to know this, but since he is acting so strangely, I feel that I must find out.

"Twenty-six," is all he says and seems oddly disturbed by this. It makes no difference to me, but I can see that he's quite agitated. I rise to my feet and watch as his eyes sweep over and down my body, flicking away just as quickly. "What the hell is wrong with me?" he asks and I can tell that he isn't talking to me, but to himself. Maybe my influence is wearing off more quickly than I'd thought. I don't have any information to tell me exactly how this works. As far as I know, no Huntswoman has ever tried to release a male from her spell. "You're just a kid. Oh, God, you're just a kid." This statement bothers me and I purse my purple lips in anger.

"I'm a woman," I say, thinking of the journey I have just overcome, feeling the ache between my legs pulse in response. "In every sense of the word," I continue, righteous anger swimming through my veins. I look up into Seth's eyes with my green ones. He pauses, fingers slowing their desperate race across the glowing square that he's clutching with a nervous hand. "The fate of an entire people rests on my shoulders. I am heir to a dying throne, daughter of a dead city. I have made hard choices to get this far and you will not diminish them by calling me a child." I take a step forward and grab the item from Seth's hand. I set it down on the windowsill and touch his cheeks gently with my nails, scraping them across his skin carefully. My dual hungers have risen with my anger and I have to take a deep, cleansing breath to fight the desires that are burning in my belly. "Do you understand, Seth?" I ask him, making sure to hold his gaze with my own.

His eyes flutter closed and from his mouth falls a moan of pleasure that tickles across my skin in gentle waves, begging for me, pleading with me to take him. I release him quickly and move away, out of the bedroom and into the kitchen. If I cannot satisfy my hungers, I must hold them off somehow. I know the black box that stands in the corner holds food, but when I open it, I am confused at the array of choices. I recognize nothing.

"Are you hungry?" he asks from behind me, slightly less coherent than before, but the shame is gone from his voice. I nod and cringe when Sarah begins to bark again. Without thinking, Seth moves to the back door and opens it.

The black and white creature trots in and romps over to me. I back up against the counter and ready my muscles; if I need to fight, to kill it, then I can do so in seconds. The venom in my veins can still a sea lion in minutes. This dog is a tenth their size. Instead of attacking me however, Sarah sniffs at the spot between my legs and then licks my bare thigh. Seth shoos her away and she trots to a dish in the corner, slurping up water with messy flicks of her tongue.

"Sorry about that," Seth says as he opens cabinets and digs through their contents. "I usually let her in before it gets dark, but Jenna really hates her, so I put her outside before I left ... " Here he pauses again and fights against whatever thoughts are making him so conflicted. "She usually only barks when she's been out for a long time. She should calm down now." Seth reaches over and grabs the plastic bag that he used to feed Sarah before. "If you want to, you can give her one of these," he says and then goes back to his cabinet search. I lift the bag up to my face and examine the brown triangles inside. Sarah sees me holding them and trots over to me, sitting down and wagging her feathered tail in wide sweeps across the floor.

"What are they?" I ask as Seth sighs and goes to the refrigerator.

"I don't have much," he says. "We may have to go out or call in." He stops digging through the plastic containers and sifts through the fog in his mind to answer my question. "They're pig ears," he says with a smile. I shake the bag and examine the bits of dried flesh. I can picture a pig in my mind, pink and fat with a strange round nose, a common source of food. I look down at the dog, who is waiting so patiently that I also have trouble holding back a smile. I open the bag and hand one of the smelly things to Sarah who takes it in her wide mouth gently, smearing my fingers with spittle. She then turns and disappears into the living room, tail still wagging in thanks. "I think she likes you," Seth says, shutting the door to the refrigerator and removing a piece of paper from its front. He glances over his shoulder and smiles at me again, brown eyes twinkling softly.

"And I think I like her," I say back to him, surprising myself. The dog is an interesting twist; I had not expected to meet someone like her. I touch the sides of my face and imagine that I must have that same look of wonderment in my eyes that Kiara had when she gazed up at the sweeping branches of the trees. If nothing else, the Feed will certainly be educational. I am filled with a sudden energy and at once, a peacefulness that tells me I have made the right decision. It may just be my heart and my curiosity that are speaking to me, but they are what makes me who I am and so I respect their decision.

"It's almost two, so there's not much that's open around here." Seth looks down at the piece of paper for a moment. "This Chinese place delivers twenty-four seven, or we could go down to Jack's though Jenna might still be there." Seth shakes his head and glances up at me sharply. "But then, you're not old enough to get into a bar ... " He trails off and I whisper softly to him.

"I cannot go out," I say. It is sad but true. I lift my hands up and spread my fingers, looking past the cuts and scrapes and at the thin webbing that starts at my knuckles and connects to the base of my hand. My scales begin there, too, fading gently into the smooth skin that begins just below my wrist. They are dry and flaky; soon I will need to submerge myself in water or suffer with the itch and the mild pain that will come. I could never pass as human, I know this, but I would like to see the world. There must be so much out there that I have never heard of, customs, animals, foods. I sigh and drop my hand to my side. "We must stay here for the entire week." Seth nods like he understands this, but I'm not sure that he does.

"Let me get my phone then. I'll call our order in. What do you want?" He walks past me and into his room, coming back with the glowing square from his windowsill. It doesn't look like the phones that the older Huntswomen have drawn for us. But I am no fool; humans change faster than the tide. I accept his words and settle back to watch, my elbows on the counter, propping me up like Seth propped himself up on the dresser in his room. It isn't a very comfortable position and I soon stand up, rubbing at my elbows.

"What are the choices?" I ask as Seth hands me the piece of paper. It is only when his knuckles brush mine that I see it. I grab his hand suddenly and pull it to me, ignoring his gasp and the rush of pleasure that settles in my stomach. The paper floats to the floor, drifting like a shell in the sea. I take several deep breaths of air, all of them sweet, comforting, swelling my lungs with oxygen. I can't even appreciate this because I'm so caught up in what I see. The symbols on his hand are letters from my language, the language of the *merighean*. "Seth," I begin, trying to keep my voice calm. "Where did you learn this language?" Seth pulls his hand away from me and turns it around, blinking slowly. He stares at the black lettering for a moment and then squeezes both of his hands into gentle fists, putting them together, and holding them out so that I can see the word that spans both his hands.

In the language of the mer, written across Seth's skin like a prophecy, is my name.

The letters across his skin say Natalie.

Chapter Eight

I release Seth's hands and take a step away from him. His eyes are dark and his hands are trembling.

"Language?" he asks and I can see from his face that he isn't sure what I'm talking about. "This isn't a language. I saw these images in a dream." I turn my head away and close my eyes. I wish desperately for Yanori; she would know what to do, what this means. I haven't a clue what to do with this knowledge. "I drew them and I … " Seth falters. "Do you still want to order Chinese food?" I look back at him sharply. I wish I could reach into his mind, wipe away the fog and have an intelligent conversation. But intelligent conversations are not what Neptune had in mind when he filled my ancestors with the magic of the Feed.

"Across your knuckles," I say, trying to bring him back to the current conversation. "You have my name written in the language of my people, the *merighean*. It is one of two languages, one that is only learned and read by the Huntswomen. It is called *Amarana,* named for the great city, the last one still standing." I reach out and point at his hands, careful not to touch him. It's so easy to forget that, but if I don't stop then he'll remain this way for the entire week and I will be left with a mystery that I cannot solve. Seth holds up his hands and looks at them for a moment.

"Natalie is just seven letters long," he tells me. "This is eight." Even he looks perplexed by this. I sigh again and fight the urge to flee, to run from the door and jump in the lake. Maybe a good swim would clear my head. This man, this Seth, I'm starting to believe that he was not just a random choice, found by accident, taken by coincidence. I will test this theory tomorrow, but for now, I just shake my head.

"*Amarana* is written in sounds, not letters. You have the symbols for *na, ta,* and *lee*. After each one is a spacer mark, used to separate the syllables when using a more complex hand. The last two ... " Again, I find myself fighting the urge to touch him. "The last two marks denote my status as heir and as a Huntswoman. Seth," I say, my voice cracking just the slightest. I am thirsty and hungry and tired, in desperate need of a soak. But this, I cannot just leave. "This is no coincidence," I continue, more for myself than for him; Seth is barely coherent enough to remember the flow of conversation, let alone understand that there is something magical happening here that even I do not fully comprehend. "You have my name, written in the royal hand, with my marks, Seth. These words, this dream, it was about me."

"I don't remember it," he says, surprising me, opening his hands and staring at his palms. "All I remembered were these designs. I drew them out and took them in; I got them done the same day." He stops and looks up at me. We stare into one another's eyes, both of us struggling to understand what is happening.

Sarah's bark breaks our concentration as she comes trotting into the kitchen, drooling profusely and smiling with her teeth. Seth tears his eyes away from me and looks down at his dog, scratching her gently behind the ears. His focus is lost and he reverts back to our previous conversation, much to my disappointment.

"I could get the orange chicken and some fried rice. Jenna always orders the sushi platter which I think is weird because it's a Chinese restaurant … " I brush his arm as I approach the front door. There is no choice for me now; I have to get in the water or I will go mad. Seth tries to follow me out. "Where are you going?" he asks, sounding downtrodden and depressed. "Please don't leave, Natalie."

"I'm not leaving, Seth," I say as gently as possible. I strip the shirt from my skin and lay it over the wet one that Seth was wearing earlier. "Order your food and I will return shortly." With that, I move forward down the grassy shore with Sarah at my heels. She joins me in the water for a moment before I dive and leave her and her strange master behind.

◆ ◆ ◆

I have lied to Seth.

I do not return that night, instead choosing to sleep

curled at the bottom of the lake. The pressure of the water soothes me and although it does not have magical properties, the wounds on my hands, knees, and feet feel much better here than they do on land. Before I fell asleep, I circled the lake and tried to clear my head, swooping down on the silver fish with an open mouth, scooping them up between my teeth and eating them as I spun and twirled through the darkness. I tried and failed to put together what I had learned, clutching Yanori's necklace and wishing for clarity. If there was any way that I could go back and see her, I would. But if I return to the city early and am caught, I will be tortured or killed by my mother, sent to Imenea for treason. If I am not caught, then I will have wasted several days of my time with Seth. As things are going, I know that I am going to need every possible second with him. I cannot go back without an understanding of the mark on his chest or the name on his hands.

I rise early, just as the sun peaks into the sky and circle the lake with my eyes above water. This time, I am looking for a man, any man. When I first heard and saw Seth, I was attracted to him. I believed this to be solely the result of the Feed's desires, but I may be wrong.

It doesn't take me long to find a man in a pair of gray pants and a loose gray shirt that is cut with sharp lines and layered over more white fabric. He wears shiny brown shoes and carries a matching satchel. As I watch him, he points something at a silver car which flashes and beeps. I put my fingers to my lips and whistle.

The man, who is just as young and attractive as Seth,

turns to face the lake. I glance around quickly, checking to make sure that we are alone, then I raise my head from the water just enough that he can get a good look at me but not so much that he will be entirely consumed. When he spots me, his brown eyes widen and he calls out. I ignore him, waiting for my body to catch up, to recognize the prey that's right in front of it. I feel it there, a burning in my belly, in my loins. There's that bloodlust and that heat for sex, but it is not the same attraction that I felt for Seth. Something there is different. It is almost as if Seth's presence draws me as mine draws him. With this new man, there is just that desire, that primal want.

When he begins to shout, to swing his satchel around, I pull back, swim to the bottom of the lake and wait. After an appropriate amount of time passes, I climb from the water and rush to Seth's door, trying as best I can to remain out of the sight of other humans. He has left it unlocked for me, so I enter without hesitation, making sure to twist the lock into place behind me. I cannot risk being walked in on.

Seth is waiting for me, sitting slumped on the cushioned seat in his living room.

As I walk around him, I'm careful not to touch him, but I do step into his line of sight, show him the full length of my body and the green of my eyes. I want him coherent, but I can't have him distancing himself from me. Once he starts to do that, he will begin to question what a girl with scales is doing in his house. I cannot have that happen.

He rises to his feet immediately, stepping forward and reaching a hand out for me. I step back and use a long, squat table to keep space between us.

"I was really worried," he says, but his face tells me he doesn't know why that is.

"I needed to think for awhile, as did you," I say, looking around for Sarah. When I don't see her, I move to the back door and adjust the curtain. Her black and white face is already lapping at the glass with a long, pink tongue. She is a good distraction, something to keep Seth from touching me. I smile at her with gentle eyes. I have been here for the lesser part of a night and already, the dog has touched me. I have always wished for a pet, but there was nothing under the sea like this. The closest thing I had found were the otters. I reach down and open the door, let her in. Sarah immediately jumps on my chest, knocks me back into Seth who catches me with expert hands.

"Sarah, on your pillow," he snaps, pointing at a round bed in the corner of the room. Sarah slinks off to it, head down but tail wagging. Still, the damage has been done. I jerk away from Seth, stumble to the back door and open it, closing it right in his face. My body is humming with his touch, with the feel of his warmth against my back. The ache between my legs suddenly becomes very fierce and I can't help but wonder if having sex with Yuri has awakened something in me or if it is just the Feed. Or just Seth.

I hold the knob between my fingers, try to keep Seth from opening it. He tries only once and then gives up, moving the curtain so that he can see me through Sarah's muddy, slobbery footprints.

"Natalie?" he asks and his voice is dreamy, full of imagined love and pretend lust. If Seth were to see me, if any man were to see me for that matter, as I am, without the veil of magic, most likely they would be disgusted. They may even find me repulsive, try to kill me like the women always do. I let go of the door and drop my face to my hands. This is all much harder than I thought. There are elements that I had not expected and those that I had, such as the pull of the Feed, are much harder to resist than I had planned.

The thing that snaps me out of my trance is a female voice calling from the other side of the fence.

"Seth, baby?" It is Jenna, Seth's girlfriend. I waste no time in opening the back door and reentering the house. This is a situation I have been trained for, one that the instructors have drilled into us again and again and again.

"Some of you may find males that already have mates; these are the most dangerous, but you can still accomplish your goals by following these simple steps."

"Seth," I say, trying to draw his attention away from Jenna. It doesn't take much; he is just happy that I have come back. My touch is still lingering in his face, in his trembling arms, in his shaking hands that bear the marks of my name. I am standing in the spot where the kitchen connects with the living room. It is not a safe place to be; after knocking briefly, Jenna's face soon looms up in the window above the sink. I push Seth back, frustrated that I'm going to be forced to touch him to keep him occupied. This will set us back several hours. "Let's sit down, shall we?" I ask, careful to keep my voice low. I could

The Feed

convince him to tell her to go away, that he never wants to see her again, but I can't bring myself to do it. If he loves her, or she loves him, then I would not forgive myself for tearing them apart.

"Should I get the door?" he asks me and I shake my head, sitting down on his lap. The tension in my skin doubles and I feel an answering response from Seth's body. I adjust myself so that I'm nowhere near the bump in his pants and touch the sides of his face, gently, carefully.

"You're not home so you should be quiet," I say, looking into his brown eyes. I take this moment to touch his hair, run my fingers through it. Seth shivers and moans, quite loudly.

"Baby? Open the door, let me in. It's freezing out here." Jenna knocks more furiously now, slams her hand into the wood. I ignore her, focusing on the soft, silky strands that glide through my fingers like the bird feathers I collect from the otter's rock. It's so smooth, almost mesmerizing, I find myself falling into the Feed's hands like a fish in a net. *I must swim away.*

I shake my head and stand up, careful to keep Seth's eyes fully locked on mine.

"That's it, Seth. I have fucking had it. I'm coming in." I hear the sound of metal on metal and realize that Jenna has a key. I panic briefly before regaining control of myself. I have to act fast. I do the only thing I can think to do. I lean forward, wrap my fingers in Seth's dark hair and kiss his lips hard. My tongue slides across his, moves around the heat of his mouth as he moans against me, reaching his hands up for my hips. I let him touch me briefly before pulling away, spinning around the edge of the wall that separates the living room and kitchen. I have to time it just right; as the front door slams shut and Jenna passes by on the opposite side, I step back and hide myself across from the refrigerator.

Sarah's barking helps hide any sounds I might make.

"Goddamn it, Seth," Jenna growls as I peek around the corner, watch as she kicks off her white heels and uses her purse to shoo Sarah away. "This dog is too damned big to just hang out in here." Seth is blinking furiously, trying to break from the spell I've just cast over him. Jenna looks down at Seth's lap and then up at his face. "What the hell were you doing in here? Masturbating? Too busy to answer the door for your own girlfriend?" Seth responds to her with a lot more clarity than I had expected.

"I've asked you time and time again not to use that key," Seth says, anger rising with each word that he speaks. He stands up from the couch and brushes at his pants like he isn't quite sure what happened. I close my eyes briefly, just to ground myself, and pray to Neptune that Seth does not mention me. If I have to, I can run to the lake and hide, but I'd rather not. It may take a long time to get him alone again.

"So, what? Am I supposed to stand outside on the porch for an hour while you finish whatever it is that's so fucking important that you can't get to the door?" Seth is shaking his head, grabbing Sarah gently by the collar and pulling her towards the back door. She's started barking again and I think, though I'm not sure, that she doesn't like

The Feed

Jenna.

"This isn't your house, Jenna. That key is for emergencies only. You can't just come and go as you – " Seth has opened the door but has yet to let go of Sarah. They've both spotted me in the kitchen. Sarah licks her lips and starts to tug against Seth's hand. He looks at me for a single second that seems to stretch out into eternity. I still my breath, wait for a response. Seth shakes his head. "You can't just come and go as you please. It isn't right." He pushes the dog out the door and closes it, standing so that he's blocking the pathway into the kitchen. "And if I can recall correctly, you're the one that said you never wanted to see or hear from me again." I hear Jenna's footsteps moving across the floor towards Seth. His eyes flicker back to me briefly and he steps forward, keeping her far enough away that I know she won't be able to see me.

"I'm sorry, baby," she says and the tone of her voice changes so substantially that I risk everything by peeking around the edge of the wall to see her. She has her arms around Seth's neck and is trying to kiss his face. He turns his head away from her and puts his hands on her hips, trying to move her back. "You know how I am when I get wasted," she chuckles at this. "You remember, right? We used to have the biggest fights, but we'd always make up the next morning, didn't we, baby?" Seth is already shaking his head. He steps away from her and sighs deeply. I can see that whatever is going on between them has been brewing for awhile. I feel a bit better knowing that the anger I hear in Seth's voice was not placed there by me.

"That's another thing, Jenna. I've asked you so many times to stop, or at least try to stop. I've asked you not to drink around me, not to bring alcohol over here and you do not listen." Seth slaps the back of his hand against his palm as he says the last three words. "If you really cared about me, you'd make an effort. After awhile, I just stopped asking; I gave in. Well, I'm not asking anymore. We're done, Jenna. I'm sorry, but I just can't do it."

Jenna's big, blue eyes fill with tears.

"No, Seth," she says and starts to cry. Seth glances over his shoulder and meets my eyes. I don't hold his gaze, instead choosing to move forward and go for the front door. I shouldn't be here for this. When he hears me open it however, things take a turn for the worse.

"Natalie?" he asks, moving forward. I pause, surprised, and see him come around the corner, eyes worried and just a bit cloudy. "Please, don't go," he begs, the full force of my kiss shining in his eyes.

"Natalie?" I hear Jenna say, sniffling. I grab the doorknob and start to pull it open, only to be stopped by Seth. He pushes his shoulder against the wood and closes it with the weight of his body, drawing the slippery metal from my hand.

"You can't leave yet; I had another dream about you." I move back, planning to run across the kitchen and escape through the back door. Events are spiraling out of control around me. *This is dangerous, very dangerous. I must stay in control.*

I turn around and come face to face with Jenna, and in

her hand is a knife.

Chapter Nine

Jenna does not hesitate.

Just as Seth cannot control his emotions or his thoughts when he's around me, neither can she. She charges me with the knife, plucked right from the block of wood on Seth's counter. I duck under his arm and scrabble down the short bit of hall, turning left into the living room. Jenna chases after me, only to be stopped by Seth as he slams her into the wall, one hand wrapped around her wrist.

"What the fuck are you doing?" he asks, displaying an unbelievable amount of clarity. "Jenna, come on." But Jenna isn't thinking clearly. She isn't just a jealous girlfriend; she's a woman whose mind is as warped by the sight of me as Seth's is, only in a different way. She will fight to protect her species with all the power she can muster. Women are true warriors, protectors of humanity. The day the humans forgot this fact, they signed the declaration that would become their downfall. Maybe there is more to all of this than just my people. The *merighean* may not be the only ones that need saving.

"Monster," she screams, swinging the knife in wild arcs. She is so frenzied and her energy is so misplaced that it takes Seth little effort to hold her down. "I'll kill you," she says, tears stinging her eyes and running down her cheeks. "He's mine; I'll kill you." I reach for the back door and watch Seth's eyes widen. He's so afraid that I'll leave that he almost loses Jenna. She scrambles forward as he drops his grip on her arms and switches to her waist, wrapping his arms around her as if in an embrace. "Freak! Monster!" she continues to shout.

"Don't leave," Seth moans as I pull open the door. "Please don't go." I want to stay, but Jenna's wild eyes and harsh shouts convince me otherwise. I say nothing that Jenna can use to remember me and step outside.

◆ ◆ ◆

I hit the lake running and swim straight to the other side, sitting in the sand in a nest of wild grasses that wave and tickle my skin. I'm so conflicted now that it hurts to think. Possibilities circle my head like sharks, all waiting for their turn to come in for the kill. I reach my hand up and touch Yanori's necklace, hoping the cool metal will help calm me.

If I wait long enough, I can go back and see if Jenna

The Feed

has gone. After a couple of hours, she will not even remember having seen me. Those few moments we had together will fade away until there's nothing but a blurry spot in her memory, a piece of time that never happened. This is why I did not speak to her. Our instructors always taught us that when facing a woman, to be as silent as the trenches below the sea. Anything we say might later be used to spark their memory of us, and their hatred.

Then there's the kiss with Seth. It was brief, but it has excited the deepest parts of me.

I lay on my back in the sand, close my eyes and think of that heat, that want. It will be hard to resist my instincts for an entire week; I am not sure if I can do it or if I want to. *Is it even practical?* I wonder, thinking of my mother. If I come back without a child in my womb, I will fail. I open my eyes again and stare up at the thin rays of sunlight that have managed to penetrate the depths of the lake.

"I can't fail," I say aloud, enjoying the bubbles that burst from my lips. Words are so much more graphic in the sea. I miss that. It's been only a day and already I'm pining away for the cool darkness of home. "I won't." I'll think of something; I know that I will. The first step I must take is to examine Seth's other tattoos. I need to know if there is yet another mystery there waiting to be unraveled. Once I've done that, once he has calmed, I will get him to tell me in as much depth as he is able where he got these ideas from, these dreams.

I close my eyes and try to imagine Yuri's face, his handsome lips, his pale hair.

C.M. Sturich

I put my hand between my legs and try to relax, try to ease away some of that hunger that comes with the Feed. Yuri's image soon fades into Seth's. Dark hair and dark eyes gaze back at me, but this time, they see me for who I am. I imagine that the magic has faded and that I am still the most beautiful creature he has ever seen.

◆ ◆ ◆

Seth is sitting on the wooden platform outside his house with a bandage on his arm and a frown on his face. Sarah is slumped at his feet, gazing out at the lake with tired eyes. If her eyesight were not so poor, she would see me skimming the water with my own eyes, coming closer with quiet strokes. Jenna is nowhere to be seen, and I believe that after the conversation she had with Seth, that she is gone. Still, as attracted as I am to Seth's physical form, I know nothing about him. He may very well have let her stay.

Seth takes another white stick from a box on the table next to him. I search my mind for the word, but cannot place it. It is similar to a cigar which I am familiar with, but there are enough differences that I know that is not right. Seth puts it to his mouth and lights it with something in his other hand, blowing smoke out across the water. I want to call out to him, let him know that I am here, but it is late afternoon and there are people everywhere. I can see them from my spot near the shore.

The Feed

They are tending gardens and walking in pairs; children, like the ones I saw at the beach play together at the edges of the lake and I smile at their pale feet and long toes.

I spend awhile looking around for a secretive spot where I might come out of the water, a bit of brush, a strand of trees, but there is nothing that will get me to Seth's house. I am about to give up and go back to the lake bottom for a nap when Seth stands up and takes off his shirt. He then removes his footwear, revealing more cloth beneath. These he also takes off. He disappears into the house for a few moments and when he comes out, he is wearing pants that stop above his knees, leaving his calves and feet bare.

"Come on, Sarah," I hear him say, dropping the lit stick in a glass jar on the table. Sarah ignores him, turning her face away and licking her lips. "Fine then, lazy bones," Seth laughs and pats her on the head before coming down the slope towards the beach, wading through the shallowest parts of the water until his waist is submerged. He rubs at his arms and shivers a bit. "Fuck, that's cold," he says as he opens his arms and pushes out into the lake, making gentle, sweeping strokes with his arms. He is coming straight towards me. I debate my options for a moment and decide to wait for him. When I feel he is close enough to hear, I quietly call out to him.

"What happened to your arm?"

Seth pauses and nearly drops below the surface. I panic and swim towards him, pausing inches away as he rights himself and begins to tread water. I raise my head a bit, casting another wary glance around to make sure that nobody else is looking our way. Seth's neighbors are all occupied with their own activities, leaving us alone to talk.

"Jenna cut me," he says, blinking furiously. He's fighting the magic again and if his words are any indication, he might be winning. He is speaking clearly and his face is relaxed but not dreamy. There is none of that fog in his gaze or glimmer in his eyes. I don't remember any of our instructors warning us about this. I would think if a man were so easily able to fight our compulsions, that they would teach us the warning signs. Maybe Seth is different, maybe the mark of Muoru gives him a small bit of protection. "She cut me and then she left. She texted me later, but all she said was that I was dick. She didn't even mention you."

"Texted?" I ask, confused. "What does it mean?" This is a new word for me. Seth doesn't respond, just floats there staring at me with his otter eyes. "You should answer me," I say, thinking of all I've ever learned about the Feed. If I ask my mate a question, he should respond immediately. *A question from your lips is an order to the male you have chosen.* I have heard our teachers utter these words a thousand times. His compulsion may be fading, but it should not be so worn down that he will not answer me, not yet. "I kissed you," I say, by way of explanation. I don't expect Seth to be coherent enough that he will care about this.

"Yes," he says, taking a big breath of air. Treading water is not easy for him and he is tiring quickly. "Yes, you did. And it's all I can fucking think about. I don't even know who you are or what you are, but you're on my mind constantly. Since I saw you last night, I could give a shit less about everything else."

"I'm a Huntswoman," I say, wanting him to know where I come from and why I'm here. "I've been sent by my people to reclaim a bit of the earth's magic, to take your baby and your essence back to the sea."

"By killing me?" Seth asks, suspicion apparent in his gaze. I nod and swallow a bit of water to calm myself. *We are having a conversation, a real conversation.* I had not expected this so quickly; I had budgeted at least two days before he would be able to speak with me like this.

"By eating you," I say.

"Fuck," Seth says, dropping into the water again for a moment. He flails his arms and floats to the surface again. His face is pink and his breaths are rapid and heavy. He will have to go back to shore soon. "You know what the weirdest part about that is?" he says, gasping and swallowing some water, too, though I think his was by accident. "I don't even care. I just want to touch you, to feel your breasts in my hands, to ... "

"Can you get me out of here?" I say, looking around again for emphasis. "Could you bring me a cloth to cover myself with so that we might go inside?" From his words, I can see that the magic has not fully left him. I use this to my advantage.

"Just a minute," Seth says, turning around and powering through the water with surprising strength. *And I had thought he was tired.* I smile as Sarah rises to her feet and starts to bounce, jumping up and down at Seth's arrival like she's been waiting centuries. *I think I like dogs,* I say to myself, floating in the gentle currents of the water like a sea bird.

Seth races inside and comes out with a large cloth, a blanket, that he folds into a square and tucks under his arm. He has some trouble with this, swimming one handed. I move forward easily, suddenly confident and proud of my abilities in the water. Being around the mers is hard sometimes; they swim so much better than the Huntswomen, maneuver better, dive better. It is easy to feel inadequate. But not here. Seth makes me feel like one of the trick swimmers my mother keeps around to entertain herself.

"Thank you," I say sincerely, cautious that our hands do not touch during this exchange. I unfold the blanket with my hands, using just my legs to keep myself afloat, and lay the cloth over my head. I let the excess trail in the water behind me and swim forward, pausing when my feet hit the sandy floor. As I walk forward, I wrap myself tightly in the orange fabric and move as quickly as I can into the safety of Seth's house where I pause, naked and dripping on the wooden floor of his hallway. Seth follows me inside quickly, dragging Sarah along with him, and locks the door behind us. "The extra key," I begin, thinking of Jenna. I was lucky that time. I may not survive a second encounter.

"I got it back from her," Seth says, shaking his head and pointing at a pile of silver on the counter. "I won't put it out there again, at least not for awhile, and definitely not in the same spot."

"I am sorry about that," I say as I watch Seth's eyes

slide down my body. "I should warn you that all women will react that way if they see me." His gaze stops at my face and he smiles. His smile is dark and wicked but in a sensual way that appeals to me.

"Then you should really stay away from my mom," he says and for a moment, I am confused. "She always acts like that around the women I'm dating." It takes me a moment, but then I laugh, realizing it is a joke. Seth has a sense of humor, how lovely. I tilt my head and bite my lip, wishing I could just give into the Feed and couple with him. I was not ready for sex, avoided it all this time, and now, I am near desperate for it. I pray to Neptune that the second time is not as painful as the first.

It takes all of my energy to turn away and move into the living room. He comes in behind me, but doesn't touch. Still, I can feel his eyes on my back, burning with desire. "You're not really fifteen are you?" he asks and sounds disgusted with himself. I spin to face him, narrowing my eyes as I turn. He's looking at me, at all of me, taking me in, absorbing my dark hair, the gills along the sides of my neck, the scales that line the sides of my face, my hands, my calves, the roundness of my hips.

"I have been sixteen for two days," I say, wondering if my fantasy in the lake is coming true. Seth is looking at me and he is not disgusted. A lack of disgust is a far cry from finding me beautiful, but it is a step. Or it could just be the magic. He is better, but I can tell from his blatant desire and roaming eyes, he is not cured. In my presence, he may never be cured. I just don't know the answer to any of these questions. I am not supposed to try and cure him, to let him see me as I am. I am here to ensorcell him, mate with him, gobble him up like the sea witch did to the *merighean* girl in my father's stories.

"That's still pretty young, Natalie," he says and I can hear some of his desire slipping away. Sarah snuffles her way into the room, nose pressed to the floor. She follows the trail of water I have left and sits at my feet, wagging her tail and licking her floppy, black lips.

"Tell me," I say, trying to distract him. I can see that I will get nowhere with this argument. "About your dream." Seth rubs at his face for a moment and then gestures with his head at the bathroom.

"Do you want to dry off first? This could take a while?" I stare at him for a moment and shake my head. He nods and tries to smile. "Of course not," he says. "You're a mermaid."

Mermaid.

That word strikes a nerve in me although I can't say why. *Mermaid.*

"I am not a mermaid," I say, trying not to sound offended. Seth opens his mouth and closes it again, unsure of what to say to that; Sarah barks and I pat her on the head, reveling in the softness of her fur.

"I'm sorry," he says, sounding genuine. "You're right; you don't have the tail." I think immediately of Yanori and Yuri and the other *merighean*. How does he know about them? Is this another sign? I shake my head at my own thoughts. Of course it is not; humans have all sorts of legends regarding the Huntswomen and the *merighean*. His words might be wrong and his images of us skewed,

The Feed

but this is where he is getting his information from. "Are you a siren?" he asks me, swallowing hard. His breathing is heavy and I can see that he is getting nervous. This is the last thing I want. I lower my voice and try to calm him with my words. I feel that the truth is best if I want to win his confidence. To give him anything else would be equivalent to rolling him under with the magic. I may as well just kiss him again and tell him everything will be okay.

"We have been called that," I reply. "But not as you know them. I am a *merighean,* a half-*merighean* to be exact. The *merighean* are like your mermaids, with long, muscular tails that shimmer with colorful scales, that can kill a shark with a single blow. My mother was a Huntswoman, like me. She came ashore, found a man and mated with him. After her week was up, she killed and consumed him, returned to the sea and bore me. This is what I am." I do not say who. I do not know who I am yet. I feel like I am getting closer to the answer with each passing day, but I am not ready to reveal that to anyone, including myself.

"Did you sing to me?" he asks. "Is that why I want you so badly?" I shake my head.

"You need but lay eyes on me, touch me, that is all it takes. My song would ... " I pause. The Huntswomen's siren songs are our most carefully guarded secret. A siren's song will call all of the men in the area to me, convince them to raise their swords against whatever enemy is at my back. It will even soothe the women, convince them to speak with me as a person and lower their defenses.

It is a very, very bad idea. I decide not to tell Seth that, not yet.

"I did not sing to you." He nods slowly before retreating into the bathroom and reemerging with a cloth that he drags through his hair to dry it.

"I don't know what to say," he tells me honestly. "I don't know what to do. I can't even think. I just ... I just want to hear your voice and touch your skin. I want to know everything about you." I smile at that.

"May I give Sarah another pig's ear?" I ask him, taking the conversation in a direction that I believe will relax him. Seth grins and flashes me white teeth.

"You sure can," he says, gazing down at his dog with loving eyes. There is real tenderness there, real concern for the welfare and well being of this animal at our feet. I like him for that, respect him even. I go into the kitchen with Sarah at my heels and grab the bag, extracting one of the smelly things and handing it to her. She takes it gently, slapping me in the thighs with her tail as she turns away and goes to the bed in the corner of the living room. Seth comes around the other side of the kitchen, in the process of pulling on a black shirt, and points at the refrigerator.

"If you're hungry, the Chinese food I ordered last night is in there. I didn't touch it. When you didn't come back, I just ... I don't know. I just sat on the couch in the dark and waited. That's all I felt like I could do."

"I'm sorry," I say to him honestly. "If I could remove the compulsion, I would." I touch my chest and close my eyes. "But it's as much a part of me as the heart that beats within my breast. I could no sooner remove that than I could a rib. If you stay away from me, the feelings should fade quite a bit." I take a deep breath and open my eyes. "Perhaps almost entirely. You are a unique man, Seth. If I had kissed anyone else, I suspect they would not have so easily forgotten."

"Oh, I didn't forget," Seth says, shaking his head. "It's the only kiss I've ever had that I can remember in high def." I don't know what he means by this, but I take it as a compliment and open his refrigerator. Inside, I search for the Chinese food only to realize that I do not know what it is. Seth comes up behind me and I tense in anticipation of his touch. But he is careful to point around me.

"The white boxes there. I'll get us some forks." He takes a step back as I bend down to retrieve the food. A moan escapes his lips and I drop the containers, spinning to face him and the foggy glaze that has just slid across his features. "Or maybe I'll get you something to wear first," he says, sounding dizzy. "A shirt and some underwear at least."

As I collect the boxes off the floor, Seth disappears into his bedroom and reappears with a shirt that's identical to the one he gave me last night. With it he brings a piece of white triangular cloth with three holes. I set the food on the counter and put the shirt on first. The white cloth, the underwear, is strange to me. I vaguely remember learning about it during our time studying human fashions. It is worn beneath the outer clothing to help the humans maintain good hygiene and warmth. I smile, glad that I'm still able to access that knowledge that feels like I learned it so long ago. *It was practically another lifetime,* I think as I bend down and put a leg through one of the holes.

Seth watches me hungrily as I do this, collecting some silverware and setting it down beside the containers.

"Can you use chopsticks?" he asks me, blinking his eyes slowly. Whatever it is that I'm doing, he finds it attractive. I pause, putting one hand on the counter and trying to get my other leg through the second hold. It is harder than it first appears.

"I cannot," I say, thinking of the long, wooden sticks that some of the Huntswomen use to make themselves seem sophisticated. They find these floating in the garbage heaps that pass by from time to time. Sometimes, bits of refuse sink down to the city. We pick through this, extracting the useful items, like plastic bottles or metal or aluminum, and the rest the *merighean* carry out several meters and bury in the sand. This is what we have been reduced to: scavengers. *We are no better than the blue crab that feasts on the leftovers of sharks.* After this thought, another pops up. *I will fix this.* I don't know how I'll do it, but the more I see, the more I am convinced that I must. I must forge my own destiny.

Finally, I manage to get the underwear onto my legs. I slide it up my body, across my scales and over my hips. It is tight around the waist and around my thighs, but the rest of it hangs loosely between my legs.

"Sorry," Seth says, not sounding like he is at all. He sounds faraway again, dreamy. I don't like the effect that I'm having on him and turn away. I was enjoying our conversation, was far from done with it. "I looked for some of Jenna's but couldn't find any. I didn't really let her leave her stuff here." With this statement, his voice clears, becomes angry. It is the strength of this emotion that I suspect is helping him fight the Feed. Anger is a powerful tool when wielded righteously.

"Why?" I ask him, turning back around. Seth collects the boxes and the silverware and gestures with his chin.

"Where do you want to sit? I don't have room for a dining table, but we could eat on the bed, or the couch."

"Either," I say, following after him. My stomach is twisting and knotting now with hunger. The little silver fish are catching onto me and I had trouble finding enough to eat. I pray that there is meat in those boxes or I may have to go out and try again. I can't be satiated without flesh in my throat.

"I didn't love her," Seth says as we enter his room and he kneels down, stacking the boxes on a squat, little table that sits at his bedside. He pauses here and puts his hands on his knees. "I didn't realize it for a long time, but when she refused to stop drinking, I knew she didn't love me, either. That's when I figured it out." He drops to his knees and reaches over, fluffing the pillows that look so heavenly to me, I can feel myself reaching out for them. He keeps talking as he straightens the blankets and smooths them out for me. "She kept asking to move in and I kept saying no. I guess it was pretty fucked up of me. I should've broken up with her when I got Sarah." As if summoned, the dog trots into the room, smiling at us both with her sharp canines. She sniffs around the floor for a moment and then makes herself comfortable on a pile of clothes.

"Why?" I ask as Seth motions for me to sit down. I kneel, following his lead, and then crawl onto the bed on my hands and knees. I make myself comfortable, sitting against the pillows and enjoying the luxury of being able to relax without consequence. There is no one here to laugh at me, to point fingers when I sit, to gasp when they see me walk. I vow not to take this treat for granted. Seth rises to his feet and approaches a series of windows that line the wall to my left. He tugs on a string and the window covering lifts away, revealing the grassy hillside and a sea of tiny white flowers that dance in the breeze. Sunlight streams into the room and illuminates the glow of the wood floors, the bright colors in Seth's blankets. I hold my hand out and let it fall across my skin. It is not often that I get to see the sun glitter against my scales. Seth repeats this action on the next two windows and his room becomes a beautiful golden jewel; the yellow walls sparkle even brighter and the paintings glow with new life. It is quite a lovely sight, one that I am so focused on taking in that Seth is sitting mere inches from me before I realize that he's there.

"Jenna never liked Sarah. When she was a puppy, Jenna put her outside in the rain. This was before I'd built the doghouse." Seth stops and hands me a container. "I hope you like it cold," he says. "I didn't think to heat it up." He stares at me for a long moment before shaking his head and glancing away. "I can barely believe I'm thinking at all."

"She put her outside in the rain?" I ask, wanting to hear more of the story. I know it's wrong of me, but I want to vilify Jenna in my head, make her the bad guy. If I can do that, then I won't feel so bad about taking Seth. If I take Seth. I still have not yet decided. He hands me a fork, being very careful not to touch me, maybe even more careful than I, myself, am being.

"Sarah got sick and almost died. Jenna never apologized for that." He digs his fork into the container he's holding and stabs a round piece of meat that's slathered in a viscous sauce. He puts it to his mouth and chews carefully before swallowing. I copy him, taking a piece of brown meat that's swimming in sauce and surrounded by green vegetables that I don't recognize. As soon as I put it to my mouth, I find myself addicted to the flavor. It's so much more complex than anything that I have eaten under the sea. And it isn't salty, not in the least. I gobble up nearly half the box before Seth continues speaking. "Once, during a fight, she told me that she wished Sarah had died, because she fucking hated her." Seth stops eating and pokes at his food. "That was a sign right there." He looks up at me again and smiles. "But she likes you," he says. "And you like her."

"Is that a good sign?" I ask him, feeling warm and comfortable in this glowing room with this person that I do not know. This person who has Muoru on his chest and my name on his knuckles. When I look into his eyes, I can see that in this moment, he is not enthralled, not in the least.

"I think it's a wonderful sign," he tells me and without knowing why, I feel my heart clench with pride.

Chapter Ten

After we eat, Seth insists on looking at my wounds again. I acquiesce to his demands on the sole condition that he does not touch me. I lift up my shirt and let him examine my belly first.

"They look okay," he says, sitting back on his haunches. "But I wish you'd led me clean them out. What about the ones on your hands?" I spread my fingers and turn my hand over, palm up. Seth gets caught on the webbing between my knuckles and spends a long time staring at that instead of at the cuts and scrapes. Instead of feeling offended, as I had thought I might be, I find myself amused. I have never before had to explain my anatomy to anyone. It is quite the strange task.

"I have it on my toes, too," I say, distracting him. He looks down and I lift my foot for his inspection. I can't wiggle my toes like a human can, so I reach down and push them apart so that he might see. The nails here are venomous as well so I make sure that I'm very careful to keep him away from them. "And my nails," I say, hoping that this won't scare him. I feel like we are building a slow

The Feed

friendship, one grain of sand at a time. I don't want any of it to be washed away. "They are poisonous. Try not to touch them or you'll die." My words are blunt but effective. Seth raises his dark eyebrows at this.

"There's no antidote?" I shake my head. The *merighean* and the Huntswomen are somewhat immune to the poison and we have little resources available to devote to the study of a cure for something that merely makes us sick.

"There is not," I say with a sigh. Seth whistles and stands up.

"Thanks for the advice," he says warily, perhaps remembering that I touched his face with them, ran them gently across his skin. "Can I ask you a favor?" he says, surprising me.

"Can I ask you one?" I return, wanting him to take off his clothes so that I might look at the tattoos. It's important that I find out if there are other symbols that I recognize, other words. Seth and I may be connected somehow or all that's happened between us might be coincidence. I can't know without this information. Or the information about Seth's dream. But we'll get to that; I try to work one angle at a time.

"Sure," he says. "No problem. What is it?"

"You first," I counter, wanting to be polite. Seth smiles and nods his chin at the hallway.

"I'd feel a lot better if you took a bath with some Epsom salt." He pauses. "Unless that might hurt you in some way. I'm sorry," he says and I don't understand at all what he's apologizing for. "I'm trying to apply human attributes to you, but I don't know anything about you at all." Seth's voice is sounding stressed again, which I can understand. I want him to trust me, but I don't know how. I try to remember Yanori's words, to let them sink into me. I can't go wrong if I take her advice. *Sometimes to change the minds of others, a test of courage must be passed. You'll have to earn their respect before you can change their lives. It's the way of the world, Natalie, in all things and not just this.*

I remember the joke that Seth made in the hallway and try one of my own. It is not a test of courage, but it's a good start.

"I do not know what Epsom is," I say smiling. "But if it has salt in it, then I should be fine. I am a mermaid, after all; I was born of the sea." Seth doesn't laugh, but he does smile.

"Right this way," he says, stepping over Sarah and guiding me to the bathroom. I pause behind him as he reaches down and spins a silver knob. Water cascades into the porcelain basin beneath it. I close my eyes, search for the right word. Bathtub. I open them again and watch as Seth tests the water with his hand, adjusting the knob to the right in small increments. He pauses and looks over his shoulder at me. "Do you like it warm?" he asks me, sounding unsure of himself. I do not blame him; I try to imagine bringing Seth to Amarana. A human in the city would certainly be strange. I would not have the slightest idea about how to make him comfortable there.

I smile for reassurance and consider my answer. Warm water is good, but rare. Sometimes, the Huntswomen go

The Feed

to the vents that empty into the sea, warming the city from beneath. They lay around in the sand and sleep the day away, hiding from our instructors behind the bubbles and the bits of molten rock that spew out around them. It is not all fun and games however. I have seen people burned beyond recognition with their carelessness.

Seth's vent however, his faucet, is much safer. I recall that the water is piped into the house, just as it was in my ancestor's days, when the Huntswomen had dry homes, rooms protected from the sea with bits of glass, where they lounged in pools of warm water and sunned themselves on patios that reached up through the depths and burst into the sky.

"I will take it warm," I say, stepping onto the smooth tiles of the bathroom floor and examining the small window that is pushed up against the hillside behind Seth's house. To my left is the sink, a bit of porcelain with a small faucet. It makes me smile to see that the humans have so many methods of accessing water. Somewhere, in their distant memories, they must know that they were born from the sea. I pause by the toilet and bend down, examining the smooth white sides and the bit of water that rests in the middle. It is the strangest thing I have seen thus far. I decide that I will continue to use the lake for that purpose, finding that far more natural than trying to squat over this. At home, we just swim to the edges of the city and find the currents that carry the water down and away. I can't help but laugh as I think of the other Huntswomen trying to use one of these and consider myself quite intelligent for choosing an area with a large body of water at my disposal.

"That bad, huh?" Seth says, turning the water off and stepping back. "I would've cleaned it better if I'd known I was having company." He tries to smile, but there's that bit of confusion in his eyes that says he still is not certain what is happening here. I straighten up and step over to the bathtub, holding my hands above the steam that radiates from the clear water beneath. "Let me just get the Epsom salt and I'll leave you to it." I frown at him.

"You're leaving?" I ask, smiling at Sarah as she sticks her head through the doorway around Seth's leg. I cannot wait to tell Yanori all about her when I get back. She will find it funny that out of all things, I had forgotten what a dog was. "You should stay." I pull my shirt off and drop it to the floor where it joins a small pile of Seth's other clothing. He swallows hard and turns away, grabbing the edge of the mirror above the sink, revealing a hidden cabinet.

"I don't think that's a very good idea," he tells me, retrieving a sealed plastic bag. Seth turns back towards me but doesn't look, pouring a generous amount of a thick, grainy salt into the water before swishing it around with his hand. I drop the underwear to the floor and step out of them, lifting one leg over the edge of the bathtub. When my foot hits the water, I groan in pleasure. The warmth seeps into my flesh, soothing muscles that ache from trying to adapt to life on land, and wetting my dry, itchy scales.

I slip into the water quickly, submerging my head and running my fingers through my wet hair. I have not gotten used to feeling it dry. It rubs across my shoulders and upper back, tickling me and making me imagine that all sorts of things are crawling there.

When I reemerge, I find that Seth has closed the lid to the toilet and is sitting on it, watching me with his dark eyes and scratching Sarah's head with absentminded fingers. She is so big that she takes up nearly the entire bathroom. I turn over and rest my arms along the curved back of the tub.

"You are so beautiful," Seth says dreamily and I worry that I've pushed him too far. "I knew it wasn't a good idea for me to stay in here. I don't know how I'm even sitting still. All I want to do is put my hands all over you." I ignore his rambling and try to distract him with something else. It seems that he has a strong mind; if I can get him to focus, there is a possibility I can pull him away from thoughts of me.

"Now for my favor," I say, turning back over and sitting up. Seth nods, but he isn't fully there, not yet. "I need you to show me your tattoos, all of them. I want to know if there are anymore mysteries written across your skin."

"In my dream last night," he says suddenly, blinking quickly and standing up. Sarah barks but doesn't move. "You said pretty much the same thing. I am having the worst case of déjà vu." Seth rubs at his forehead with a nervous hand and stalks out of the bathroom. I rise to my feet, spilling water across the floor and across Sarah's back. She wags her tail and stands up, trailing me as I walk after Seth, licking my calves and ankles with her warm tongue.

"Tell me all of it," I say as he walks into his bedroom and turns around, eyes suddenly scared.

"Is this really your name?" he asks me, pointing at his knuckles. I nod and Seth curses, tearing off his shirt and throwing it to the floor. The mark of Muoru winks back at me, almost beckoning. Seth pushes his shorts down his hips and reveals all of himself to me. My breath catches strangely in my throat as I try to look away and fail. Instead of hiding in a slit that pulls back before coupling, Seth's male organs are situated between his hips, surrounded by the colorful, sweeping lines of tattoos. It is just as I have been told to expect but no less shocking to look at. "And is this the mark of Neptune?" he asks, pointing to a spot just above his member. I come closer though I don't want to. The temptation to take him is overwhelming. I reach my hand up and cup Yanori's necklace for strength.

"It is," I whisper, noting the rounded blue curves of the moon, crossed with a segmented line that ends with a tail fin on either side. It is inverted which is not good. Neptune's mark should never be placed horizontally; it is a sign of bad fortune.

"And this," Seth's hand rises to his hip. "What is this?" I reach out, hover my nails across his skin. There's a fish there, a pink tetra. Its dark eyes are cloudy and the corner of its tail is missing. *Yanori.*

"Where did you get this?" I ask, wishing I could touch him, run my fingers over the marks as I take them all in. Some, like the ones on his neck are meaningless, at least to me. If there is any significance to them, their purpose does not lie within the depths of my knowledge. But hidden in the curling waves that line Seth's right arm, are the symbols of Amahna, the giant sea snake, and Kua, the sea dragon, wrapped around the body of his mate who I can no longer remember the name of.

There are so many shapes there that beg familiarity. I know that I recognize them from somewhere, but I can't think where. It is like the Feed, like this energy has been put into my very soul, and I have no control over it.

"And this," Seth says, panting, whether from my proximity or his own fear, I don't know. He reaches out and lays his fingers across one of the rectangles that hang from the necklace. "This was in it, too." I step away from him and mimic his touch, fingering the silver gently.

"Describe it to me in detail," I tell him, hoping that his words will make everything clearer. Seth shakes his head and pulls up his pants.

"I can't think with you around," he says, moving to his bed and sitting on the edge of it. The muscles in his neck are tight and I can see that he's coming unwound. I want him coherent, focused, but I can't have him stressed out. I step up to him and run my nails gently through has hair, careful not to nick his scalp, and then lay the back of my hand flat against his forehead.

"It will be alright," I tell him, hoping that my words are true. I did not expect all of this strangeness. I came here to forge my own destiny, not be drawn down the path of another. If there is something here that I am to learn from, I will do it, but I will not be pushed into another series of events that I cannot control. *If this is a message,* I tell Neptune with a prayer, *then it was a poorly placed one. Guide me, but do not instruct me, I beg of you.*

Seth relaxes substantially, reaching out for me. I let him touch the sides of my thighs briefly before stepping back.

"Tell me," I say softly.

"I can't think with you around," he says again, much more gently this time. "Maybe that's why I dreamt about you." He looks up, eyes cloudy but focused. "We made love," he says and I hold his gaze, unashamed. "And you studied me, my body. You asked me if I was hiding any mysteries from you and I said no. You called me a liar. You told me about your sister and her house of coral and you were wearing that necklace, only it was silver, not black." Seth shakes his head like he's having trouble remembering. "You touched every part of me, told me about ... things ... monsters, I guess, or gods, that lived under the sea and then you ... " Seth looks over at Sarah who is sitting in the doorway with her ears taught and her tail still. "You ate me, slowly, piece by piece, and I loved every minute of it. I tried to convince you to save my head for last, but you refused." Seth looks nervous again, but I stay away this time, watching him use his confusion to fight the Feed. "You know how dreams don't make sense?" he asks me suddenly and I nod, colorful memories flooding my head as I remember snippets, bits of stories that I've told my sleeping self over the years. "You asked me if it was wrong to change your destiny, even if you knew it was right. And then, from inside your stomach, I watched you go back to the ocean." Seth sighs. "It doesn't make anymore sense to me than the ones I had before, the ones where I saw this, and this." He points to his knuckles and then his chest. "None of this makes any sense."

I stare down at the wood floor and think the same thing. But it's okay, it doesn't have to. I look up at him and decide. Whether our meeting was by chance or by destiny, it doesn't matter. The decisions I will make in the next few days will not be swayed by this. I have to use my mind and my heart to decide, only then will I be able to live with myself, no matter what the future holds, no matter what consequences I face. When I get back to the ocean, I will talk with Yanori, I will study the old texts, and I will find out who sent these messages and why.

Chapter Eleven

I decide that Seth has had enough for one day and leave him, fleeing to the lake with my thoughts. I am careful to be quiet so that he doesn't realize I've even left. I feel so guilty that I can't stand it. The magic of the Feed is supposed to make this easy for him, take away this confusion and this pain. In my mercy, I am causing him agony.

I will fix this, I decide as I swim in tired circles. The lake has quickly become boring. With the sea, there is always something new to learn, to do, to discover. I swear that I have memorized the pattern of the lake bottom, the green grasses, the swimming cycles of the silver fish. I will go back and kiss him again, just kiss him. I will let him trail me, touch me with questing fingers, until I can figure out my next step.

I take this energy with me when I go back to the house, using the orange blanket to get in the door the same way I used it to leave. I throw it on the floor of the hallway in a sopping mess and turn to find Seth in the kitchen.

"I was hoping you'd come back," he says, standing over a silver pot that sits above a tiny blue flame on his stove.

"Were you?" I ask, wondering how deep the magic has penetrated him. What if I were to disappear now, choose another man, go back to the sea? What would happen to Seth? How would he remember me? What would he do?

"I was," he says, stirring the contents of the pot. He turns back to me and smiles. "I don't know who you are, what you are really, but I think I like you."

"Why?" I ask, perplexed.

"Because you make me think," Seth says, turning his smile into a grin. "Well, when I'm not imagining us in bed together." He shakes his head. "No, no, that's not what I

The Feed

meant to say. God, what is wrong with me?" He turns a knob at the front of the stove and the flame gets bigger, licking at the silver sides of the pot. "What I'm trying to say is that you're interesting, unique. I like that." I stand there and stare at him, wondering if his words are coming from the Feed's magic or his own heart. Still, I find myself changing my mind about my decision. Maybe I won't touch him again. Maybe I'll let him say what he has to say, feel what he has to feel. He has a right to. "I found some cabbage and pancetta in the back of the fridge. There isn't much, but I could throw it together with some beans and some bouillon cubes, make you a soup." Seth bites his lip. "I need to go grocery shopping, but I just can't bring myself to leave the house. I don't even know how I'm going to get to work tomorrow."

"You can't go," I say, not ordering him, but asking him. I don't want Seth to leave. We have precious little time together, precious little time for me to learn about him, understand him, understand this world, so that I'll know what to do. I did not plan this far, so all I can do is try my best to get through the Feed without breaking either of us. "I'm sorry I picked you," I say, cutting him off before he can speak. I want him to know how I feel, just in case. "I wasn't going to, but then I heard you laugh. I don't know why, but it drew me to you." Seth smiles at this.

"It's okay," he says. "I think you made a good choice. I'm probably the only bachelor my age who can cook with a fridge full of nothing."

◆ ◆ ◆

I come to find that Seth makes a lot of jokes. I don't know if it's a coping mechanism or if it is just part of his personality, but I like it. There are not many *merighean* at home that are as wanton with their words as he is. He curses a lot, and he knows how to handle food. His hands remind me of my father's, sure and strong as he chops vegetables, seasons the dish, tastes it. These are the only things I know about him, but I am pleased.

"I hope you're not too picky," Seth says, putting a bit of green, leafy vegetable in his mouth. "I don't have all of the ingredients, so it's a little bland." I shake my head at this.

"At home, we eat most everything raw. There are only a few people in the whole city that can or will do what you do. Food preparation is not a skill that has survived well in our culture." Seth looks over his shoulder at me. I can see questions in his eyes, but he doesn't ask them. He turns back to the stove and continues to stir the food with a plastic spoon, raising it to his lips for another taste. "And we certainly don't have access to fire, so anything that you cook over it will be exciting enough for me." Seth laughs, nice and smooth, confident. He knows who he is inside, I can see this. I can see it in his face, the way he holds his shoulders, the way he decorates his house. There is something very particular about this man. I wish I were the same way; I wish that I knew who I was inside. If I did, it would make things a whole lot easier.

I had told Yuri to remind me of who I was if I came back and had forgotten. I see now that it is impossible to forget something that you don't truly know. I will have to find myself on this journey, embrace it, and take it back with me. That is what I have come here to do.

Sarah wakes me from my thoughts with a whimper, scratching at the back door with her nails. The white paint is already gouged through, showing me that this a ritual that she has repeated often. Seth moves to the back door and lets her out, pausing to look up at the round fullness of the setting sun. I move over next to him, sidling around him carefully so that I am standing outside with Sarah.

I have seen precious few sunsets in my life and all of them have been memorable. This one is no different, pink and orange and yellow. It's as if the colors of the sky are bleeding into the earth, melting with them, becoming a single, glorious entity. I sigh.

"So beautiful," I say as Seth steps up next to me. He studies my face for a moment and then follows my gaze to the rolling hills, covered in thick swathes of dark green trees. I follow the horizon with my eyes, over the perimeter of the fence and look at the lake. It is sparkling like a jewel, its dark depths a secret to all of the world except for me and the silver fish.

"If you want," he says. "When it gets dark, I could get you into a sweatshirt and some sweatpants. Maybe we could walk Sarah up the hill and down the road a ways. There's a mountain path that's not a bad climb and the view, especially at night, is pretty incredible. You can see all the way to the city." I jump at Seth's offer, desperate for a chance to go out and see more of this world that I have been taught to fear since birth. There must be something special about it though, for Neptune and my mother to want us to bring back a bit of its magic.

"I would like that," I say as Seth moves forward and starts down a small flight of steps.

"There's some wild basil out here along the fence," he tells me as I follow him, stepping into the grass with my bare feet. It is much thicker back here, more lush than the scraggly stuff that grows at the edge of the lake. It's soft, too, and it tickles my skin with gentle fingers that don't bother my cuts or scrapes in the slightest. If I had walked on this the whole way here then I would be much less sore than I am now. "This might just be the answer our poor soup is looking for. There," Seth says, pointing at a clump of purple flowers that are nearly hidden in the growing shadows of the fence. I follow him to it and bend down next to him, examining the long stems and the rounded leaves. Flora here is so much different than it is at home. I find myself fascinated with it. I reach my fingers out and brush them over the tops of the plants. "Try to pick some that aren't flowering yet," he says, pushing aside stems and examining plants. "The ones with flowers will be more bitter. We want some that look like this." Seth pinches off a bit of green plant and shows it to me. It's half as long as my forearm and covered in bright leaves. I take it from him and bring it to my nose, enjoying the fresh scent that comes with it.

The Feed

"You know," I begin, mimicking him by plucking off a bit of plant. "When I first crawled from the sea, I lamented life on land, but if there are more experiences like this then I must say, I grossly underestimated it." Seth chuckles at this.

"I'm glad that a bit of basil could change your opinion of us," he says. "I wonder how you'd do with a whole herb garden?" I think Seth is making a joke, but I don't understand it. I smile at him instead and rise to my feet, taking a handful of basil with me. He follows suit and leads me back into the house, leaving the door open for Sarah.

"May I help you add this?" I ask, stepping over to the pot and gazing in at the contents.

"Sure," Seth says, pulling a knife from a block of wood that sits on the counter. It reminds me of Jenna and I shiver. Somehow, I think Seth knows it. "Could Jenna have killed you?" Seth asks and I'm not entirely sure what his question is getting at. "Are you immortal?" I shake my head.

"I'm not." He sets his bit of basil down on the counter along with the knife. I take it my hand and test the weight of it. I am quite skilled with a knife when it comes to fighting underwater. On land, there is a whole different method to it. I can see that without even trying it. The earth is doing what it does best, tugging my hand and the weapon down as best it can. It's even more obvious to me now that my training in the ocean has in no way prepared me to fight here. If I had to, it is very likely that I could die.

"Will you be?" he asks, stepping aside for Sarah. She looks up at us both and wags her tail furiously, oblivious to the conversation. "After you sleep with me?" I know without clarifying that Seth is not talking about sleeping; he's talking about sex. "I read something online while you were gone. It said that a siren becomes immortal after sleeping with a human. Is that true?" I turn away from him and press the blade against the stem of one of the plants, severing it in two.

"It is not," I say, wondering if I'm doing the right thing with the knife. Seth doesn't say anything about it so I continue what I'm doing, cutting the stems in half, shredding the leaves with slow, purposeful strokes. *This is actually quite fun,* I realize, moving onto the next bit of plant. *Maybe I will encourage the merighean to explore food more.* My father would make a great teacher. Something about the way he makes his *kimtazi* tells me that he'd be more than happy to try it. "I know of nothing that is immortal; everything can die, including gods." Seth steps up next to me and reaches for another knife, pulling a bit of basil in front of him with the blade.

"Have you met one?" he asks me, voice dark and serious. "A god?" I watch him cut the plant with rapid strokes, severing the pieces with an experienced hand. "Is this one, Muoru, is he a god?" Seth gestures at his covered chest with the back of his hand. I consider my answer carefully. He is looking for something in my words. I don't know what it is, but this is important to him. Even knowing him for just a single day I can see that.

"Muoru was not a god, not in the sense that Neptune is. But he was close enough. They say he was so powerful that he could form tsunamis with the tip of his tail." I set the knife down and scoop the shredded plant into the palm of my hand. "May I add this now?"

"You sure can," Seth says, taking his own basil and tossing it into the pot. He lets me stir it and leans back against the counter, crossing his arms over his chest. "So Muoru is dead?"

"I don't know," I say, trying to be as honest as I can. "I thought he was, but now I can no longer be sure."

"Why's that?" Seth asks as I step back and allow him to take over the cooking again.

"Because," I reply, watching him carefully. "I am finding out that not all things are as they seem."

◆ ◆ ◆

After we eat, Seth finds me some clothes to wear. He hands me a pair of thick, dark pants that are as soft as the blankets on his bed, another pair of underwear, and a heavy, black shirt with long sleeves and a piece of fabric that he pulls over my head.

"I don't think you should have any trouble now," he says, examining me carefully. I have told him my fears about going out, about what might happen if we encounter another person, especially a woman. "Now they'll just think you're a pretty girl," he tells me and I smile. Seth then brings me some footwear, some shoes. They are smaller than his, and white with pink sparkles. A series of purple laces tie up the front and make me feel suddenly claustrophobic. I had liked the idea of wearing clothes, but now that I have so many on, I feel hot and cloistered. There always seems to be a piece of fabric that is rubbing against my skin in an irritating manner; I don't know how Seth stands it. "Those are Jenna's," Seth says with a bit of anger in his voice but also a bit of sadness. He may not have loved her, but I think he misses her, even if it's just a little bit.

"I think I prefer being nude," I tell Seth honestly. When I walk, my feet sink into the rubber that lines the bottom of the shoes. I imagine that it is supposed to be comfortable, but I just find it strange. I like to feel the earth beneath my feet. I would think that humans would be the same way, but they are not. It's almost as if they do everything they can to stay apart from it. Seth's laugh is strained, almost forced.

"I think I prefer that, too," he says, and then, "Shit." He walks away from me and grabs a long, purple rope from a hook on the wall. At the end of it is a metal clip which he attaches to Sarah's collar. "Do you want to hold the leash?" he asks me, holding out his hand. "It's just for show really; Sarah never pulls." I nod my head and walk over to him, trying not to trip on the shoes. There's an awkward moment between us as I try to take the leash from him without brushing our hands together. Seth finally just drops it into my palm and we make our way out the front door.

Night has dropped into the sky while we were inside, so I lean my head back, address the stars and moon with wide eyes and a smile. I then drop my gaze down and scan the lake. Most of the houses have lights on, but I don't see anyone around. My heart is pumping furiously in my chest, but I'm as excited as I've ever been. I may be the only Huntswoman to have ever participated in something like this. *I'm forging my own destiny,* I realize, following Seth down the wooden path where I first spotted him last night. He then takes me up the flight of stairs that are built into the hillside and over the metal railing where Jenna sat and waited for a car.

The road stretches out before us in a gray line, snaking away into the distance and disappearing into the horizon where the mountains meet the earth. I don't see any cars yet but secretly wish that one will drive by so that I might get a closer look at it.

"We don't have to stay on the cement for long," Seth says, starting off down the road with Sarah and I in tow. He slows down and I catch up to him, walking in line with his shoulder. "It's just a little ways on this and then we can climb over the railing and take a shortcut to the trail. There's some pretty thick brush up there, but it's nothing you can't handle."

"Thank you," I say and Seth stops briefly to look at me.

"For what?" he asks, eyes dark, dressed in a sweater that matches mine. It fits him nicely, stretching across his chest and draping gently over his shoulders; I am drowning in mine. There seems to be fabric everywhere. It hangs from my flesh like Tejean's skin, billowing around in the breeze.

"For listening to me, for trying to understand, for taking me out." I pause. "And for the soup," I add. "It was the best I've ever had." Seth smiles at this.

"You think so?"

"I do," I say, hoping that my next attempt at humor doesn't fall flat. "But since it is the only soup I have ever eaten, I will have to reserve my judgment." Seth laughs loudly at this, shaking his head and starting up our walk again; Sarah barks and we both reach down to pet her at the same time, pausing just before our fingers touch. Seth drops his hand and lets me scratch her behind the ear.

"I'll make all kinds of soup this week if you want," he says, tucking his hands into the pockets of his black pants. "I'll make you whatever you want to eat so long as you promise not to add me to the menu." I think he is trying to be funny, but his statement sobers us both up. He knows that I may kill him, eat him, and yet he doesn't try to retaliate. I had been afraid that he may attempt to end my life before I had a chance to end his, but Seth's shown me no aggression whatsoever. This I attribute to the Feed; there is certainly no other explanation for this portion of his behavior. Still, he has done his utmost to treat me as he would another human being and that I can genuinely appreciate.

"You don't have to worry about that," I say suddenly. "Because I'm not going to kill you." Seth glances over at me sharply.

The Feed

"You're not?" he asks, sounding as surprised as I feel.

"I'm not," I confirm, wondering how I'd even considered it before. I can't kill Seth. I barely know him and already, I'm disgusted at the idea. *There must be a better way,* I think again. I shouldn't have to kill him to accomplish my goals. Death begets more death. If the *merighean* want to have a prosperous life, to rise from the ashes of our fallen cities, then we must be like the phoenix. We must breathe new life into our traditions. Still, I wonder how I'm going to pull this off. There is so much that could go wrong that it frightens me. My mother will ask me, under Neptune's oath, if I have completed my tasks as outlined. I don't know what I'll say or how I'll get through the tests that await me as an accomplished Huntswoman. If I do not kill him, she will know. My body will be tested for the essence of his flesh.

"Will you be in trouble with your people?" he asks me as he gestures at me to follow him. We step over the metal railing that lines the road and begin to walk through an area with short, dark green grass. Feet have worn a thin path through the center of it leading to a strand of trees and heavy bushes ripe with large, white flowers.

"I may be," I say as Seth leads the way, lifting aside branches and knocking away small, orange spiders that cling to delicate webs as beautiful as anything I've seen under the sea. "But I'm the heir. If I'm not willing to break the cycle of tradition, then who will?" I follow Sarah through the bushes, full of hope and anxiety both. There's so much to see in that moment that I'm overwhelmed, eyes scanning the sky, at the trees that are becoming increasingly frequent, at the leaves that surround us in a sea of green.

"That's beautiful," Seth tells me, pausing. Sarah doesn't stop, instead choosing to go around him. I have no choice but to drop the leash so that we don't bump into one another. Seth puts his fingers to his lips and whistles, drawing her back. He picks up the leash and glances over his shoulder at me. "I think you might be the most mature person I have ever met," he tells me and I can see in his eyes that he's serious, but also that he's speaking from the heart. There is none of the Feed's magic in his face right now.

Seth smiles and turns away, drawing us out of the brush and onto a wider trail, one that's been manicured just enough that there are no overhanging branches or plants in our way. Trees surround us on both sides, punctuated with small bunches of flowers and little patches of brown mushrooms. It's very dark in here and full of shadows, but the moon's brightness manages to penetrate in places, highlighting the area without illuminating it. It's quite stunning.

"It's gorgeous," I say as Seth turns back and watches me admire the scenery. Sarah barks and Seth steps forward, unhooking her leash and letting her gallop ahead of us. "Will she be okay?" I ask, just the slightest bit nervous. If anything were to happen Sarah, I'd feel like I'd lost a friend. I can easily see why humans decided to form a bond with dogs. They're incredibly easy to fall in love with.

"She knows this trail pretty well," he says, tucking the

leash into his sweater pocket. "And I doubt we'll run into anybody up here that can write us a ticket. I just use it around my neighbors because they're all dicks." He cringes like he's said something horrible. I can tell the word is an insult but am not entirely sure that I know what it means.

"You don't like them?" I ask as we start up the sloping trail in a brisk walk. Seth shakes his head.

"I don't."

"Why not?" I ask, feeling my muscles protest this newest endeavor. I have not taken a *hike* before. The word is strange to me, but the idea is even more foreign. Walking for the sake of walking. Incredible.

"They don't like me," he says simply. "I came into their perfect, little community and had the audacity to be different." Seth grimaces and digs around in his pocket. "I sound bitter, don't I? God, I hate that." He takes out a white stick and puts it between his lips, readying the plastic rectangle he uses to light it. Then he pauses and pulls it out of his mouth. "Do you mind if I have a cigarette?" I shake my head, glad to finally get the word down. Cigarette. I had been close with my guess of cigar. "Maybe I'll quit this next," he says with a sigh, lighting the tip and tucking the object back into his pocket. "Anyway, they have this, oh, I don't know what you want to call it, this club, I guess. It's for everyone that has a piece of lakefront property. They take turns hosting barbeques and having the neighborhood over for dinner." Seth sucks in a big breath, drawing the burning line of the cigarette closer to his lips and then blows it out into the night air where it drifts up and away. "When I bought the house, I had an invite waiting in my mailbox. I filled out the card and sent it in and then, nothing. I kind of suspected something at that point because I'd seen the neighbors talking about my car."

"What's wrong with your car?" I ask, unable to repress the feeling of relief that washes over me when Sarah comes trotting back, grinning from ear to ear. She falls into line between Seth and I and keeps pace with us.

"I drive a hearse," Seth says and he smiles gently. There's yet another word that I don't know. My training has left me sorely unprepared for our conversations. It's so frustrating that it makes me want to scream. Before I can ask, Seth supplies me with the answer. "It's a special car used to transport dead bodies." That's an entirely new fact for me. I bite my lip and process this, trying to recall if we were ever taught what the humans do with their dead. *They bury or burn them,* I remember, thinking of our own tradition of dragging the deceased out to sea and leaving them for the ocean to feed on. It isn't very dignified, but it is practical. There is a cycle to life in the sea and none of the *merighean* are ashamed to be a part of it.

"Is that not acceptable?" I ask to let Seth know that I am still listening.

"Not really," he says with a smile and pauses, bending down to push his cigarette into the dirt. Sarah licks Seth's cheek as he stands up and I'm glad to see that he's still carrying the remnant in his hand. He tucks it into his sweater pocket and leaves the earth as he found it. "So I called the director of the group and asked about the schedule. He told me to fuck off." He cringes again and shakes his head. "Sorry," he tells me though I don't know why. I don't completely understand his last sentence, but I'm guessing he means something offensive by it. I wait for him to clarify. "I don't mean to be crude, but those were his exact words. Fuck off. It means," Seth mulls this over for a moment. "Fuck off is a rude way of telling somebody to leave you alone. And I would have." As I listen to Seth's story, I find it increasingly hard to breathe. The exertion of climbing up this hill is making the muscles in my legs burn and tingle, and my lungs feel hungry for air. I copy Seth by taking bigger, longer breaths as we near the summit of the trail. "But his kid spray painted some shit on my fence and when I went over to talk to him about it, he told me to fuck off. Again. I'm not good at taking a lot of crap." Seth pauses and even stops walking for a moment. "You're easy to talk to, you know that?"

"Nobody's ever told me that before," I say, trying to think of Yanori and Yuri and Ira. I miss them already and it's only been a few days. I think it's because so much has happened since I left, that it feels longer. It's as if time is passing in events, rather than minutes or hours. If I were to use that estimation, then it feels as if it has been weeks. "But I appreciate the compliment." Seth smiles at me again and we continue walking. "So what happened?" I ask, prompting him to continue his story. Seth doesn't know it, but this simple conversation is one of the most interesting I have ever had, and informative. Everything Seth says is educational. I'm absorbing his slang, his dialect, the way he holds his mouth, his facial expressions.

All of these are important communication devices and ones that I am lacking.

"I punched him in the face," Seth says, sounding chagrined yet proud. "And he pressed charges. All of my lovely neighbors watched me get hauled off in a squad car and when I came home the next morning, I had a petition on my door telling me to move. That was a few months ago, but it still pisses me off."

"It hurts your feelings?" I ask, trying to grasp the full context of the sentence. Seth pauses again, just as we are about to crest the hill. I'm excited to see what's on the other side, but I wait with him as he studies my face and thinks carefully about his answer.

"Maybe a little," he admits and then smiles. "But it mostly just pisses me off." I laugh with him, although I don't fully understand. The night is so beautiful and different, full of strange sounds and new sights, that I just don't care anymore. All I want to do is laugh. "Are you ready to see the city?" he asks me, moving forward and over the top of the hill.

Through the trees is a glittering collection of lights that wink and sparkle like jewels. I find my feet pulling me forward without realizing it, until I'm standing near the edge of a cliff that falls away and disappears into darkness. There's a bench behind me that I drop onto. Seth sits next to me and Sarah flops onto his feet.

"Do you like it?" he asks me and I nod, unable to find the right words to say. All I can think about are the other Huntswomen and how much they're missing. They're spending all of their time trying to accomplish a single, limited goal with a bloody end and a preplanned future.

I glance over at Seth again and find him watching me.

I will change this, I say, finding a bit of myself, hanging onto it with steady fingers. I stare into his dark eyes and make a promise. This is the last Feed that will ever take place this way. Next time, it will be different.

Chapter Twelve

By the time we get back to the house, I'm so tired that I can barely keep my eyes open. I glance longingly at the water of the lake as we pass by. The clothes have irritated my skin and made my dry scales even more painful, more itchy; I could use a quick dip to refresh myself.

"Is that where you sleep?" Seth asks me, unlocking the front door. I turn around and look at him, fighting another surge of desire. Now that I've spoken with him and am starting to appreciate him as a person, the magic of the Feed is getting more difficult to resist. I want to couple with him so badly that there's a nearly painful ache between my legs. I don't think about my other desire, the other hunger that I have sworn off completely. That will get worse, too, and I will have to deal with it. It will test my limits of self-control, but I believe I can do it. I have that strength inside me.

"I want to sleep in your bed," I tell him, watching as he blinks his own, tired eyes at me. This day has been as challenging for him as it's been for me, maybe even more so. "I've always wanted to try one. At home, my mother is the only one that has that privilege. The rest of us sleep on the floor, or in hammocks." Seth yawns and I find myself following suit; we smile at one another.

"The princess sleeps on the floor?" he asks and I can see that he's trying to make another joke, but that he's too tired to deliver it successfully. "Of course you can. I'll take the couch." Again, I have trouble comprehending the exact meaning of that phrase, but I understand the most important part. *I get to sleep on a bed.*

"I need to get into the water for just a moment," I tell him, looking around for the neighbors that Seth has made me so averse to.

"They're all asleep," he says, letting Sarah off of her leash. She darts into the darkness of the house without waiting for us. "Or if they're not, they can't see much. I skinny dip all the time. Haven't gotten the cops called on me yet." Seth smiles wide. It's another joke that I don't get so I just nod. "I'll see you inside then?" he says, sounding worried. I nod again and he turns away reluctantly, following after Sarah. The lights in the kitchen flicker on and spill out the door, casting bars of yellow light across the ground. Seth leaves the door open for me which I appreciate and waves to me through the kitchen window as he passes. With one last look around, I strip off my clothes and dive into the comforting arms of the lake.

I relish the feeling of weightlessness, spinning and twirling, chasing the silver fish who now suspect me of murder at every turn. I cannot get the image of the twinkling city out of my mind. It was so vast and thriving; it makes me nostalgic for days that I don't even remember when Amarana would've dwarfed that city three times over. There are ruins that stretch for miles, hiding beneath the kelp forest, crumbling into the trenches, disappearing into the dark arms of the sea. I want to rebuild them, watch the bones of the ancients rise above me, and see them filled with lights and activity.

"You get more and more ambitious with each passing second, Natalie," I say to myself, listening to the currents of the water and the way my voice carries across the lake bottom. Yanori would help me, as would Yuri, maybe even Ira. But I know it will take more than just my friends to restore the health of the city. It will take the efforts of all of the *merighean,* every last one. Even my mother.

Her purple lips flash in my mind and I see her standing over me, Spindled Blade in hand.

"The things that you do, Natalie," she says and I shudder, curled on the ground in a ball beneath her. Already she has punctured my skin with the blade, let the poisons course through my veins. I can hardly keep my eyes open. "They frighten me. Something isn't right about you, daughter." And then she stabs me with it, again and

again and again.

I spent the next few days in my room throwing up. The only reason that I did not get any sicker is because Yuri and Yanori were there, bringing me food and cleaning up after me. Without them, I may have died. My mother doesn't even realize how far she had taken me. Aleria is blind to everything around her, a bad mother and an even worse queen.

I gasp suddenly and bubbles explode from my mouth, spin in circles and rise to the surface.

I can't believe the thoughts that I'm having. They're treasonous at best, truthful at worst. I sink to the sandy ground and cross my legs, fingering my sister's necklace. Change may not be possible with Aleria on the throne.

Yanori has said as much on several occasions. I know she is my biggest champion, but I know that what she wants is almost impossible at the moment. To take the throne, I must wait until either my mother passes away, steps down (which will never happen), or until I return from the Feed, marry a *merighean* and bear two children. Even with that option, I will have to wait until the second baby survives its first three years: a frightful task under the sea. At least a third of all *merighean* babies die in their first year. As things stand, it will be a long time before I ascend the throne.

Still, the seeds of change have been sown in my mind and they will not be easily forgotten.

The Feed

◆ ◆ ◆

Seth is sitting on the end of his bed, shirtless and dressed in a pair of fuzzy, gray pants. He looks up when I come in and smiles.

"Enjoy your swim?" he asks me as I spy Sarah in the corner, curled up on the large pillow that was previously in the living room. I nod at Seth's question and watch as his eyes follow mine to the black and white dog. "If I didn't put her in here," he says with a grin. "Then she would've just gotten up in the middle of the night and joined you on the bed." I smile at this.

"I wouldn't have minded," I say wondering if Seth will care if I crawl into his bed wet. The water feels so good on my skin that I'd rather not dry off, but if it is the way things are done here, then I will comply.

"Will you be okay if I have to go to work tomorrow?" he asks me suddenly, as if he's been thinking about this while I swam. I nod but don't comment on it, trying to follow along with my own decision to let Seth do what he wants to do. If he chooses to go to work, I will have to let him. After all, I don't fully understand human society and don't have any idea what sort of consequences he might face. "I'm probably the only idiot who *would* go to work with a beautiful, mermaid girl staying at his house." It's another joke, one that I can appreciate. I smile at him and decide to let him sleep with that thought in his head. Maybe he will change his mind.

"May I?" I ask, gesturing at the freshly made bed. Seth has even changed the coverings on the pillows for me.

"Be my guest," he says, moving away to the door and pausing with his hand on the light switch. I like that phrase. Guest. Seth sees me as a guest, not an intruder. I bow my head in thanks and bend down, climbing onto the bed on my hands and knees. When I reach the pillows, I pull the blankets back and slide my feet under them. It's so comfortable that I find myself burrowing into the cushions, rubbing my legs along the softness of the sheets. I moan in pleasure and hear Seth cough in response. The lights turn off, leaving me in darkness with nothing but tiny stars on the ceiling. "Sleep tight," he says in a strained voice, moving away and disappearing into the living room. I hear rustling and then those lights, too, shut off.

I listen to the sounds of Sarah's breathing and the gentle breeze that ruffles the grass outside Seth's windows. It's as if the whole world has gone to sleep, leaving a gentle quiet that masks the energy of this place. I close my eyes and am asleep before any other thoughts can cross the threshold of my mind.

◆ ◆ ◆

Morning comes much quicker than I had expected,

The Feed

reaching her golden fingers across the blankets on Seth's bed and opening my eyelids with her light. I stretch and sit up, feeling my muscles protest at the movement. Sarah is awake and is looking up at me from her spot on the floor, head lying across her massive paws.

"What shall we do today?" I ask her, smiling. She raises her head and her tail thumps against the floor happily. I want to go on another walk, see what the city looks like during the day, but I know that even with the clothing I was wearing, it is too risky. If I find myself in a large crowd, pandemonium could ensue and the only thing that might save me is a siren song which I refuse to use, knowing the consequences are too great a price to pay. I decide to get up and check on Seth, see if he is still here. If he has gone to work, then I will be left alone for the majority of the day, a thought that I find very disappointing.

But Seth is not gone. He is sleeping on the couch, curled on his side, blankets tangled around his legs. When I move into the living room, he opens his eyes slowly and blinks up at me. His face registers surprise for just a moment before he remembers who I am and what I am doing in his house.

"I thought I might've dreamed you up," he says without moving. I shake my head and smile as he groans, sitting up and running a hand through his hair. His phone is sitting on the edge of the couch and he grabs it, staring at it for a long moment before starting to curse. I take a step back and he cringes again. "Sorry," he says, putting it to his ear and standing up. He paces down the hall and opens the only door I have not been in. It's another room with a desk and a large window whose curtains are currently closed. It is not until I turn around that I see its main purpose.

It is a library.

I gasp as my eyes catch on the bookshelves that line two of the four walls in the room. They are made of a dark wood, smooth and polished, and stretch nearly to the ceiling. Every shelf is filled with books, most of them small and thick with colorful spines and big, English words. I reach out before I even think to ask permission and extract one.

"Hey, Bob, it's Seth," my host says from behind me and I spin around, hands clutching the book. The tomes at home are old and very rare; they are a special commodity that cannot be taken for granted and here I am, clutching one of Seth's to my chest. I search his face for anger but find none. "Yeah, yeah. I feel like shit and slept in pretty late." Seth pauses and sees me holding the book, looking guilty and staring at him with wide eyes. "Of course. No problem. Thanks Bob, I owe you. Yeah, you, too. Talk to you later." Seth hangs up and breathes a big sigh of relief. "Dodged a fucking bullet," he says and then looks down at the book in my hands.

"You have a beautiful library," I tell him honestly. He has at least a thousand books, maybe more spread across the four bookcases. Seth laughs at this and then when he realizes that I'm not joking, sobers up immediately.

"You don't have books at home?" he asks. "You seem like a reader to me." I close my eyes and caress the

The Feed

smooth, dry pages. Seth is right; I am a reader. I could easily spend the rest of the Feed in this room, sitting cross legged on the floor, consuming one after another. I haven't read anything new in years. The thought makes me so giddy that, combined with my hunger, I feel a bit dizzy.

"There are thirty-one tomes in the library at home," I say, opening my eyes. "Three of which are almost entirely unreadable. All of them are damp, flaking apart and fading with age." I turn and hold out my arm, trying to encompass his books with a wave of my hand. "I have never seen anything like this before." Seth stands there staring at me with his phone clutched in his hand.

"This isn't a library," he tells me, stepping back and dropping it on the desk. "God, I wish I could take you to a real one." Seth looks up at me and smiles. "Since I now have the day off, maybe we could work something out?" As soon as he says this though, I know that it will not happen. A central library would have a lot of humans, too many. It would be too dangerous, but I smile anyway, appreciating the thought.

"This is your own personal collection then?" I ask him, turning back to the shelves and holding out the book in my hand. I crack the pages open and stare at the sharp lines of dark print. I will have to read one of these before I go, just one. Since the books are not in my native language, it could take me the better part of two days, but I promise myself that I will do it.

"Yeah," he says, stepping up beside me and running his fingers along the spines on the highest shelf. "I've never really seen it as that impressive, but I guess I do have a lot of books." He takes one down and examines the figures on the cover. "I just sort of collected them over the years. I'm a big sci-fi/fantasy fan. How about you?" I swing my gaze back to the books quickly. I don't know what sci-fi is, but I do know what fantasy means. Pretend. Make believe.

"These are all leisure books?" I ask, thinking of the ones at home. Most of them are historical or filled with information about humans, save a couple. Those precious few are all tales of fantasy, of heroes in ancient times and depictions of the great creatures of myth, the ones that Seth has tattooed all over his body. He nods.

"I keep everything else on my e-reader," he says and upon seeing my look of confusion, heads back to his desk and pulls out another phone. Or at least, it looks like one. "Do you know what a computer is?" he asks me as he hands the device over. I spin it around in my hands for a moment and then give it back to him.

"In a sense," I say, digging through the facts in my memory. "It is like a television, with a screen and speakers for sound. Used to store information and connect with others. Am I correct?" Seth laughs but nods, playing with the device in his hands and handing it back to me. On the screen is the page of a book. I read a few words and look at up him, surprised.

"An e-reader is basically a small computer that you use to read books," he says, reaching down and swiping his fingers across the screen. The page changes and I repeat the action, watching the flow of words and ideas across the little screen with amazement. "I have a couple hundred

The Feed

books on there and room for plenty more." I read the page in front of me and see that it is some sort of medical text.

"This is amazing," I say, wishing I had more than a week, wishing I had years. It would take me that long to absorb everything there is to learn here and even then, I'd be left wanting more. I hand Seth back his e-reader, knowing that I hardly have time to learn even a fraction of human technology. "You are an incredible people," I say, holding the paper book in my hands. It is the first one I grabbed and so it is the one that I will read. I don't even really care what it's about. "You should be proud of your advancements. You step forward while we slide back." But then I think of the garbage in the ocean and the way the humans separate themselves from the earth. There must be a happy medium somewhere in there. I don't correct my compliment though, not wanting to upset Seth.

"Well," he says with a sigh and in his eyes, I can see that he thinks some of these same things. "We could debate that all day." He bites his lip and I can see that he doesn't really know what to do with me. I am the guest here, one that came uninvited. I will have to guide Seth, keep him occupied so that he does not find my visit awkward or bothersome.

"I am sorry about your job," I say genuinely, wondering what he has done to get out of it and what will happen to him for it.

"It's okay," he says and then adds with a laugh, "I hate it anyway." I cock my head to the side and study him carefully.

"You don't enjoy medicine?" I ask, curious. Seth

shrugs and I can see from the set of his shoulders that for whatever reason, this is a sensitive subject for him.

"It's not that. I just don't like the twelve hour days or the assholes that fill them." He shakes his head. "I'm so sick of being a free taxi for people who don't give a shit about the tax dollars that pay for it." He tries to smile at me but fails. Seth's eyes draw me in, absorb my face. "If I hadn't caught Bob stealing from the truck then I might've gotten fired today. He owes me a favor." Seth shakes his head and walks from the room, patting Sarah as he goes. "In fact," he continues, pausing with his hands on the counter. I follow him and stand in the hallway, still holding the book. I just can't bring myself to put it down. "Maybe I won't go in at all this week." He looks over at me. "When do you have to leave?"

"Today is the third day of the Feed," I say, providing him with the name of our strange ritual. "I have to leave on the morning of the seventh."

"The Feed, huh?" he asks and then shivers. "Okay then." Seth stands up straight and grabs the bag of pig's ears, tossing one of them at Sarah's feet. "Fuck it. I won't go to work." He stands there staring at me for a moment. "So what do you want to do today?" I look down at the book and then back up at Seth.

"If it's okay with you," I say, feeling a smile slide across my lips at the same time one crosses his. "I'd like to read."

The Feed

◆ ◆ ◆

Seth leaves me for awhile to go out, but I hardly notice.

The book I have chosen is fantastical. There is a character by the name of Acacia that reminds me so much of myself that I find that I am drawn into the pages, pulled away from the demands of the Feed and my fears for the future. Acacia's confidences become my confidences and her fears, my fears. But it is her love that thrills me most. Her romance is a forbidden one, a wild test of passion, respect, and understanding. I squeal and drop my head against the pages.

"This," I tell Sarah, who is a rather good listener. "This is what I want. Freedom, love, passion, purpose." I breathe the words against the paper, get lost in strange ideas that twirl around my head, teasing and beckoning. This book has awoken something in me. I don't know what it is, but it feels good. I hear footsteps and glance up suddenly from my place on the floor. I am lying across a pair of round cushions that Seth calls beanbags. They are both decorated in animal patterns that I feel I should recognize but don't. One is brown with black spots and the other is white with black stripes. I want to steal them away when I go back home, keep them for myself. They are wonderfully comfortable.

Seth steps into the living room with bags hanging from

each of his hands. His face is thoughtful and contemplative.

"I'm back," he says by way of greeting and lifts the plastic bags. I can't help but frown briefly at these. They are a menace in the sea; there are far too many of them and they have a habit of tangling around animals, leaving an unsavory mess for the *merighean* to clean up. Seth most likely does not know this, so I smooth my features. "I got all kinds of good stuff, lots of meat like you asked," he says, reminding me that I am hungry. My stomach roils painfully, begging for the taste of sweet flesh. *Seth's* flesh. I push those feelings down and stand up, using the strip of paper Seth has told me is a bookmark to remember my page.

"This is wonderful," I tell him, holding the book tightly against my chest. "You're lucky to have so many of these to read." Seth smiles.

"Thanks," he says, and then, almost as if he's afraid to ask, adds. "Was that your native language?" He is referring to my words to Sarah. I nod and follow him as he heads back towards the kitchen. I trail closely behind him, hoping that whatever he has in those bags is as good as the soup he cooked for me last night.

"It was," I say. "Did you like it?" Seth sets the bags down on the counter and removes a small, plastic sack. He opens it and the smell of meat wafts out, teasing my nose and moistening my lips.

"It was beautiful," he says, reaching in and pulling out a dried, brown piece of meat. He hands it to me and I put it in my mouth, whole. The scent of it is stirring my belly and making me desperate; I find that I'm starving. "Was that what's written here?" he asks, holding out his hand, palm down. "Was that *Amarana*?" I shake my head and reach for another piece of meat. Seth doesn't stop me and steps back, emptying more containers and packages onto the counter.

"On your hand is the language of the Huntswomen. What I was speaking is *Tersallee,* the language of the mers." Seth gives me a look that must mimic what I am always giving him. "The mers, the *merighean,* the ones with tails that make up the whole of our city. That is the language they speak, what we all speak for the most part. *Amarana* is just there to separate the Huntswomen from the rest of our people." I didn't realize this until I said it, but now it bothers me, sitting in the back of my mind like a clue.

"Maybe you could teach me a few words?" he asks and I can see his interest is piqued.

"I will," I promise, feeling excitement course through my veins. I can finally share something of my people with Seth instead of it always being the other way around. I watch him fetch a bowl from beneath the counter and place it next to a box full of white eggs. "Would you mind if I helped you cook again?" I ask and already, he's shaking his head.

"Not at all," he says, stepping back. "Please do."

Seth then shows me how to crack the eggs which he tells me are from a chicken, a white bird that is often used in human cuisine. We mix this with milk, a powdered grain called flour, a bit of salt, and a splash of yellow oil.

When the time to cook it over the stove comes, Seth pulls out a black pan and greases it with more oil, showing me how to pour the batter and flip the flat pastry he calls a crepe. When we're finished, Seth cuts up a slab of pink meat which he heats quickly in the pan and puts on a plate next to some yellow cheese. On another plate, he slices up tiny, red fruits and what I know is called a banana. He then pulls a plastic jar out of one of the shopping bags and warms it up, setting it down on the counter with everything else.

"There," he says, smiling at me and tossing one of the rolled up crepes to Sarah who gobbles it up in midair. "We have a make-your-own crepe station with ham and cheese for the savory and strawberries, bananas and chocolate-hazelnut spread for the sweet." I don't really know what to do with any of it, so I watch Seth make his plate first and copy him.

When I take my first bite, using the silver fork that he hands to me carefully, I am blown away. There are so many flavors that it takes my virginal palette a moment to catch up. I finish both crepes in record time and go back for more. Seth waits for me on the couch, still only halfway through his first one. I sit down next to him and hope that I'm not being rude. Human food etiquette was not taught to us by our instructors; I would be surprised to find if any of them had even sat down to a meal with their lover. More than likely, they just convinced the men to bring them food and ate it while the human swooned away in a stupor.

"This is incredible," I tell Seth honestly, feeling a bit of pride since I have helped to create this dish. It is similar to eating after a big hunt, when I know I have helped to bring down whatever animal is on the menu for that night, especially when it is something dangerous like a shark. "You have a real talent for bringing food alive." Seth opens his mouth and then stops, whatever he is about to say lost on the end of a low chuckle.

"Wow," he says and sets his plate down on the floor for Sarah. She gobbles up what is left of the crepes and then sits patiently, brown eyes silently begging for more. "I've never actually heard anyone say that to me before. Thank you." Seth leans back and examines me as I eat. I imagine that he's still getting used to me, still waiting for the practical side of him to accept what the magic has already forced the whimsical part of him to embrace.

"Am I being improper?" I ask as I finish another crepe and wish for more. It's the hunger of the Feed that's making me so ravenous, but I know that I can partially sate it by filling this rumbling in my belly with the ham and cheese. It is better than the alternative, better than eating Seth. He shakes his head.

"Not at all." Seth smiles as I stand. "Normally, when I cook something like this, Sarah gets it all." He rubs the dog behind the ears and her tail thumps the wood floor with pleasure. "Or I end up throwing it all away. It's nice to see someone actually eat it." I smile back and return to the kitchen for a third helping.

As I'm dishing myself another portion, I look out the window and watch the shimmer of the sun across the surface of the lake. Already, it is midday and it feels as if I have just woken up. *Time passes quickly here,* I realize. Having the sun in view, and then later, the moon, is a constant reminder of time. Below the sea, it is not like that at all. There are days marked by the time keepers in my mother's palace as well as a general sense of when things are to be done, an energy that passes amongst the citizens, but there are no clocks, no sun dials, no lightening of the sky or brightening of the moon and stars. Just a cool, darkness that soothes the soul, slows down the body and brings none of the sense of urgency that the humans exuberate. I can see positives and negatives in both lifestyles. Again, the idea of a middle ground comes to me although I can't quite decide how it might be accomplished.

Seth comes in the kitchen and stands beside me, looking down at my necklace with curious eyes.

"I was thinking," he says, holding up his arm so that I can see not only the tattoos that have brought me such confusion but also a silver bracelet that sparkles brightly, bringing attention to how tarnished mine truly is. "If you want, I could help you clean your necklace off. It wouldn't take long and it might be kind of fun. What do you say?" I nod as he unhooks the clasp of the bracelet and sets it on the counter next to me. "This used to be black, too. I actually found it on the beach, but it cleaned up nicely. I was going to give it to Jenna, but I just never found the right time. If you'd be interested, I'd like to give it to you. You can take it back to the sea where it belongs." I smile and pick up the piece of jewelry, draping it across my wrist gently and admiring the tiny links and the little silver plate. *Sailor* it says simply.

"Thank you," I tell Seth genuinely, knowing that this is yet another thing I will have to hide from my mother. "It's beautiful," I say and almost step back when he reaches down and lifts the ends of the bracelet.

"May I?" he asks politely. "I'll be careful not to touch." I nod and Seth loops the chain around my wrist, fastening the tiny clasp with steady fingers.

"I would very much like to know the story of this piece," I say to him, lifting my arm and letting the bracelet slide down my scales. "Who *Sailor* was and why he or she had this at the ocean." I drop my arm and pick up my fork, looking at Seth out of the corner of my eye. "I imagine that it would make a fine novel. Perhaps you should write one?" Seth laughs at this and moves over to the stove, bending down to retrieve a large pot.

"I don't have the patience to write," he says, rising quickly and pulling out a long, cardboard box from the drawer next to him. "But you seem like you'd be good at it. All of the great writers I've met in my life have been compassionate and empathetic. I think it comes with the craft." I ponder this a moment, savoring a big bite of the chocolate-hazelnut spread.

"I'm neither compassionate nor empathetic," I say honestly. "If I had to evaluate myself, I would say that I was practical, sometimes logical, perhaps a bit reckless." Seth laughs at this as he opens the cardboard box and reveals a cylinder wrapped in thin sheets of metal.

"You're not really sixteen, are you?" he says, but this time, he doesn't sound disgusted with himself. In fact, I think he may be making a joke. "You're way too smart, too honest for sixteen. When I was your age," he begins, cringing slightly. "Fuck, I sound old." Seth shakes his head and unrolls a bit of the metal, slicing it off on a row of silver teeth that line the edge of the box. He then proceeds to pad the bottom and sides of the pot with it. "Anyway, when I was your age, I spent most of my time playing guitar and chasing after girls." Here he pauses and then shakes his head again. "That sounds god-fucking-awful, doesn't it?" I finish the last of my crepes and place my plate in the sink next to Seth's other dishes.

"Why did you have to chase them?" I ask, hoping that I'm being at least a little amusing. Seth laughs and puts the cardboard box back in the drawer, turning with the pot in his hands and leaning his hip against the stove as he thinks about his answer.

"Because I was a really ugly kid?" he supplies and we both laugh. Seth steps forward and sets the pot in the sink, turning on the faucet and testing the temperature with the back of his hand. "I think I was trying to find something in myself that was worth living for, some trait that made me special. I just didn't want to be the kind of person that my brothers and my cousins were." Seth fills the pot with water and sets it on the stove, turning on the burner beneath it by twisting one of the black knobs that lines the front. "I guess I figured that the girls I was seeing could show me that somehow. If I had known that they were using me, I never would've bothered. I would've run away to Thailand and become a monk." Seth laughs at this, but it is not the same kind of laugh from before. I can see that this still bothers him.

"Did you ever find it?" I ask him, wondering if I'm doing the very same thing, searching for a special something within myself. *I know I'm different from the other Huntswomen, from the merighean, but why? What is it that makes me this way and how do I know that it's right?*

Seth reaches into a cabinet above and to the left of the stove, withdrawing a small yellow box. He opens it and pours a bit of white powder into the water, stirring it around with a metal spoon that he's retrieved from the hooks above his head.

"I don't know," he replies honestly. "Sometimes, I think I know why I'm here and other times ... " Seth doesn't finish his sentence, lets it trail off into silence. I don't ask anymore questions; it is obvious that Seth has gone as far as he wants to go right now. After all, I am not only a stranger, but a creature of myth, something that should not exist. I am surprised he is sharing any of himself at all. He turns to face me and points at my necklace. "The water's ready if you want to take it off?" he says this like it's a question, as if he isn't sure how I feel about the jewelry that graces my neck. Yanori has given it to me so in a way, I suppose, it is special, but I have seen others with such an attachment to their jewelry that they will not remove it, regardless of the circumstances. I suppose Seth has seen this behavior in others. I reach up and unhook the necklace quickly, letting it pool in my palm, and hand it over to him.

He holds out his hand and I drop the silver in, watching

as he rinses it quickly in some water, scrubbing gently with some soap that he gets from a bottle on the counter. He uses only his fingers to clean it, moving them in slow circles, trailing them down the decorative rectangles. All the while, I can see his eyes taking in the gold flecks, the bits of serpentine, the designs that are so crusted and dark that they cannot be seen properly through the tarnish.

When he's finished, Seth turns towards the stove and motions me forward. I stand as close to him as I can get without bumping his shoulder. I would hate to touch him now, to take away that contemplative look in his eyes. Seth is turning out to be quite the interesting character. Before I close this book, I am determined to learn more.

He moves the pot off the burner and turns off the flame. When the roiling bubbles subside a bit, he lays the necklace in the spoon and drops it gently into the water. Since I haven't the slightest clue what Seth is doing, I watch in silence, absorbing every step in this process. One can never be sure what the future holds and any information is valuable, just in case.

"Shouldn't be long," Seth says. "The aluminum foil is already turning black." I watch in wonder as little black flakes begin to float in the water and the necklace becomes lighter and brighter. My heart is racing now though I'm not sure why. Maybe it is because Yanori does not do anything without a reason. She gave me the knife, the necklace, and the crown with a purpose in mind. Perhaps I'm about to find out what that is.

Seth scoops the tangle of silver out with the spoon and lays it on a clean, white cloth. This he uses to carry the hot metal to the sink where he rinses it with cool water, using the edges of the cloth to scrub away at the few remaining spots of black. As he moves his thumb in gentle circles, what I see takes my breath away.

The first design that we have uncovered is the one that lives in the middle of Seth's chest.

Muoru.

Chapter Thirteen

I can't be bothered with prophecies. There are *merighean* that believe in them, even some that claim they are privy to such things. I have never seen any good come from one, whether it was true or not. Still, what can I make of the symbols on this necklace if not a prophecy?

On Seth's body is a match to each one: Muoru, Amahna, Kua, and the others who I cannot name.

I'm sitting on the floor in Seth's living room with Sarah pressed against my back. The necklace lies in my hand, limp, silent. What I really need now is Yanori's guidance, but since I don't have that, I make do with the thoughts that swim through my head in schools.

I ask for guidance and you give me quiet commands cloaked in secrecy? I ask Neptune, wondering what I have done that he has felt I should be put in such a position. Yanori knows something, too, or else she wouldn't have given the silly thing to me. I lift the necklace up to my throat and clasp it behind my neck. I admit, it looks much prettier against the pale blue of my skin now. The silver suits the shimmer of my scales much better than the black.

"Is everything okay?" Seth asks, a glass of water clutched tightly in his hand. I nod my head but don't respond; I'm so caught up on trying to solve this mystery that words seem like too much trouble. "I'm sorry," he says and now I'm forced to look over my shoulder at him. "If I had known, I wouldn't have done it." His apology is silly.

"If we had not cleaned the necklace," I say. "Then there would still be the issue of your dreams and your tattoos. This is just another piece of the same puzzle, not a new one entirely. It can only help." I sigh as I say this, knowing that my words are true but not yet how to interpret them.

"It doesn't change anything?" Seth asks and I hear a hint of fear in his voice. *Maybe he thinks that I will eat him now, gobble up the bright lines of color that are etched into his skin and forget all about it.* I smile; that is not like me at all.

"It changes nothing," I say and rise to my feet with Sarah. "I have come here to forge my own destiny and so that is what I shall do, prophecies be damned." Seth raises his dark brows. He hasn't heard me curse before.

"Forge your own destiny?" he asks and then sips the water. "I like that." He pauses and takes a step forward, placing his hand on the top of Sarah's head. "How can I help?"

I glance longingly at my book which now sits on the edge of the couch, an extravagance that I will have to pay for with time, but can I afford it? I look back over at Seth and see that he has finished the water and is gazing into the bottom of the glass with a desperate expression. Then he sighs, straightens his shoulders, and looks up at me.

"Teach me something," I say, not caring what it is. "Anything. You choose." Seth thinks about this for a moment and sets his glass on the little table next to the couch.

"I was wondering," he asks and I can see that whatever it is that he's about to say, he has been thinking on it for awhile. "If I could take your picture. I could show you how to use the camera and you could even take one of me or Sarah." He smiles gently. "Like a souvenir or something."

Pictures. Photographs. Video.

These are deadly words under the sea. One of the first things drilled into us by the instructors is to never, ever allow ourselves to be caught on film of any kind. Drawings are okay; humans don't consider drawings as evidence. But physical clues of any kind are forbidden – a bit of hair, a bit of scale, anything that we might leave behind that could be examined. That is the first rule. The second is to remain clear of any human media. I consider this for a moment.

"Are you planning on selling it?" I ask and I look directly into Seth's eyes, hoping to pull the truth from him. His intentions are an important consideration to me. Already though, he's shaking his head.

"It would be just for me. I wouldn't show it to anybody; I promise." I stare at Seth carefully, examine the lines of his face for betrayal. He has not tried to harm me thus far, has only been nice to me, welcoming. I am already taking so many risks, what is one more? Besides, some risks are worth taking. I only hope that I am smart enough to determine which ones those are.

◆ ◆ ◆

"Okay," Seth says as he kneels, hands wrapped around a square of black plastic. "Put your hand up to your face." I do as he asks, trying to appreciate his artistic vision. I am sitting in the patch of basil at the edge of the yard, trying to keep my eyes on the camera. It's difficult; even in Seth's relatively small backyard, there are a million things I have never seen. There are so many flying insects, most of them in bright colors, and birds, too, that sing and flit from the edge of the fence, to the house, and back again. Sarah is barking at something in the tree that grows at the back of the yard, shadowing the grass around it with big, beautiful branches. "I might have to go get something better than this piece of shit," Seth says with a sigh, examining the images on the screen. "It isn't capturing you at all."

I rise to my feet and walk over to him, maneuvering myself carefully so that I can see the pictures. I look strange on the glowing screen, that is for sure. Not like me at all. My skin is dry and my scales are flaky; my hair hangs limply on my shoulders and my eyes are dull.

"It's not your camera," I say as I lift the arm with the bracelet. It twinkles softly, shaming my skin with its beauty. "I should be in the water." Seth looks at the camera, then at me, then at the camera again.

"You're right," he says, handing it over to me. His eyes are sparkling now, lost in thought. Perhaps he's imagining the possibilities. I can see an artist hidden in Seth. Whether he knows it or not, there is a creative part of him fighting to get out. It's in his cooking, in his pictures, in the set of his face as he looks up at me. "Would you mind if I went out and got an underwater camera? Maybe we could take some pictures in the lake tonight?" I raise my brows but nod. This is getting interesting.

"I would like that," I say, turning the camera around in my hands.

"Great," he says, tucking his hands in his pockets and whistling for Sarah. She comes racing over to us, black ears flopping, and runs in tight little circles around us, barking. Seth shakes his head at her. "Newfies aren't supposed to bark so much, Sarah," he tells her in an amused voice. "It's why I picked you out, you silly girl." Seth turns to go back in the house, motioning the dog to follow along behind him.

"Wait," I say, smiling. Seth pauses and turns back. In his face, I can tell that he knows what I'm about to say.

"I'm not getting out of this, am I?" he asks and I shake my head.

"I don't need an underwater camera to capture you," I say and wonder what Seth would look like with his black hair billowing around his face, brown eyes reflecting back the dark depths of the sea. It is enough to make me shiver, so I turn away and pretend to be more interested in the scenery. I think I would like to see him against the tree. If he were to lean against it casually, close his eyes ... No. I want his eyes open. They're quite pretty and very deep. I can always see something turning in there, some idea that's beyond the scope of the situation. Seth likes to think a lot. "How do I operate this?" I ask, examining the myriad buttons on the back of the device. Seth points to a silver button on the top.

"It's pretty easy," he tells me. "I've got it set up for this lighting, so all you need to do is point and click." I nod and point at the trunk of the tree with my nail.

"I want you there," I say, imagining the image in my head. If taking photos is in any way similar to carving busts then I may very well fail at this. At home, we take bits of stone and tools that date back before my mother's birth and shape one another's likenesses. I cannot even remember the name of the Huntswoman I was instructed to sculpt, only that she did not smile when I presented her with my final product. "And if you would," I say as Seth moves into position. "Remove your shirt." Seth's brows rise substantially, but he complies. I want to capture as many of his tattoos as I'm able. I am most interested in Muoru, but I cannot miss the images on Seth's arms or his hips. I haven't asked Seth yet, but I am hoping that he will print me these pictures to take back home. I can't show them to Yanori, of course, as she is blind, but if I have them in my hands, I can describe them to her. She will ask questions that I will not have thought of it. It's more important even than Seth may realize.

"Is this good?" he asks, leaning his back against the bark of the tree. He motions for Sarah to lie in the grass before him which I appreciate. I may not need her image to solve this mystery, but I would certainly like to have it. Just because. Little things like that make life worth living.

I frown thoughtfully as I adjust my position and scoot forward. I can't see the pink fish on Seth's right hip nor the symbol of Neptune below his belly button.

"Unbutton your pants as well, please," I say, trying to use a severe enough tone that he does not mistake my requests for seduction. Seth chuckles deep and low in his chest and shakes his head.

"You really know how to get a guy going, don't you?" he says and I think hear the slightest hint of flirtation in his voice. I pretend to ignore it and wait until he's done what I've asked. Despite his words, I can see that Seth understands where I'm coming from. He peels the denim of his pants down so that both symbols are visible. I ignore the beating of my heart and the desires of the Feed as I look around for something to stand on. If I were a bit taller, I think I would be better equipped to capture the details that I'm looking for. "Try one of those wine barrels," Seth suggests, once again anticipating my thoughts before I have a chance to say them.

I follow the line of his pointing hand to a pair of wooden objects filled with dirt and little, green balls that, from the teeth marks, I can guess belong to Sarah. I empty one of them out and drag it closer to the tree, turning it over so that I can stand on the bottom. Once I find my balance, I tilt the camera to the side and try to grab the whole of Seth's body on the screen.

At first, I struggle to keep my hands still and end up with blurry washes of color instead of the clarity that my eyes drink in hungrily. Seth is beautiful; the tree that towers over his head is beautiful; his dog, with all her drool and her growling barks, is beautiful. The pictures do not capture that at first, shaken by my nerves and the fear that, like the sculpting, I will fail in this, too. Soon though, I find a rhythm inside of myself, and I follow that melody all of the way to the trunk of the tree. I glance up at Seth and capture one, final shot of his face.

"I'm think I'm done," I say, knowing somehow that I have gotten the images I was looking for.

"I think so, too," Seth says and he takes the camera from me. We stare at each other for a moment before he turns away and bends down to retrieve his shirt. "Lunch?" he asks as he whistles for Sarah and moves towards the back of the house. I pause for just an instant longer, taking in the white clouds that drift overhead and the sound of children playing in the water.

I did not expect to fall in love with this world, not so quickly, but with the blueness of the sky and the shimmer

The Feed

of the sun on the lake behind me, I am spellbound.

◆ ◆ ◆

Seth and I have sushi, which he makes from scratch, slicing thin filets of fish and layering it over rice wrapped with nori. This is a dish that I am somewhat familiar with. *Kimtazi*, the food that my father makes so well, is very similar although we cannot boast rice or dried anything under the sea. After we eat, Seth retreats to his library and I curl up against Sarah on the couch, book in hand. It's such a peaceful thing, reading, that I am caught up in the pages until the very end. Acacia, the main character, finds herself queen of a nation she never loved, in charge of a people she never loved, but at the side of a man who makes her heart beat and her talents come to life. Together, they shape their country into a message of hope, into a symbol of proof that people can and will change given the right opportunity.

When I finally finish it, laying the novel against my chest with a sigh, the sky outside is dark and Seth is standing in the doorway of his bedroom, a sweater and a pair of pants in hand.

"Want to take another walk?" he asks me and I nod, stretching my arms above my head and giving Sarah a scratch. She lifts her head from my lap with a soft sigh and jumps down from the couch, shaking her fur and splattering the edge of the furniture with drool. Seth says nothing, just smiles.

I dress myself as quickly as I'm able and practically race Seth to the edge of the cliff where the city shimmers brightly in the darkness.

"I think we should do this every night," I tell him as I stand a little too close to the edge. Somehow though, it feels as if I cannot fall, as if, were I to drop from this spot and plummet into the black sky, that I would grow wings and fly. This is, of course, not true in the least so I breathe in a big breath of air and take a step back so that I'm in line with Seth's shoulder.

"I would love to," he says, examining the cigarette in his hand with distaste. I can see that he both loves and despises it. He sees me looking and glances over, meeting my eyes with a challenge. "Want to help me quit?" Seth asks. I turn towards him and reach out, taking the glowing stick between my fingers. The smell makes it something that I would most certainly not want to breathe in, but I have to ask.

"What are the benefits?" Seth stares at me for awhile before answering, glancing over his shoulder briefly to check on Sarah.

"I guess," he starts and then takes the cigarette back from me when I show no intention of smoking it. He puts it between his lips and inhales deeply, chest expanding beneath the orange sweatshirt that he's wearing. "It relaxes me. Oh," Seth snaps his fingers. "And haven't you ever heard that phrase, 'With a cigarette, I am never alone'?"

The Feed

"Are you lonely, Seth?" I ask, meaning only to clarify, but there's something behind his eyes that tells me that this is true. He doesn't answer and I don't ask him to.

"It's like a reward, you know? Like, if I finish this project, if I get this shit done, then I can have a cigarette. It used to be that way with alcohol, too. If I do this one thing, then I can have a drink, and another, and another." Seth throws the cigarette down angrily and crushes it with the toe of his boot before using one of the bags he brings to clean up after Sarah to grab it and stuff it in his pocket. He smiles, but the expression is not a happy one. His face is so bitter right now, harsh and dark in the light of the moon. "I only started smoking to meet Jenna," he says and I wonder if he misses her. I ask him that and he doesn't respond right away. I look back at the city and try to imagine living there. What does a person do in one of those high rise buildings? Don't they miss the touch of earth beneath their feet? If I were them, I would only want to visit their glowing city. I would want to live in a place like Seth's where the earth, and the water, are at my fingertips.

"Only the idea of her," Seth says finally and it takes me a moment to pull myself out of my thoughts. His voice is so melancholy that I decide to keep the rest of my questions to myself. After awhile, he starts to ask some of his own. "What about you?" he begins, trying to soften his face into a more pleasant expression. It works and I return the favor, smiling back with my purple lips that he doesn't seem to mind so much. "Do you have a boyfriend or a husband or something at home?" I look back at the city, considering my answer carefully. I had thought he might ask something like that and I have been trying to decide how I might respond. My words will be for more than just Seth's informational purposes; they will be for my own as well.

Yuri.

I sigh softly and let my gaze travel across the rise and fall of the tallest towers, drop down to the houses that trickle out from the center, disappearing into the blackness of the forest that we're standing in. At least they have left this bit of nature untouched; gentle and wild it sits, like a reminder of what was here before the lights of the city drowned out the darkness.

Unconsciously, I let my hand drop to my belly, trying to still the flutter that whispers there, begging me for another taste of what Yuri had to offer. The ache between my legs has finally subsided, but the hunger may never go away. I glance over at Seth and try to imagine sleeping with him. *Do I want to? Do I have to? If I don't, what will my mother do when she finds I am without child?*

"I don't know," I decide to say. I'm being as honest as I can. I haven't thought much about Yuri since I left; there hasn't been time. When I get back however, it will be all I have to think about. Yuri will expect things; the other Huntswomen will expect things; my mother will expect things. If I don't marry him, the *merighean* will wonder. "I want love," I tell Seth, keeping my eyes on his face. He stares back at me, mouth serious and listens closely. I think he understands this, desires it as much as I do. "I don't know if I've found it or not." Seth doesn't respond to that, just turns his own gaze back to the city.

"We're a lot alike, you and me," he tells me, and I know that this is true.

We don't say anything more to one another, just stand in companionable silence until the breeze that teases our brows gets frosty and the moon dips lower in the sky. Without another word, Seth and I turn as one and head back to his house.

Chapter Fourteen

As per Seth's instructions, I take the pile of cigarette boxes that he's presented me with and hide them while he waits in his bedroom with the door closed. He says that if they're not easy to get to, that he's less likely to smoke, but that he can't bear the thought of throwing them away, just in case. I decide to take them outside and stash them in the dirt that lines the bottom of the second wine barrel. I am careful to wipe my hands off before going in to retrieve Seth, not wanting to give away my hiding place.

"Thanks so much," Seth tells me honestly, rubbing at

his messy hair and yawning. I enjoy Seth's couch as a seat, but I think for sleeping, it would not be nearly as comfortable as his bed. I feel guilty for taking it and wonder if I should ask him to join me next time. It would present us with an awkward scenario and then there's the chance that he might touch me on accident. I decide that I can't make that suggestion but promise myself that when night rolls around again, I will offer to sleep on the couch. "I think I'm going to take a shower and then head out and grab that camera for tonight. If you want to take a car ride, I could dress you up in another sweat suit." I bite my lip as I consider this. I would love to go with Seth, even if I can't leave the safety of his car. Still, I know it is dangerous. As of this point, it's just a matter of deciding if it's worth the risk.

"I think I would like that," I tell him, following him into the bathroom. I have heard of showers. The instructors rave about them, tell us that they're like miniature waterfalls, warm and soothing to the muscles. I sit down on the toilet seat and wait for Seth to turn on the water. I didn't make it into the lake last night and my skin is so dry that it's nearly painful.

Seth stares at me for a long moment and I realize that perhaps I'm not welcome in here after all. I have no problem with my nakedness, but I know that humans often do. I rise to my feet and make as if to leave.

"You might as well stay," Seth tells me with a smile, bending down to twist the silver knobs. Water cascades from the faucet for a moment before he pulls on a central knob and the flow switches to a second faucet, positioned on the end of a metal pipe that protrudes from the floor and reaches nearly to the ceiling. "I've already seen every inch of you; it's only fair." I smile at Seth's joke and sit back down, crossing my legs and watching as he tests the water with his hands.

When he's satisfied with the temperature, Seth reaches down and pushes his pants to the floor without looking at me and climbs into the tub, pulling the curtain closed behind him to prevent the water from splashing on the already wet tiles. I don't know if he realizes that I plan on joining him, but I decide not to ask, fearing that he will tell me no and that I'll be left with flaky scales and itchy skin.

I move around to the back of the tub and peep in, wanting to make sure that I don't touch Seth by accident. He's facing away from me, running his hands through his hair and letting the steam rise around his muscled form.

He's quite beautiful, I realize as my heart thumps painfully in my chest and my body begs me to reach out and touch his naked skin. I step over the edge of the bathtub and join Seth before he even notices that I'm looking. When he spins around and finds me standing there, he slips on the slick surface of the porcelain and I come very close to reaching out and grabbing him. Luckily, Seth finds his balance with the help of the shower curtain and stands there staring at me.

"Well hello there," he says and I think he's trying to be funny. All I can hear in his voice, however, is shock.

"Is this inappropriate?" I wonder. I have not been taught human etiquette when it comes to sex and nakedness. No such thing exists under the sea, and for our purposes here, it is not necessary to learn. Still, I am quite aware that there are boundaries that exist. I can only hope that I don't stumble across them and offend Seth.

"To be honest with you, I don't really know," he tells me and I can see that, at least physically, he is happy that I'm here.

"I could leave?" I suggest, wondering if my presence in the close confines of the steamy shower is too much for him to take. After all, the magic of the Feed is still at work, still drawing him to me, making him desire me with each beat of his heart. Seth shakes his head rapidly and glances down at Sarah who's stuck her head underneath the shower curtain.

"No, no, you never got to swim last night, so I guess you're probably ... " Seth stops talking for a moment and I watch as his eyes sweep my naked form carefully. He's been looking at it for several days now and I had thought he'd gotten used to it. His expression tells me that he's just been ignoring it. Not so much right now. He's as hungry for me as I am for him; I can see it in his eyes. I take a step back and consider leaving. If he reaches for me, touches me in any way, then I will fail to fight my desires. I will become a slave to destiny. All of my choices now must be conscious ones. "You're probably pretty uncomfortable, huh?" I nod my head and show him some scabs on my wrist.

"Last night," I say, moaning as the water sluices between my scales. "Last night, this is where my scales rubbed off while I was sleeping." Seth reaches out like he's about to touch me and then drops his hand.

"God," he says and I can tell he feels somewhat responsible for my condition. "Maybe tonight we'll both take a swim." He pauses. "Is it painful?" I shrug my shoulders like I've seen him do. It's an effective way to communicate uncertainty.

"Not anymore than these," I respond, gesturing at the scratches on my belly and hands that are only partially healed.

"Where did those come from anyway?" he asks me, trying to distract himself from the demands of his body. He turns away and reaches for a green bottle that's resting on the edge of a metal rack.

"When I climbed out of the sea, I came up the rocks of Muoru." Seth pauses and looks over his shoulder at me.

"The rocks of Muoru?" he asks and then his eyes widen in shock. "Captain's Cliff?" he says with disbelief, turning all of the way around to stare at me. "You climbed up Captain's Cliff?" I presume that Captain's Cliff is the name for the rocks so I merely nod.

"I did," I say recalling the fear that clung to my heart and weighed me down. But I made it. I made it here to this warm shower with this kind person and a hundred revelations that I wasn't quite ready for. "Along with one other Huntswoman, Kiara. The others refused to follow me; instead they opted for the beach. Many of them are likely dead." Seth is staring at me now and I can see that some of the information I gave him in the beginning was lost in the thrall of the Feed.

"How many more of you are there?" he asks, sounding quite surprised.

"One hundred and one, including myself," I say and then remember the dead Huntswoman I saw in the sea. "It is probable however that at least a third of them are dead by this point," I add. Seth continues to stare at me for awhile before opening his mouth. He pauses and closes it again. "By the time we return to the city, there will be less than fifty. This is my guess anyway."

"Wow," he says and shakes his head. "That's harsh. And a pretty piss poor return. What happens to them?"

"Sharks," I say, thinking of the girl in the sea with her insides laid out for the crabs. "Cars, women mostly."

"Yeah, well, that part's not all that unusual. A lot of my friends died that way, too," he says and I can see that he's making another joke. I don't quite understand it so I nod. Seth laughs at my ignorance and lathers up his hair with soap from the green bottle. "Never mind," he says, trying to smile. "I was being a sexist ass. And insensitive." He frowns briefly. "I'm sorry about your friends. I was just trying to lighten it up. I didn't mean any disrespect."

"None taken," I tell him honestly. The whole situation is funny in an ironic sort of a way. It makes absolutely no sense to me. I think I have finally come to the root of one of my problems with the Feed. It is ludicrous bordering on insane. "I hope I am wrong about that number though or we will have to initiate the Hunt." I frown severely and try not to think that far ahead. The Hunt would topple any plans I might make for the future. In effect, it would render all of my risky decisions pointless. I can see that Seth is about to ask me about it, so I change the subject quickly in an attempt to distract him. "I was wondering if we might watch a movie today," I say and watch as he closes his eyes and rinses the white lather from his hair.

"Do you have anything in mind?" he asks me and I can see that for just a moment there, he'd forgotten that I wasn't human, that I am something else entirely. "Or I guess I should be asking, have you ever seen a movie before?"

"I haven't," I say, thinking of the plays at home. They are grand affairs, to be sure, with scripts passed down orally from the older generation to the younger. Sometimes a particular story will be acted out over several weeks or even months, drawing in the audience more and more each day. Occasionally, they are fabulous, but most often, I find them dull. Much of the time, the plays are chosen based on my mother's whims, and the only ones she enjoys are tales of destruction where the *merighean* rise from the sea and crush the humans. Every once in a while she will select a tale of old, something that says how great we were, that displays, in horrible clarity, how far we've fallen. If Seth's movies deviate from these themes in the slightest, I know I'll be pleased. "Pick me something without mermaids," I say and then add, "And without the sea."

Seth wipes water from his eyes and scratches Sarah behind the ears. She's lapping droplets up from the edge of the tub, switching to Seth's skin when he gives her the chance.

"Not a problem," he says and then smiles. "The only two movies I can think of with mermaids are *Splash* and *The Little Mermaid,* neither of which I would want to watch on a date. Or ever at all for that matter."

"A date?" I ask, missing the context of the word. *Date, day, a specific time.* Seth's smile droops for a minute as if he's deep in thought. He misunderstands my confusion at the specific word and tries to explain the context of his statement.

"I feel like this whole time, we've been on one, big, long date. Maybe it's because I feel like I want to please you, show you a good time." Seth stops and takes a breath. "Or maybe it's because we're having so much fun together. At least, I am." I smile back at him.

"I'm having fun as well," I say, still missing the meaning of the word. Seth grins back at me and steps out of the shower and onto the black rug that graces the floor in front of the tub.

"Good, then it's a date, officially," he says and gestures at the faucet with his chin. "Stay in as long as you want; when you're done, just holler. Okay?" I nod, still confused, but before I can ask another question, Sarah is leaping into the bathtub and the shower curtain is following after her, caught on her back legs. With a groan, the metal rod that holds it separates from the ceiling and crashes down around us, smashing into the floor with a spray of white dust.

For a moment, there's complete silence as the faucet, now crooked, sprays water in an arc across the room and all over the wall and window behind me. Seth, still naked, is standing with his back against the sink and Sarah is barking.

"Are you okay?" he asks, voice shaky. I look up and

examine the holes in the ceiling.

"I am," I say, glancing down at the dog who's still wrapped in bits of torn curtain. Her tail is wagging and she doesn't seem the worse for wear. "And I think Sarah is as well."

"Good," he says, and moves forward to turn off the water. Then, as he surveys the damage above us, "Crap." Seth grabs a cloth from the rack behind him and tosses one to me without thinking. I hold it against my chest and wait to see what he will do. "I knew I should've hired someone to put that thing up," he tells me as Sarah escapes from the curtain and trots out of the bathroom, not in the least bit ashamed at her destruction. Seth watches her go with a sigh but says nothing. "I guess we can stop at the hardware store and get some stuff to fix it," he tells me, shaking his head. "I was going to paint the bathroom anyway." He dries off his hair quickly and wraps the cloth around his hips. "Maybe you could help me pick the color? I could bring some paint chips out to the car." I look around at the white walls and nod, glad that Seth has not lost his temper with the dog.

"I would like that," I say and I watch as Seth holds out his hand. I think he is intending to help me out of the tub and over the debris that's strewn across the floor, but I can't take it. He realizes this at the same moment I do and drops his arm at his side. For an instant, I wish that I'm a human girl, that I could take Seth's hand and paint his bathroom and kiss his lips, all without fear that a voracious magic will sweep down and wipe the emotions from his face. Then the desire is gone, leaving me slightly empty.

C.M. Stunich

Even if I had that chance, I would not take it. I have to help my people, at all costs, even if it means never setting foot on land again.

◆ ◆ ◆

I borrow yet another sweatshirt of Seth's with a wide hood that droops into my eyes and hides my face. I forgo his offer of underwear but take another pair of pants in gray to go with a pair of dark glasses and the same shoes he loans me for our walks. When Seth is ready to go, we put Sarah in the backyard with a bowl of food and a couple of pig's ears. She's looks awfully sad to be left, but I can tell that Seth, although he doesn't blame her for what happened, is a bit irritated.

He opens the front door and surveys the grass and the lake in front of his house. When he decides that the coast is clear, he motions for me to follow and takes me to a gleaming, black car with a square roof. Seth opens the door for me and shows me how to strap myself in with what he calls a seat belt.

"My brother went through the windshield," he tells me by way of explanation. I'm not sure what he means, but I don't have to ask. Seth starts to elaborate as soon as he climbs in the other side. I think something about me inspires him to talk. He doesn't seem like a person who readily empties his thoughts for all the world to see. "I was sixteen, he was eighteen and we were driving home from a party." Seth inserts a silver key into the car near a round wheel that I know from my teachers' diagrams is used to steer. The vehicle rumbles and I find myself clutching the edge of the door and curling the fingers of my other hand around the seat. It sounds a bit like the boats that I've seen near the surface and the remote beach where I spotted my first humans. I don't think I like it at all. Things get even worse when Seth backs the vehicle into the gravel behind us. My stomach is lurching and I feel the slightest edge of nausea.

Seth turns the rear of the car towards the house and lets us drift back until we are pointed up a gravel road that circles the lake and then turns a sharp left, disappearing behind the crest in the hill.

"We were both drunk, of course," he says with a sigh and turns back around until he's facing the front. Only then does he see my discomfort and stop the car. "Are you okay?" he asks me, trying to look at me behind the flop of hood.

"I am," I say, although that's a lie. I relax my hands and put them in my lap, folding them gently. "Please, continue." I can tell that Seth wants to tell his story and I want to hear. He stares at me for another moment before accelerating slowly. Soon, the lake is whizzing by on one side and houses are spinning away on the other. I lean back into the seat and close my eyes, confident that Seth will not be able to tell behind the glasses. I have never traveled so fast before and the flickering scenery is making me dizzy.

"Anyway," he says with another sigh, turning us left at

the hill and steering the vehicle up a ramp of cement that leads to the big road behind his house. "My brother hit a parked car and flew through the window. I've never seen so much blood." I don't ask if Seth's brother is dead; it's quite obvious that he is. I open my eyes and try to concentrate on the stillness of his face.

"My sister, Adora, died in an accident as well," I tell Seth and he glances over at me sharply.

"I'm sorry to hear that," he says softly. "What happened?" He tries to smile, but the expression flops and he just looks sad. "I'm assuming it wasn't in a car … " I smile back at him, but mine is more genuine, not as sad. I didn't care for Adora much. Although she was my sister, she was the spitting image of my mother in personality. She was abusive, rude, and careless. These are the traits that got her killed.

"She took a group of *merighean* out to a shipwreck," I say, letting the memory of that day wash into my mind. "It's something we do often, to look for things," I explain to Seth. "We have almost nothing so we scavenge for everything." He grimaces when I tell him this but says nothing. "Do you know what a *maruna* is?" Seth shakes his head and I try to explain. "It's a black and white whale." I open my hands wide although the gesture is pointless; *maruna* are longer than Seth's car. "At least," I calculate distances in my head, try to use something that Seth is familiar with. "At least six meters long."

"You mean an orca?" Seth asks. "A killer whale?" I don't know either of these terms, so I shrug.

"Perhaps," I say. "Although they are hardly killers. At

least in most circumstances. My sister stabbed their baby with a harpoon and that is the only reason they killed her. It's just another example of how disrespect for the sea will bring a person to her knees." Seth chuckles and then immediately apologizes.

"Sorry, I didn't mean to laugh at your sister's death. It's just, you sound a lot like me." I smile.

"You apologize too much," I tell Seth firmly and he laughs again, much more loudly this time. I have been so engrossed in our conversation that I have missed much of what has passed by outside my window. I suspect however that I would've been much too nauseous to look at it anyway.

The car is slowing down now, maneuvering into an area of cement with several others, all of them still and empty. Seth moves his car between a pair of yellow lines and removes the key. The engine quiets and I feel my stomach start to settle.

"Wait here for me, okay?" he says and takes off his seat belt. "I'm going to run in real quick and get some paint chips then I'll be back." I nod and reach into the pocket of my sweatshirt. From it, a pull another novel.

"I borrowed this without asking," I tell Seth. "I hope that was okay." The book is burning my fingertips, begging me to crack the cover and dive inside. I see that this one is about fairies, a creature I have heard tales about but have never seen. I had told myself that with my time restrictions, I would read only one book; I have lied.

"Of course," Seth says with a soft smile. "While you're here, anything that's mine is yours. Make yourself at home." And then he climbs out of the car and disappears into the glass doors of a massive white building teeming with people. I hunker down and hope that none of them see me. If one spots me, they may draw the attention of the others and I could have a riot on my hands. It's something I can't afford, so I allow myself only a quick look around. There isn't much here besides the cars and the people. Out Seth's window, I see a massive road with speeding vehicles and beyond that, the mountains.

Satisfied that there isn't anything new to take in, I lie on my back with my head resting on Seth's seat and start my book.

There were only two things that pleased the Great Fairies: food and sex. Of the latter, it was the burden of the village's most beautiful men and women to supply it. The ornery fae would accept no others.

I read on hungrily, desperate for more of a story that unfolds with a scene of wild sex the likes of which I have never imagined. There are acts written of that I have not heard of and I find myself convinced that Yuri was being kind with me. We had not touched on most of what I see in the pages I consume.

A knock at the window startles me out of my story and I find myself looking up at Seth's smiling face. I sit up and scoot back to my side, curious to see what it is that he's clutching in his hands.

"I was thinking," he says as he climbs in next to me and holds out two pieces of paper. On them are rectangles of color that start light at the top and get progressively darker as they reach the bottom. "We could do something that mimics your colors." Seth hands me the papers and then points at the scales on the back of my hand. "Maybe a light blue for the ceiling, since I have to repaint it anyway, and a silver color, like this," he gestures at a square of blue-gray. "For the walls. What do you think?" I examine the color palette for awhile and then look up at Seth's brown eyes.

"I inspired you?" I ask, touched that he would think to model his home after me.

"Absolutely," he says and smiles. A thrill teases my body, makes it hard to breathe for a moment. I hand Seth back the papers.

"Then I think that's a wonderful idea," I tell him, trying to keep my voice steady. There are feelings in my belly now that have nothing to do with the Feed. I like Seth, as a person, as someone completely unrelated to the magic. I can see that now.

"Which blue do you think would work best for the ceiling?" he asks me and I point to the lightest color. It reminds me of a clear sky with white clouds and a breeze that smells of flowers.

"This one," I say and he nods his head like he's had the same thoughts.

"I liked that one, too," he says and then grins. "Alright, let me just grab the paint and some stuff to patch up the ceiling and I'll be back. I think the place next door will have the camera I'm looking for, too. Just give me twenty minutes." I nod my head and wait for Seth to leave. I know that if I have feelings for him, any at all, then making rational decisions will be that much more difficult. I close my eyes and finger the necklace through the fabric of the sweatshirt. Sleeping with Seth would be the wisest decision, but the most difficult for me to follow through on. I like him too much to make him a part of the Feed. I want my own destiny, and I'm willing to pay the price, but I'm not sure how much I'm willing to extract from others.

I don't have to decide anything yet, I tell myself and pick up my book again, wanting to distract myself from my thoughts. I turn the page and read the next line three times before it settles into my heart.

She did the things she knew she had to do, although in her heart, she wanted something different.

◆ ◆ ◆

When Seth and I return back to his house, I retreat inside and watch him put the cans of paint on the wooden platform that I have learned is called a deck. When he's finished with that, he drags in several large bags of items that he deposits on the couch with a sigh.

"How hungry are you?" he asks me. I touch my stomach and think about it for a moment. Seth has been very good at keeping me supplied with enough food to hold back my hunger for flesh, but it is getting stronger with each day. I decide that it's best if I eat again.

"Very," I tell him and follow his back into the kitchen where he digs around the refrigerator for a moment. I watch him excitedly, eager to learn another culinary technique or discover a new ingredient, a taste I never before knew existed.

"I could broil a steak real quick, maybe whip up some mashed potatoes." He looks up, and when he sees that I'm removing my clothes, looks away again rather quickly. "I could throw in a small side salad, too, if you're ravenous." I smile at his choice of words.

"I would like that," I say, not knowing what mashed potatoes or a salad are but trusting in Seth's cooking talents. He stands up and tosses a plastic wrapped item on the counter. "Would you mind if I joined you again?" I ask.

"I would love that," he tells me and then pauses.

A ringing sound is echoing through the house, like the tolling of a bell. It's followed soon after by a series of loud harsh knocks. Someone is at the door.

Seconds later, I hear a woman's voice.

"Shit," Seth curses violently as Sarah starts to bark. "It's Jenna." A brief shiver of terror travels down my spine as I move into the doorway of Seth's bedroom. If she looks in the window or somehow manages to open the door again, I don't want her to see me. This time, though, Seth is on my side and is fully aware that I am here. I am confident that he will keep her from seeing me. He looks at me with dark eyes for a long moment before speaking again. "Hide in there," he tells me. "And keep the door shut. I'll come get you when she's gone." I nod and do as he says, closing it as quietly as I can. I don't want to eavesdrop but decide that I should know what's going on.

If I have to run, or fight, it would be better to have a moment's warning; Seth's room does not have a lock. I press my cheek to the wood and wait.

The first thing I notice is the anger in his voice. Whatever transpired between them after I ran for the lake has made Seth furious. His words are clipped and harsh.

"What the hell do you want?" Jenna is crying; already I can hear that.

"You don't answer my calls or my texts. I called you at work and you weren't there. I'm worried about you, Seth. God, I miss you so fucking much." I hear movement and the sound of the front door. At first I think that Seth has shut the door in Jenna's face, but then she starts to speak again, much closer to my position. They're moving in the living room now. "Three years, Seth," she says and her voice is strained. "You can't throw that all away because of one, little fight." I hear something, like the tearing of paper, and Jenna starts to sob. "It was an accident," she says and I think that perhaps Seth is flashing her the knife wound on his arm. He hasn't shown it to me, but since he still keeps it wrapped, I am assuming it is fairly deep. "I didn't mean to threaten you," she says and I can tell that she has forgotten all about me. I have mentioned this to Seth, so I hope he plays along. From my position behind this door, there is nothing I can do but wait.

"Jenna," he says with a sigh. "It isn't about that fight. It's about a hundred and one other things that have piled up over the years and I – "

"I can see you chose some paint for the bathroom," she says suddenly. "I saw it on the porch." Seth doesn't respond. "Did you take a look at those paint chips I left for you?" More silence. "Seth, god, Seth." Jenna is nearly to the point of wailing. "We could have a home together, a family." Sarah's barks increase in frequency and I hear her scratching at the back door. Neither Seth nor Jenna acknowledges her.

"Just leave, Jenna," he tells her quietly. "I'm done, okay? I'm just done."

"I'm pregnant," Jenna barks and my heart freezes in my chest. I don't know why, but I feel suddenly alone. If Seth decides to get back with Jenna, what will he do with me? Will I have to fight for my life? Will I have to run?

"No," Seth says sharply. "You're not; you're drunk right now. So don't fucking lie to me. I hate it when you lie." A large crash resounds in the living room and I hear the sounds of a struggle. I debate opening the door but decide against it. It's too dangerous for me to be around Jenna if she's already feeling violent.

"I hate you," she screams at the top of her lungs. "I hate you!" Seth grunts and I hear another crash.

"That's it, Jenna," he says quietly. He must be right next to the door now because I can hear the sounds of labored breathing. "If you're going to get violent with me, then I'm calling the cops."

"Fuck you!" she screams and I hear the sound of her shoes stomping down the hallway. She pauses for a moment. "You're a fucking creep, Seth. Go to hell." And then the front door slams violently, shaking the whole house. I wait for Seth to come and get me, but when he doesn't, I open the door and peep out.

Jenna has broken some of Seth's things including the lamp that graced the table next to the couch. I move out of the room quietly and pause next to him.

Seth is sitting on the floor with his face in his hands. On his arms are scratch marks and his knife wound is bleeding freely onto the leg of his pants. I kneel down beside Seth and hover my hands over him, wanting to touch him, to help him.

"Are you okay?" I whisper and he looks up at me with dry eyes. He tries to smile, but his lips won't cooperate.

"Yeah," he says and rubs at a bit of blood that's leaking from his nose. "I am." I move back and allow him to stand. Seth stumbles into the bathroom and washes his face before bandaging up his arm and putting some of the clear ointment he used on my scratches on his arms. "Bitch," I hear him mumble as he walks out and surveys the damage to his living room. I say nothing, certain that this cannot be easy for him. Although rare, when *merighean* mates separate there is always drama. I have learned not to interfere; it will only make things worse. "I'm just glad she didn't try to kill you again," Seth says, letting Sarah in. The dog sniffs in circles around the living room before coming to greet me, burying her nose in my hand and twirling around my legs.

"As am I," I say, standing still as I wait for Seth to say something more. He goes into the kitchen and I hear cabinets slamming. I wait for a moment and follow him; I go around the opposite side and stand in the hallway, watching Seth through the archway that separates us. He's standing over the sink with his head down and he looks

The Feed

tired. I take a step forward and pause. Seth looks up at me and runs his tongue over the split in his lower lip.

"She punched me in the face," he says. "Can you believe that?" I shake my head but say nothing. *Merighean* women can be quite mean to their mates. Abuse like that is something I have seen before although it is nothing I would ever condone. He spits in the sink and curls his fingers around the edge of the counter. "I'm glad you came here," he tells me. "Or I would've never had the courage to leave her." I swallow hard and put my hand to my throat. I don't know how to respond to his words, so I merely wait, my fingers curled in Sarah's long fur. "I went from fucking a bunch of girls to drinking to dating Satan." Seth sighs and moves over to the plastic package on the counter. He unwraps it quickly and pulls out a slab of meat which he sets on a metal tray and sprinkles with some spices. "I'm such a mess, Natalie," he tells me as I take a step towards him.

"I don't think that's true," I respond as he looks over at me.

"It's true," he tells me as he puts the tray in the oven and turns one of the knobs on the front of the stove. "There is nothing in my life that I have ever gotten right."

"You treated me with the utmost respect," I tell him. "Even in the face of death. You take good care of Sarah, shower her with love. And you respect the earth," I add, thinking of the cigarettes he picked up off of the ground. It seems like such a small thing, but it means a lot. "You work to save people's lives, even though you don't like it. That's noble." Seth chuckles and grabs an orange bag from under the counter. From inside of it, he pulls out brown fruits, or maybe vegetables, that he sets in the sink and rinses off. After he does this, he stops and turns to face me, drying his hands on a decorative cloth. "I don't think you should be so hard on yourself. That special thing inside of you, the one you've been looking for all along," I say. "I see it and it's more obvious than you might think." Seth says nothing, but he does walk over to me and stare down into my eyes. Without a word, he leans down and presses a kiss against my lips.

For a moment, neither of us moves and I find that my body is frozen. I am held in place by the gentle touch of his lips, the warmth of his body radiating just inches from mine. When he pulls back, I watch his face in fear, terrified of the hazy glaze that will fall over his eyes, but his touch, although intimate, was brief and he's still holding onto some of his anger from the fight. Both of these things keep everything but a smile off of his face.

"Thanks," he says and moves away, pushing one of the brown vegetables towards me along with a metal tool. "Want to learn how to peel potatoes?"

The Feed

Chapter Fifteen

I don't think about my kiss with Seth; I *can't* think about my kiss with Seth. Whatever it was, it is over and neither of us is acting any differently. We peel the potatoes which are indeed a vegetable, boil them in water and mash them up with milk and a solidified cream called butter. Seth removes the meat from the oven and tells me it needs to "rest" while we get the salads ready. These he makes by shredding bits of lettuce with his fingers and sprinkling them with cheese, dried bread cubes, and a clear sauce he says is olive oil mixed with vinegar. After that, he slices the meat into strips and lays more than half of it on the side of my plate.

"Bon appétit," he tells me with a smile. His lip is still split and painful looking and I can see a purple bruise sneaking down his cheek. I ignore his injuries, certain that he doesn't want to talk about them, and head into the living room. Seth has promised me a movie while we eat and although the smashed lamp and the broken plastic objects near the television are disturbing to me, I pretend not to notice for his sake. But they are bothering Seth, too. I can see that from the look that crosses his face when he joins me. "Why don't you start eating?" he suggests as he sets his plate next to me. "It's best while it's hot." And then Seth heads into the kitchen and returns with a broom. "I'm just going to clean this up a bit," he says, sweeping the glass into a pile. There are brooms all over the palace at home, leftover relics from the drier days of my ancestors. Never before have I seen one in use. I watch Seth clean up, rather effectively, and bend down next to one of the plastic squares I noticed when I very first entered his home. I had thought they were stereos, but as I see Seth pick them up, I am not sure. "She trashed my fucking 360," he says with a groan, pushing Sarah away with his other hand and watching her to make sure she doesn't go for his plate. I block the dog with a hand on her muzzle. "And the Wii is toast, too," he says with a sigh. I haven't the slightest idea what he's talking about, neither the terms nor the phrasing. "At least the PS3 is alright. I thought you might like to play some games."

"The 'we' is toast?" I ask, confused. I feel like a moron, but the sentence means nothing to me. Seth rises to his feet with a chuckle, the broken equipment clutched in his arms.

"The Wii is a type of video game," he says. "Along with the PS3 and the 360. They're like computers, but just to play with. I was hoping to show you some of my favorites, if you're interested." I nod my head and press a kiss to Sarah's nose. She licks my face with vigor and attempts to use her affection as cover to get to my plate. I push her away like Seth did and pat her back gently.

"Absolutely," I say, curious to see more of what humans do to entertain themselves. They are certainly not lacking in options, from what I have seen. "At home, our most exciting games happen in the arena." Seth's eyebrows lift in surprise.

The Feed

"The arena?" he asks as he heads down the hallway and disappears into the library with his video games. He returns shortly, arms empty, and pauses, surveying the living room carefully. When he's satisfied, he looks over at me. "What's that about?" I finish my bite of meat, nearly swooning at the taste. The food is as good as usual and the smell of it is intoxicating.

"The arena is an old building where my ancestors once tried prisoners. Now the Huntswomen use it to spar. Sometimes the matches get very heated."

"So," Seth begins, moving over to the back door and closing the curtain that hangs above the window. "Are you trained in combat then?" He repeats this action around the room and into the kitchen until the light is banished and we are left in dusky darkness.

"I am," I say and start to list off weapons on my hand. "Spears, knives, axes, harpoons, ropes." I stop there as I can see from Seth's face that he is sufficiently impressed. "I know now though that my training is useless on land. The gravity and the pull of the earth is so different; I can't say for certain that I'd be able to defend myself. Although, if I had to, I could certainly poison someone with my nails."

"You could've killed Jenna," he says, looking down at me with a strange expression on his face. "When she came at you with the knife. You could've killed her, but you didn't." I nod and hope that whatever it is that I am seeing in Seth's eyes is respect. I think it is, but I'm not sure and I don't want to find myself disappointed later. I turn back to my food and put a piece of lettuce in my mouth. It is almost tasteless; if it weren't for the cheese and the sauce then it would be. "Time for our movie?" he asks suddenly, effectively changing the subject.

I nod and wait for him to sit down beside me with another electronic device clutched in his hand.

He presses a button on it and the television brightens to life, presenting us with a menu full of options that I cannot even begin to decipher. He scrolls through these and selects one quickly, moving us to another page: a list of titles whose pictures pop up on the right side of the screen as he scrolls through them.

"Hey Natalie," he says and I watch as his eyes follow Sarah to her pillow where she curls into a ball and sighs tiredly. "I just wanted to say I'm sorry for what happened in the kitchen. I kind of had a breakdown, you know?"

"Stop apologizing," I tell him with a smile. "I'm not as easily offended as you might think." Seth smiles back and returns his gaze to the screen. I can't tell if he's apologizing for kissing me or for his words. Either way, I decide to forget all about it. He hasn't though; I can tell.

Neither of us speaks however and soon our attention is on the television. Once the movie starts, I see that it is essentially a recorded play, much like looking through a window at the actors and actresses. It is interesting to be certain but not as life altering as I had been led to believe by the older Huntswomen. I watch carefully though, wanting to drink in the experience like any other.

Seth has chosen a movie about human relationships. I don't know if he selected it for himself or for me, but I pay attention, watching the interactions between the characters

The Feed

with interest. Before I know it, I've emptied my plate and am starting in on what Seth couldn't finish. The film has taken a turn and drawn me in so fully that I don't see Seth watching me for a long time. When I finally notice, I turn to him and stare into the gentle depths of his eyes. He doesn't say anything and after awhile, we both turn back towards the screen, but I can tell, from the set of his lips to the lines of his face, that Seth is interested in me.

The Feed has suddenly become a lot more complicated.

◆ ◆ ◆

When the movie ends, quite happily I must add, I am left with a smile on my face and a thousand questions in my heart. The characters in the film made references I did not get, used slang I did not understand, and did things that baffled me. When I tell Seth this, he just laughs.

"Half of the jokes in there are pop culture references. I didn't get any of them either," he says with a chuckle as he searches around the couch cushions for something. When he comes up empty, I can only guess that he is looking for a cigarette. "It was number one in the box office a few months back, though I can't say why. I mean, it's not as bad as some, but it wasn't great either." I have nothing to base my opinions on, so I take Seth's word for it, glad that at the very least, the movie has left me in a positive mood.

"Ready for our walk?" Seth asks and Sarah raises her head as if she knows what he's saying. I nod and we dress quickly, leaving the house in record time. This is my favorite part of the day and the thing I will miss the most when I leave. The thought depresses me, so I push it away in favor of taking in the scenery.

This time, Seth takes me in a different direction, away from the city and deeper into the forest. Convinced that he has a reason for doing this, I trail after him, my hand tangled in Sarah's leash.

"Where are we going?" I ask him as we come upon a small road that cuts through the forest like a wound. We cross it quickly and once again are surrounded by foliage.

"There's a native plant garden not too far from here," he says, hands tucked in his pockets. He's holding a lot of stress in his face; once again, I guess that this is because he is used to having a cigarette at this time.

"Is it hard?" I ask him and Seth turns to look at me, his breath puffing out in small clouds. It is much colder tonight than it has been previously, a sign of the turning seasons. I wish I could stay to see the transformation. "To fight an addiction?" Seth smiles tightly and nods his head.

"It is," he says. "Because to have one in the first place, a person has to be weak enough to get hooked. Fighting it is almost a joke. Sometimes, it's hard to find the strength." Seth is beating himself up today. The argument with Jenna is almost certainly to blame, but I find it difficult to watch.

"I don't think that's true," I say, holding my head sideways so that I can look at him and watch Sarah at the same time. "We all have weaknesses, some just manifest differently than others. The fact that you're even trying to put up a fight shows strength. You underestimate yourself, Seth." He pauses as we emerge from the foliage and find ourselves in a grassy area with wooden benches.

"What the hell did I ever do without you?" he says as he turns to me with a genuine smile on his face. "What am I going to do when you leave? I've gotten used to having so much optimism in my life. You've got infectious strength, Natalie."

"You'll do what you've always done," I say and hope that Seth doesn't hear the sadness in my voice. "I see the power inside of you to change; whatever it is that you want, I know you can do it." He shakes his head and bends down to let Sarah off of her leash.

"If you keep talking like that," Seth tells me as he stands and looks me straight in the face. "Then I might have to kiss you again."

◆ ◆ ◆

Seth refuses to let me sleep on the couch, insisting that a princess who's slept on the floor her entire life deserves a week on a bed. I don't argue with him. I tell myself that after I go, he'll have his bed back again for as long as he wants it. In all honesty, it is just because I am selfish. I am getting used to some of these comforts that I have found ashore. Going back to the sea now will be a challenge. Still, I plan to make changes, perhaps I can even adapt some of the things I've learned here to work at home.

In the morning, I find that Seth has risen early and fixed the shower curtain. The ceiling is painted the beautiful blue we selected and three of the walls shimmer back at me in a silvery gray.

"These were the perfect colors," he tells me when he sees me standing in the doorway behind him. Seth takes a step back and admires his handiwork. "I've been looking for a palette for awhile and just haven't found anything that's inspired me." He pauses. "Except for you." I ignore his words the same way I did last night. I suspect that Seth is trying to court me. It was only after I'd gone to bed last night that I'd finally realized this. Outside the magic of the Feed, Seth has come to like me as I have come to like him. I smile at him and don't bother to say that a romantic relationship between the two of us is impossible, maybe even catastrophic. Forbidden romances are lovely in books but painful in real life. Besides, it's only been five days since we met. Whatever he thinks he sees in me may be entirely misplaced.

"I think it's wonderful," I tell him instead, finally catching a scent in the air that starts the hunger pains in my empty belly. Seth watches me as I breathe in the smell and puts down his paintbrush.

"I've got some cinnamon rolls in the oven," he says as he wipes his hands on the front of his already dirty pants. There are blue splotches everywhere, even on the side of his face. "I was thinking I could add some sausage and scrambled eggs to go with them."

"Besides the eggs, I have no idea what you're referring to, but I trust you." Seth smiles and I move out of his way so that he can get into the kitchen. I don't follow him right away and instead hang back.

Today is day five of the Feed; I will be leaving the morning of the seventh. This gives me just two days to make my final decisions. I reach up and grab my hair, twisting it in front of my neck. I feel like I need the pressure in my scalp to help me think. This whole time, I have been imagining sweeping change, seeing my people rise from the ruins and become great. I have yet to decide how my refusal to eat Seth is going to accomplish this. I have high ideals but little in the way of a plan.

I must go back, see Yanori and tell her about Seth's tattoos, his dreams, the necklace. I ponder this for a moment. All of that is important certainly, but it may be just a coincidence or a tangle of fate. Who's to say that any of that will help me change a time honored tradition that my mother, and most of the other merighean, see as our last grab at hope. I sigh and release my hair before moving into the kitchen.

Seth is in the process of removing a tray full of baked goods that smell heavenly. He smiles at me and sets them on the counter.

"Let me just get that sausage in the pan," he says and I bite my lip. I told him that I was going to leave on the morning of the seventh day, but that could be interpreted in many different ways. I need to let him know that we have just two full days left. And I have to ask him a question, a very, very important question. I have to ask Seth if he will couple with me. More than once.

After our walk last night, I skipped the lake and took a shower instead. It wasn't as peaceful as a good swim, but it did help me think. I laid the facts out in my head like Yanori is always suggesting and came to the conclusion that I should sleep with Seth, but only if he himself allows it. If I return home without doing so, I will have a few months at the very most before my mother sees my flat belly and knows that I have failed. Knowing her, she will kill me herself and if she hasn't initiated the Hunt yet, then she will. Her strongest Huntswomen will go to the shore and drag back men for the others to rape. I shiver and lock eyes with Seth.

He's cracked some eggs into a bowl and is mixing them with a fork.

"Penny for your thoughts?" he asks. I've never heard the phrase, but I get the gist of it. I stare at him for a moment, unsure of how I should phrase what I'm thinking. I know I've made the right decision. Leaving Seth alive will have consequences, too, I am sure, but that is something I could never live with. He doesn't deserve to die and I know I don't have the heart to kill him. But with Seth's permissions, the other desires of the Feed don't have to amount to rape. If he wants to, if he allows it, then it's no different than what I did with Yuri. And besides, taking a daughter of Seth's to the sea would not be a bad thing. I was not lying when I told him I saw something special in him. Perhaps she would grow to have a bit of his strength. At the very least, I would be one step closer to the throne and if I raised her right, I would have a strong warrior at my back.

I look Seth straight in the face and say none of this.

"What's a cinnamon roll?" I say instead and he smiles.

I will get the courage to ask him tonight; I promise myself that.

◆ ◆ ◆

Seth shows me his video games which are like movies but with controllable characters. They're quite complicated and colorful and loud. I think they're fabulous. I brush hair from my face and realize that I've broken into a sweat. The sounds and the sights were so realistic, I can believe Seth's claims that some people become addicted.

"Wonderful," I say, handing Seth the controller. He smiles at me and sets it on the edge of the couch.

"I'm impressed," he says with a smile. "There are humans that don't catch on that quick." I incline my head and try to stay modest. However I seem unable to keep a grin from crossing my lips.

"Are you certain you didn't allow me to win?" I ask him as I pull my legs up and cross them. I turn to face Seth and recline into the pillows that grace the back of the couch. He shakes his head vigorously and turns off the television with a touch of a button on the device that I saw him use last night.

"If you'd seen me play before, you'd know that wasn't true. I don't really have a knack for video games. I'm the first person to cheat," he says and grunts when Sarah jumps into his lap, knocking both controllers to the floor. "God, Sarah," he groans as he tries to push the dog into the empty space between us. "You're not a puppy anymore, let up." I whistle and Sarah immediately loses interest in Seth, kicking him in the groin in her frenzy to get to my side of the couch. She rolls on her back and flops into my lap in a single, clumsy motion. Seth puts his hands between his legs and lies with his head against the cushions, eyes closed. "Stupid dog," he mutters, but I can see that he is just joking.

"Do you have any other games?" I ask him, thinking of the tamer ones we have at home. "Or some rope, a few sticks, and a large body of salt water?" I actually manage to get Seth to laugh at this; he opens his eyes and turns his face to look at me.

"Well, since Jenna ruined the Wii, which you would've loved," Seth begins as he rises to his feet with a groan. "All I've got is some stuff on the computer and an old copy of Monopoly in the closet." I watch as Seth stretches, muscles sliding beneath the fabric of his dirty T-shirt. He has paint and flour and some of the icing he used on the cinnamon rolls smeared across the front.

"I think I've had enough technology for today," I tell him honestly. I would love to delve further, dig into those plastic cases and see what makes them work, but I can tell from the complexity of the game we just played that there are years invested there. Since I have only days, I decide that I've had enough. I'd rather play with Sarah or cook with Seth, maybe take a longer walk. "What is 'Monopoly'?" I ask instead. Seth grins and moves into his bedroom. I'm still weighed down by Sarah so I wait for him, listening to the rustling and the light curses that filter out to me. "I'm going to miss you," I tell her in the language of the *merighean*. I don't bother to keep my voice quiet. Instead, I hope that Seth hears. He had said he liked it after all.

When he comes out of the bedroom, Seth is grinning and has a rectangular box clutched in his hand.

"You did that on purpose," he accuses me as he kneels down and puts the game in front of him. He removes the lid and pulls out a blue board, revealing little red and green trinkets as well as a pair of dice and colorful bits of paper in neat stacks.

"And if I did?" I ask again, still speaking in *Tersallee*. Seth laughs and sits back, crossing his legs in front of him and looking up at me.

"I wish you could teach me," he says sincerely. "I never learned a second language. It's one of my biggest regrets." I stare down at him as he unfolds the board and lays it out on the wood floor.

"You're not dead yet," I tell him, trying to be as gentle as I can as I push Sarah off of me and stand up. "It could be a dream instead of a lost opportunity." I sit down across from Seth and watch him watching me. Now would be a good time to tell him when I'm leaving. "Seth," I start, but he either senses what I'm about to say and changes the subject or he doesn't hear me.

C.M. Stunich

"Maybe I'll learn French," he says absently as he holds out a handful of metal objects. "Here, pick which one you want to be." I examine the pieces carefully before reaching down and plucking a dog from Seth's hand with my nails. If I make him nervous with their proximity, he doesn't show it. "I have to warn you about something before we start," he says in a serious tone. I look up at him sharply and wait. "This game takes forever; we could be here all day." I smile.

"There's nowhere else I'd rather be," I tell him and it is the simplest of truths.

◆ ◆ ◆

Monopoly takes even longer than I had anticipated, but once I come to understand the rules and the purpose more fully, I close the gap between Seth and I, and ultimately, I win.

"You really are something," he tells me as he scoops up stacks of cards and places them back in the box.

"That wasn't what you were calling me when I stole your 'Boardwalk,'" I say referring to one of the squares on the game board. Seth chuckles and places the lid on the rectangular box.

"It's what I should have said," he tells me as he pushes it aside and looks up at me. "Is there anything you can't do?" His question sparks all sorts of thoughts in my head and I look away. There are all sorts of things I can't do. *I can't figure out the meaning of the necklace or the tattoos; I can't change the minds of my people; I can't decide what it is that I really want when it comes to Yuri.* Instead, I copy Seth by attempting another bit of humor. I think it's a skill that I'm rapidly improving, but also one that will likely not come in handy under the sea.

"There are a few things, I'm sure," I say with a smile. "But I have yet to find out what they are." I had thought my joke was a good one, but Seth doesn't laugh. Instead his face is as serious as I've seen it.

"What happens when you go back?" he asks me and I can see that he's been thinking of this for awhile. It's understandable, I suppose. I have been absorbing everything there is to know about his world, asking questions, enjoying experiences. Seth has not asked me for much and I feel obligated to tell him the truth.

"I hope I can fool my mother enough that she does not suspect that you are still alive," I say first. This will be the hardest part. After returning from the Feed, we will all be tested in secret in the dark room at the back of my mother's palace. Nobody but the older Huntswomen know what this will entail. "Then I will talk with my sister," I point at Seth's clothed hip. "The one that is represented by this tattoo." His eyes widen and I realize that we have not talked much about the tattoos although he must be at least as curious as I am, if not more. "She is blind," I continue, wanting to tell him all that I know. He has a right to that, at the very least. "And her tail is pink," I add with a smile. "Yanori is also missing part of her fin, just like your fish."

"Wow," Seth says, running a hand through his dark

hair. "That's a literal interpretation if I've ever seen one. Fuck me." He pauses and touches a hand to his chest. I can see that he's thinking about the mark of Muoru now, but I have no more to tell him. I, myself, have no idea what that represents.

"When we have a queen that sits the throne, that realizes this, then we will be great again. Muoru will wake up and the sea dragons will come back." I swallow my fears down my throat.

"Then what happens?" Seth asks as he drops his hand to his lap. Even I don't truly know the answer to this question.

"I decide if I'm going to marry Yuri," I tell him, mentioning my friend's name for the first time to Seth.

"Yuri?" he asks curiously, brown eyes on mine.

"Yuri is my lover," I say, not knowing if that's even the right way to phrase our relationship. I know that he thinks of it that way, but I am still not sure. "Or he was once." I frown and tap my nails against the floor. It reminds me so much of my mother that I draw my hand back in disgust. "I didn't want to go on the Feed as a virgin." Perhaps this is more information than Seth needs or wants, but I tell him anyway. "He will expect me to marry him when I get back, but I just don't know." *I want love*, I repeat to myself again. If I go back and don't find that with Yuri, I will have to say no. I will have to, for my sake as well as his. Seth says nothing, so I keep talking. "I want to stop the rape and the murder," I tell him. "Next year, when the younger Huntswomen go out for the Feed, I want it to be like this, like you and me." I touch my chest and gesture at Seth. "I want them to experience life, make friends, decide their own fate."

"How will you do that?" he asks me and I can see that there is one question that is conspicuously missing. *What are you going to do with me?*

"I don't know," I say, answering just the one question but refusing to acknowledge the silent one. I know that it's important, but I know that I will also wait until the last possible second before I respond to the other.

Seth is the first one to move, standing up and stretching again. His face is pleasantly blank, masking the myriad thoughts that I know he has in his head. He's a very intelligent person and I would be a fool to think otherwise. I rise to my feet as he moves down the hallway and glances out the window in the front door.

"It's a bit overcast today," he says, as if our conversation had never happened. When he turns back to me, he's smiling again. "We could wrap you in a blanket and get into the lake for those pictures. I don't know if it'll work at night, might be too dark." It's a dangerous proposition, but I agree to it anyway, wanting to fall back into the routine I've been living for the past few days, into the fairy tale.

"That sounds lovely," I tell him as he moves into the bedroom and finds Sarah on his bed with a shoe in her mouth. We both stare at her and she cowers guiltily, dropping her head to her paws with a sigh. Seth copies her by sighing, too.

"Stupid dog," he says again, but leaves her where she is, moving to his dresser and withdrawing a pair of short legged pants. "Swim trunks," he says to me by way of explanation and I watch as he removes his shirt, flashing the bright colors of his tattoos. "I'd rather go skinny dipping," he continues as he drops his pants with barely a moment's hesitation. "But I think we'll have enough trouble trying to keep you hidden." I try not to stare at his naked form, but the Feed seeps into my blood and intoxicates me, making me turn away and stare at the wall. It is getting stronger, that's for certain. I imagine that it must reach a sort of frenzied peak on the final day. It will take all of my self-control to keep my decisions my own. *Seth must give his permission, remember that,* I remind myself.

When I turn back around, Seth is dressed in the swim trunks and nothing else. He smiles at me and moves to his closet, retrieving a brown blanket which he wraps around my shoulders carefully.

"Let's get the camera," he says and I follow him down the hallway and peep out the front door. There is nobody in my view and I am glad that Seth's neighbors are spaced fairly far apart. If someone does see me, it will be from afar and I can always dive. That break in sight should be enough to keep them from remembering that they even saw me. The only thing that worries me, and I don't tell Seth this, is Jenna. Somewhere inside of myself, I am more afraid of her than I am of any other woman. I tell myself that it's because she came at me with a knife and hit Seth, but I think it's even worse than that.

I think that I am jealous.

I downplay this thought as soon as I have it as part of

the Feed. The magic wants me to want Seth and Jenna wants to take Seth, therefore, it is only natural that I should feel this way. But I know that isn't true. Other Huntswomen have chosen men with families, children, loving wives, and none of them have ever reported feeling this way.

These thoughts are enough to propel me out the front door and into the lake. I drop the blanket just before I dive, wondering as soon as I hit the coolness of the water if my lack of swimming is what has been making me crazy.

I move through the water and spot the silver fish. I may not have seen them in days, but they have not forgotten me. They shimmer as they move, zigzagging through the darkness of the water and disappearing into the depths. I let them go and sink to the bottom, using the muscles in my thighs to push off and propel me in a spin towards the surface. I don't break through however, turning so that I'm heading straight towards the shore. I slow myself with my arms and enjoy the way my hair floats in a cloud around me. I have been adjusting to having it sit on my shoulders all day, but this is much more comfortable.

I float to the surface and bob with my eyes above the water. Seth spots me right away and waves, the camera clutched in one hand. He's moving into the deeper waters slowly, shivering and cursing at the cold. It's something that I barely register; the ocean is much colder than this. But I wait patiently for Seth, knowing that it is only by Neptune's good graces that my people can survive the darkness of the sea.

When he finally steps off the shelf of sand and starts to swim, I move up beside him and smile.

"Isn't it lovely?" I say and cannot help but gush. Two days without a swim was not a good idea. Water is as much a part of me as my heart; I cannot live without it. Suddenly, I ache for the sea. The urge passes quickly, but I can still feel it there deep inside, waiting, pulsing. I can entertain all the thoughts I want about what it would be like to stay, but I could never do it. I feel myself coming alive when the water slides across my skin, awakening my senses and beckoning to me. It's so much harder to remember myself and my purpose here when I'm surrounded by such cool, comforting hands. The water makes me feel a part of something larger, takes me away from myself. But right now, that is exactly where I need to be. I need to be fully aware to make this work.

"Fucking perfect," Seth says as he tries to adjust to the temperature and then smiles. "If you're a mermaid." I laugh at his joke and dive, spinning in circles around him while I wait to have my picture taken. When I surface again, Seth is fumbling with the buttons on the top and cursing again. "One good shot," he says as his teeth chatter involuntarily. "Just one good shot is all I want." He looks up at me and I can see a sort of desperation in his eyes. He wants to remember this, no matter what. The memories we have made together are important to him, and I hope for Seth's sake that the magic is gentle with his mind. There is a very good chance that I could become nothing more than a blurry dream to him in the days after I leave.

"If you want," I say, holding out my hand. "I could dive and take some of myself, if that would be easier." Seth nods his head as he struggles to tread water with just the power in his legs.

"That would be nice," he says. "But I want one, just one from my own hands." I remember how I felt in the yard when I was holding the camera and trying to capture a bit of his soul inside of it. I understand where he is coming from. Seth takes a big breath and without warning, drops below the stillness of the surface. I follow after him and am surprised at the thrill I feel at seeing him underwater.

He's in my element now, and it feels good. I wish that I could take his hand, show him the fish, the sandy bottom, the way the sun can penetrate the water on a pretty day and the way the moonlight makes it glow on a clear night. All I can do now, however, is tread the water gently with my arms and still my breath, letting my gills absorb all the oxygen my body needs. I want to be as motionless as possible so that Seth can get his picture quickly. I know that it isn't easy for humans to hold their breath for long.

Seth's cheeks are full of air and his eyes are blinking furiously as he lifts the camera and focuses on my face. I wait, my green eyes catching his and holding them as he presses the button on the top. But he doesn't stop at just one. Once he gets started, he goes crazy, capturing me a million times over as I float before him and watch his short, dark hair whisper around his face. The tattoos on his neck, arms, and chest are even brighter down here, despite the gray cast of the sky above. It's as if the water is enhancing every line, every color, drawing the art from his skin like a line pulls a fish from the sea. Seth releases the bubbles in his mouth and clamps his lips shut. Just as I'm starting to worry about him, he kicks his legs and explodes through to the surface.

I chase after him and come up just inches from his face.

"Did you get what you wanted?" I ask Seth as he takes huge breaths and fumbles with the camera. After a moment, he hands it to me carefully.

"Not sure," he says between gulps of air. "But we'll find out tonight."

Yes, I think as he turns towards the shore and starts to swim away. *I know that we will.*

Chapter Sixteen

I swim around the lake for awhile and take pictures of the lake bottom, the fish, my feet, hands, nails, belly, face, hair, anything that I think might help Seth to remember me because I want him to; I truly do. When I think I've got

The Feed

enough, I let myself drift to the sand and lay on my back for awhile. I don't know when it became so important to me, but I feel like if Seth forgets me, I will be failing him and myself somehow. Memories make up who a person is inside; they help define an individual and shape their future. I try not to fool myself with delusions of grandeur, but somehow I can see that Seth needed me here. I have changed him in a way that he was looking for. I don't know how or why, or even if I was just a catalyst to something he already had inside, but what I do know is that he can't forget me or it could all be for naught. That much is clear.

I sense a splashing at the edge of the lake near Seth's house and look up to find white paws pinwheeling through the water. An orange ball of some sort floats above me and I watch as Sarah moves towards it and retrieves it in her mouth before turning back around. I follow after her and rise slowly from the water, eyes searching around the neighborhood for wandering eyes. The gray sky above has sped the descent of night and I see that most of the houses are already lit, sparkling like jewels in the distance.

"You look like a gator," Seth calls out as Sarah bursts from the water and shakes her fur, splattering the dry clothes that Seth has changed into with droplets. His mood is much lighter now than it was after we stopped playing Monopoly. I didn't quite realize how heavy his face had been. *You think too much*, I say to him silently as he comes forward and soaks his pants to the knee. Seth tosses the blanket to me and I catch it, wrapping myself up as best I can and racing for the front door.

When I arrive inside, shedding puddles of water in my wake, there's something in the oven and the house smells of food, reminding me that it's been awhile since I ate.

"Sorry for disappearing like that," Seth says. "The water was so damned cold; I wasn't thinking straight." I drop the blanket to the floor as Seth and Sarah come inside and Seth closes the door behind them. I set the camera on the counter with a smile and watch as he opens the oven and checks our food.

"It's alright," I say, wondering how long I've been out in the lake. Time passes so much differently; I had forgotten that. "I forgive you." I pause. "What's a gator?" Seth chuckles and spins to face me. He is definitely different now; he has made a decision while I was swimming. His face is so happy that I can't help but feel a returning warmth swell in my chest. Behind it though is a bit of fear. I don't know what it is that has made him so happy, but what if it's something to do with me? What if it's something I can't deliver on. I try not to think too much about it. Seth will tell me soon; I can tell. He is bursting with the effort of holding it in.

"An alligator," he says. "A big, green lizard sort of a thing. They sit with their eyes above the water when they're hunting." I tilt my head to the side.

"I would like to see one," I say, unsure if it is a food item, a pet, or just a wild creature. Seth laughs again and leans against the stove. He pats his pant pocket briefly and almost frowns when he realizes there are no cigarettes there. Still, whatever news it is that he has for me puts the smile back on his face.

"Then you'd love the zoo," Seth says with a sigh and I can see that he's a bit disappointed that he can't take me out. I think he likes to show me new things. I can understand that; sometimes seeing the wonder in another's face can remind you how special something is. It can show you a new angle on something you had stopped seeing as interesting or unique. I remember Kiara's face when she looked up and saw the trees for the first time. I hope she found at least one other thing on the Feed that made her eyes sparkle like that. "Maybe next time I'll figure something out," he says and I'm confused. *Next time?*

Oh no.

My breath catches in my throat as Seth moves forward and passes by me, just inches from brushing his whole body along mine. *He doesn't think that we can see each other again. He doesn't; he can't.*

I follow behind him slowly and try to keep my face neutral. Maybe I misunderstood him. Perhaps he misspoke. I keep myself calm as Seth grabs a stack of items from his desk. When he hands them to me I see that they are pictures tucked inside of a plastic bag. I open the top and pull them out, shocked to see the images I have taken of Seth transferred to glossy paper. Knowing what a photograph is and seeing one in person is quite different, especially when it is one you have taken yourself. I flip through them quickly and admire the sunlight on Sarah's fur, the emerald green of the tree, the beauty of Seth's gentle smile.

"These are amazing," I tell him, thinking that even if I

did not intend to use these to solve the mystery of the tattoos, that I would want them anyway. I don't want to forget either. I look at Seth and see that he is still smiling. This was not his big surprise; there is more.

"I was thinking that we could go out tomorrow and get them laminated," Seth says and then explains without my having to ask. "That means they'd be coated in a thick layer of plastic; it's probably the best chance we have of making them waterproof."

"I think that would be perfect," I reply, realizing that I had not yet decided how I was going to keep them safe from the sea. Seth is moving again. He goes into the living room and gently pushes Sarah off of a bag that's sitting on the couch. The top is open and I can see already that it is filled with books. Seth turns to me and brushes some hair from his forehead.

"I picked you some of my favorites," he says, touching the bag with his hand. "I thought you could try to take them with you. This bag is waterproof so I figure if we stuff it inside of a couple garbage bags or something you could transport it to wherever you keep your other books." My throat has closed completely now or at least it feels like it. I appreciate Seth's gesture, but I know that it is leading up to something else. "If they get ruined, it's not a big deal. We could always try again next time."

"Next time?" I ask and my voice sounds strange even to me. Something is happening here and it is taking me too long to understand it. I know in my heart it is because I don't want to. I am protecting myself from hurt. In five days, I have given the human the power to hurt me. I realize then that I have truly broken off from the destiny that was laid out for me. If I am feeling these pains inside, then I have succeeded. I have learned something; I have discovered more of myself. Seth still doesn't see it. Maybe he's blinded himself, too.

"This has been the best first date I've ever had," Seth tells me by way of explanation. On his face is a smile that could charm a Huntswoman. I decide to interrupt him, to get out what I should've told him this morning.

"Tomorrow is my last full day," I say clearly, ignoring Sarah's wet nose against my thigh. "I have to leave the morning after, very early, before the sun rises." Seth nods and I can see that he's disappointed to see me go, but not sad, not depressed.

"I know," he tells me and his smile stays where it is. "But I can't wait for our second." I drop my chin to my chest and try to calm myself. It's as I had feared. He believes we can court one another. I don't know how he came to that conclusion, but I have to banish it quickly before the pain gets worse for either of us. I tuck the pictures he's given me back in the plastic bag and try to breathe slowly. My heart is racing so quickly that it's nearly painful.

"There won't be a second date," I tell him, trying to keep my voice steady and neutral. "Once I leave, I can never come back." Seth shakes his head like he hasn't heard me correctly.

"What do you mean?" he asks, sounding suddenly panicked; his smile is fading. "We can't meet up once in awhile? I could go to the beach. I could even drive you to the coast tomorrow night to see you off."

"No," I say trying to be firm, trying to keep my eyes off of his. I can't look at Sarah either so I turn myself to face the wall.

"We can't keep in touch?" Seth says and I can see that this is now as painful for him as it is for me. The two of us have become good friends, and I had no idea how hard this would be. Still, I can see that he's been laboring under the impression that there would be some way we could communicate; there is not. I feel my chest tightening with emotion and have trouble choking out the words.

"No," I say as I touch the bag of books. There are so many of them; I will not be able to carry them back to the sea, much as I might want to. I can take a few, perhaps, if I am careful to hide them in the sands outside the city. "Once I leave," I say and then feel softness against my leg as Sarah squeezes past me and rubs herself along my skin. "Once I leave," I say again, trying to control myself. I am not usually prone to so much emotion and rarer still, tears. Especially knowing what I have to do. I have ask Seth to sleep with me; there is no alternative to this. "You will never see me again." Seth doesn't speak, just puts his hands on his hips and curses lightly under his breath. I look over my shoulder at the darkening sky and lament the idea that it is all or nothing. If I stay here, then I must stay forever. I will never see Yuri or Yanori again and my body will never again grace the sea. The *merighean* will fade away and die; I cannot, in good conscious, let that happen. "Seth," I begin, knowing that if he refuses me, I will be putting my life on the line for my beliefs. I am willing to do this, true, but I feel like I can get so much more if I buy myself the time. The choice, though I believe it to be the right one, is hard. Once I touch his skin, press my lips to his, then all of the friendship and the respect in his eyes will fade, replaced with lust and forced love. He will not be able to say no.

"Yes," he says before I even get the words out, looking down at the floor and then back up at me with a sigh. "I knew you were going to ask, and I want to thank you for it. I know you could just, you know, do whatever." He runs his hand through his hair and shakes his head again. "I don't know how it happened, but something about you has woken something in me, Natalie. You're a good person," Seth says with another lamentable sigh. He lifts his chin up and slides his fingers down the front of his shirt, pulling the fabric up and over his head.

"Maybe we should wait," I say, turning around and taking a step back. "Once I touch you, you'll be under the spell of the Feed and when you finally come out of it, I'll be gone. We could spend tomorrow together, too. There's always tomorrow night for this." I want to go on another walk, cook another soup, play another game. I don't want to use Seth, run away, disappear like a dream.

"I've waited long enough," Seth says and in his voice, I hear a melancholy that matches my own. He takes a step forward, runs his hands down the smoothness of my back and brushes my lips with his own. The magic I've been denying all along rises to the surface, takes over me, draws my hands up and around his strong shoulders. My mouth tastes his and my heart beats a requiem of despair.

C.M. Stunich

◆ ◆ ◆

Sometimes, when you meet a person, however briefly, you know that they are going to change your life. As I look down at Seth's sleeping face, I know that he is this person for me. Tears I did not know I could shed drip down my face and splatter his.

"I'm sorry," I tell him, brushing my fingers gently across his lips, down his throat. "I was selfish. I used you the way the Feed always wanted me to. It wasn't about the sex or the seed or the flesh. It was about capturing your strength, your energy and taking it into myself. And I have done this. I don't know how, but I have."

Seth's eyelids flutter open and he looks at me with eyes clouded by love. It's all fake, of course, all a byproduct of the magic. I sigh and drop my face to his chest.

"Is it morning?" he asks me and I nod my head. We spent all night coupling, tasting each other's bodies. The sun has just risen into the sky and started to spill across the blankets. I have not slept though I know that I should. Tomorrow morning, I will head back to the sea and it will be as hard a journey as the one I took to get here. Harder, maybe, because once I return home, everything will have to change. I have a duty to take what I have learned here and apply it to my people. I can do no less than try to save them from themselves. And try to save more people, like Seth, who are killed in the pursuit of power. But I know

The Feed

that if all I have done is save one life, saved Seth's life, then I have accomplished something important. "That was wonderful," he tells me and I ignore him. Whatever he has to say to me now will be tainted by false dreams and a haze that hides the truth.

Seth rolls me over and looks down at me, head propped by his elbow.

"Are you alright?" he asks me and sounds, for the briefest of seconds, almost like himself.

"I am," I say simply and close my eyes as Seth presses a perfect kiss against my lips. The Feed rears its horrible head again and desire sweeps over me, taking me in its hand and telling me to do what I have been sent here to do. I wrap my legs around Seth and pull him into me to ease the ache. I weave my hands in his hair, ever so careful to keep my nails from scratching him, and allow him to move inside of me. Laying my head back against the pillows, I try to breathe, try to remove myself from the magic.

Remember who you are and why you're here, I tell myself as I stare at the ceiling and try to imagine that I'm doing this because I want to, because I like Seth as much as I've ever liked anyone before. I pretend that our bodies are joining not because of tradition or power but because we've grown to respect one another. The frenzied feeling in my gut relaxes and I find myself wrapped with pleasure. I can see now why the other Huntswomen were so interested in coupling. Now that I have gotten used to it, I no longer feel any pain, just euphoria, pure and simple.

I take Seth's face in my hands and kiss him.

Everything will work out, I tell myself, convinced that

this was the right decision, that there was no other. *I did this because it makes sense; it was the most logical choice.* As Seth kisses his way down my neck, I know that perhaps that isn't entirely true.

◆ ◆ ◆

After Seth and I climax, I finally fall asleep. When I wake and find the bed empty, I panic. The other Huntswomen have told horror stories of men who have wandered off whilst they slept and nearly got away. I fling back the covers and am even more worried when I see that it is dark. I rush into the living room and find Seth sitting on the couch, naked. His lap is covered with a blanket and in his hands is a plate of whatever it was that he had tried to cook for me. I feel myself flush with shame as I move slowly into the living room and stand watching him. Sarah raises her head and thumps her tail at me, drawing Seth's eyes over to mine.

"Hi," he says and that's it. He starts to eat again, the fork clinking against the white china of the plate. My stomach rumbles and I close my eyes against a wave of hunger. Now that I have slept with Seth and the final day of the Feed draws near, the desire for flesh is trying to overwhelm my thoughts. But I thought about this, too, while I lied awake yesterday. My mother will test for the power of the earth inside of me and although I believe that I have found it in Seth's strength, she may be more literal.

The Feed

I will have to take a piece of him, just a small piece, so that no matter what tests I may face, I will pass them. I decide though that once again, I will ask Seth's permission. As of this moment, he is under the thrall of the Feed so it is not entirely fair, but I can't wait for him to come out of it. There isn't enough time. I clench my fists and berate myself for not thinking of this earlier. "Are you hungry?" he asks me, as if, once again, he's sensing my thoughts.

"I am," I respond, surprised. Seth rises to his feet and keeps the blanket wrapped around himself with one hand while he carries his plate with the other.

"I'll go get you some food," he says, cursing when he bumps his foot against the edge of the wall. He's neglected to turn on any lights and the house is full of shadows. "Though it's a bit burnt. Thank God I turned off the oven before we ... " He doesn't finish the rest of that sentence. "We could've had a house fire on our hands." I sit down heavily on the couch and try to pretend that I don't notice the pictures laid across the squat table in front of me. There are pictures of me, beautiful pictures. I have never seen myself so lovely as I do in Seth's photographs. Without much of a fight, I give in and pick them up. I wish I could ask Seth to turn on a light so I might see them better, but it doesn't seem right. A light would ruin whatever ambiance it is that I feel in this room.

As I lift the pictures of myself up from the table, I see that the ones I took of Seth are lying beneath them. They are surrounded now by a thick layer of plastic that very well may keep the ocean away from them for a short time. After awhile, the sea claims everything, but it's always worth the effort to try. Perhaps I could even hide them on the otter's island. The strangeness of the situation takes a moment to sink in. The fact that Seth had the clarity of mind to take the pictures and laminate them is strange. I look up at him sharply when he walks in and hands me a plate.

"Au gratin potatoes and roasted pork loin," he says with a sigh. His face is heavy and sad again, not dreamy, not clouded by lust. *He's recovered?* I wonder as he sits down besides me and doesn't bother to keep his skin from mine. He even lays his head against my shoulder with a sigh. The fork in my hand is shaking and although the food smells incredible, I'm not able to find the strength to eat it.

"You're," I pause. I don't know how to say what I need to say. I try a different tactic. "Seth, look at me." He lifts up his head and turns to face me, but although we have just touched, his mouth stays in a frown and his eyes are dark. I lean forward and kiss him fiercely, forcing my tongue between his lips until he tastes me back. When I pull away, I examine him again.

"Natalie," he says and sounds sad. Seth should not sound sad, not with the magic of the Feed, not after a kiss like that. I lean back against the couch and set the plate in my lap. The bracelet that Seth gave me is sparkling in a stray shaft of moonlight. I stare at the word *Sailor* and wait for him to speak. "If we have a ... " Seth stops talking and pulls away from me so that we're no longer touching. That is also strange behavior for a man who should be in a thrall. The only explanation I can come up

The Feed

with is that in the same way Seth's anger helped him to fight the Feed before, his sadness is doing it now. It doesn't make sense with what I know, but I don't know what else to think. "If we have a child together, will you do something for me?"

"I will," I say. Seth has done great favors for me, and I can't imagine refusing anything he might ask. He looks over at me and I see in his eyes that he is fully there. I can ask for a bit of his flesh and know that I will get an honest answer.

"Make sure that she lives her life the way she wants to," he says. "Not the way anybody else does. Make sure she chooses her own destiny." I can't respond to that with words so I merely nod and dig into the food which is, as always, incredible. Much as I like the taste of fish and mussels and clams, I will miss Seth's cooking.

"You are a good friend, Seth," I tell him as I finish my food and set the plate on the floor for Sarah to lick. "So I hate to ask this of you, but I've been thinking about my return home and I think my position would be more secure if I took a bit of ... " I struggle to get the word past my lips. "A bit of flesh." I turn towards him quickly, prepared to explain. "I won't take much and it won't hurt if I do it while – "

"Yes," Seth says. "Go ahead. Do what you need to do." He looks down at the pictures on the table and smiles. "That's a quality I respect. You have the strength to follow your dreams. You wanted your own destiny, you're taking it. I'd like to be able to do the same."

"You'll be okay," I tell him although I'm not sure why

I'm doing it. "After I leave, you'll forget about me."

"No," Seth says firmly. "No I fucking won't." He pauses and looks back up at me. "I think I could've fallen in love with you, Natalie," he says and my heart nearly breaks in two. *Love.* It's one of the two wishes I had for myself, but that was before I thought I could save my people. *Freedom.* I can get that only by relieving myself of my duty to the *merighean*, by giving them the tools to change. *Or perhaps you're locking yourself into a different destiny?* I wonder. But no. I'm making these choices, these decisions. It might be a destiny, but it's of my own choosing. I made it and I could change it at anytime. "I wish we had more time to get to know each other," he says sadly, reminding me that I'm running out of that particular commodity.

"Come with me," I say, holding out my hand. "And I'll make you forget all about it." *Or at least I hope so,* I think as I watch Seth's face. It may very well be that he's broken out of the thrall of the Feed and that is a simple something that could change everything.

As soon as we step through the doorway into the bedroom, Seth takes charge and pulls me against him, kissing me hard and angling us so that we're pressed against the wall near his dresser. My experience is limited enough that I don't mind. Seth did everything that I demanded of him last night, so I allow him to lift me up and enter me from a standing position. At first, my body is tense and sad, making his thrusts little more than a reminder that I have betrayed his trust. Soon though, he soothes me with gentle kisses to my neck and sighs of passion that draw me in and relax me. I let myself enjoy this for awhile before duty comes crashing down around me in painful clarity.

The hunger is back again.

This time, instead of pushing it away completely, I let a bit of that desire seep into me so that I have the strength to lean forward and put my teeth against Seth's neck. I apply just a bit of pressure, just enough to bite down and pierce his flesh. Seth doesn't scream, just moans in pleasure and keeps moving his hips. A bit of Seth, just a small bit, slides down my throat and crashes into my stomach. My eyes open bright and I find myself filled with a strange power, a sense of accomplishment that is almost too good to resist. I calm my breathing, hug Seth to me and try to relax. He is bleeding from his neck and red is trickling down his chest although he hardly seems to notice.

"Thank you," I tell him and am surprised when this is the thing that stops him, slows him down.

"Don't mention it," he tells me and in his words, I hear nothing but clarity of mind and the person that I have been doing my best to get to know. Seth starts to move again and I push him back with gentle hands until he pulls away from me and sets me back on the floor. I look into his eyes and ask him the one question that will tell me the whole truth.

"Why are you doing this?"

"Because it's what you wanted," Seth says. That is not the answer of a man in the Feed. He might've said that he loved me, that I was the most beautiful thing he had ever seen, that we were meant for one another. Any of those would've worked. But not that.

"I'm leaving," I say to him, trying to swallow the difficulty of leaving behind a seed that, if watered, might've grown into a mighty tree. Seth and I could've been something special; I can feel it.

"Please don't," he says and reaches out to take my hands. He's gentle with my nails but not afraid of them. It's a gesture that shows he doesn't think of me as an *other,* an intruder, a *merighean.* Seth sees me now as just a woman. "Stay with me tonight and I'll drive you to the coast tomorrow."

"Okay," I say, wanting to soothe the disappoint in his eyes. "I will." I kiss Seth's lips gently and try not to let him see that I have lied.

Chapter Seventeen

After I am sure that Seth is asleep, I sneak into the living room and take the pictures, stuffing them in the plastic bag along with a single book. It is the one I had started about the fairies. I decide that it's the only room I can spare and slip the *Sailor* bracelet and Yanori's necklace in beside it. I will have to hide all of these things before anyone spots me, and I decide that it is better if they are all together. It increases my chances of recovering them later.

As I move down the dark hallway, I hear movement behind me and freeze.

But it is Sarah, not Seth. She trots up to me, nails clicking across the wood, and wags her tail in anticipation as I reach for the front door. Perhaps she thinks that we are going on another walk. The thought depresses me more than I care to admit. I pause and turn around, bending down just enough so that she can lick the air near my face.

"I will miss you, too," I tell her in *Amarana*. It is such a rough, guttural language that the sound of it isn't so sad. No matter what I say in the language of the Huntswomen, it will sound strong. I need that now more than I ever have before.

I give Sarah one last kiss and leave before I can change my mind.

The sound of the door closing behind me holds such finality that I can't bear it. Without hesitation, I move forward and dive into the darkness of the lake, the bag clutched tightly against my chest. I don't need my arms to swim and I feel better knowing that I have it in two hands. If I were to lose it, it would cost me greatly.

I move through the water quickly, not bothering with shortcuts or spins, just a straight shot from one side to the other. I do keep my eyes peeled for the silver fish, however, and when I don't see them, decide to at least wish them a silent goodbye and a thank you for filling my body with energy. My thoughts are a jumbled mess, but as I kick my feet and maneuver through the quiet waters, I start to feel myself calming down. It is only after I emerge from the dark depths that I have second thoughts.

I pause next to a cluster of bushes and sink to my knees as I take big, gasping breaths of the night air.

Nothing is forcing you to go back, I tell myself. *You could stay here and make a life of this. You wanted freedom and the ability to make your own choices. Here one lies right before you. What will you do?*

But I know that as nice as these ideas are, as tempting, that they are impractical. I cannot live among humans forever. Yes, Seth has fought through the thrall of the Feed, but for whatever reason he is a special exception. All it would take was one woman to spot me over the fence and I could be dead. Beyond that, if my mother ever were to discover that I was still alive, she would send the Hunt after me and Seth. It would be death for us both. I can't put either of us at risk.

I decide that these thoughts are nothing more than overexcited emotions and press on. I am so wrapped up in my own head that I hardly feel the needles of the trees beneath my feet or the touch of the icy air along my skin. I am not quite certain where I am going, but I let my instincts guide me, trusting that the blood of a Huntswoman will always find the sea.

I am right.

Hours later, when the sun is just starting to lift into the sky, I come to the rocks of Muoru. It seems as if it's been weeks since I was here although it has been merely days. I approach the edge of the cliffs and peer down. I have thought briefly about how I will get back in the water. Climbing down is not an option; I was lucky to make it up alive. I move along the shoreline secretly hoping that Kiara will appear here although I know that there is a slim chance of that happening. I have waited until the last possible moment to leave. In fact, there may already be Huntswomen arriving in the village as I stand pondering my dilemma.

I step towards the edge of the cliff and look down. It is a straight drop here, a sheer wall of rock and mud and the branches of scraggly trees. I could dive down, slip into the water like a seal. It would not be a problem; the Huntswomen are built for feats such as this. The only problem with my idea is that there very well may be rocks hidden beneath the waves. If that is the case, I will impale myself and die at best, become maimed and vulnerable to the sea at worst. I should have scoured the coast better before climbing up, but now it is too late to lament lost chances.

I had told Seth that I was reckless, but I am not stupid. I sigh and look around, wanting to disappear beneath the waves before any humans stumble upon me and cause a scene. I decide that my best course of action is to reenter the sea where I had warned the other Huntswomen not to go. I will head to the area just west of here where the rocks are smaller. If I can catch a rip current out, then I will save myself a lot of time and energy. The risks are as I'd warned the women before, but it is the best choice to me now. The beach, although the easiest spot geographically, was never a choice. Humans – especially women – are still the most dangerous obstacles between me and a safe journey home.

I backtrack a bit through the forest and find a trail that winds down the side of the mountain quite a ways before ending in a grassy area with a sign describing the movements of the sea and a plaque dedicated to a human who was unfortunate enough to have been swept off of this vista point during a storm. There is a sign of warning and a chain hooked between two poles that I ignore. I step over it quickly and work my way around stunted brush that clings to this earth with stubborn fingers.

It is not long before the sparse growth turns entirely to rock and begins to disintegrate into the sea. I step into the water, placing my feet as carefully as I'm able. If I get too cut up by the rocks then my swim home will be comprised by predators; I have not forgotten the Huntswoman who was killed by the shark and do not wish to share her fate.

My eyes scan the rocks for awhile, trying to map out a route. The waves are not as fierce today as they were the day I left although I wouldn't call them quiet. I tuck the bag under my right arm and walk as deeply into the water as I can, making sure that I am careful to stay as close to the center of the cove as possible. When I near the spot where the water empties into the sea, I want to get out as quickly as possible. If I linger, I may very well get thrown backwards against the rocks. With a deep breath, I press forward and submerge myself.

My view from beneath the waves helps me to understand the layout of the area and it isn't long before

The Feed

I'm spinning and diving, twisting past eddies and bursting through scattered clumps of seaweed and piles of driftwood. The current is begging me to return to the shore and I soon find that the loss of my right arm is going to cost me in strength. As I get closer and closer to the exit, I become more and more fatigued and switch the bag to my left side, but I refuse to lose it. Even if it doubles the time it takes to get home, I will not relinquish the items inside without a fight. Thankfully though, it doesn't come to that and soon I'm at the inlet, climbing over a grouping of rocks that make it impossible to swim past. On the other side though, the sea stretches out to the horizon in one, perfect blue expanse. I tilt my head back, close my eyes and let the spray of the waves splash against my face. Despite my feelings for Seth, it is good to be home.

◆ ◆ ◆

The rest of the swim back is uneventful and I'm pleased to discover that this far below the surface, I am able to return to holding the bag against my chest with both hands. I don't encounter any other Huntswomen – dead or alive. For this, I'm grateful. I would hate to have to explain my items to another person at this point, especially one that I haven't determined is on my side yet. And there will be sides. If I am going to stand against my mother, the *merighean* will be forced to pick. I haven't been as social with the people as a whole and I know that as of right now, they would pick my mother in a heartbeat. They see her as experienced, strong, and wise. As I swim, I decide that if it's to come to something as drastic as that, then I have two options. When new Huntswomen return from the Feed successfully, they are seen as heroes to the rest of the city. If I play off of this, I could very well gain the support I need. On the other hand, it may be better to wait, to socialize, to bring the *merighean* and the Huntswomen to my side slowly.

I'm so embroiled in finally making plans for myself that I don't see Yanori waiting for me outside the city.

"I think this would be a good place to bury your things," she tells me as I adjust the position of my legs and kick backwards in the water, trying to still my forward momentum. I pause and turn to look at her, unsure if she is merely making the assumption that I had taken the items she gave me along or if perhaps she heard the way I was swimming and suspects that I am holding something. "Welcome back," she says with a smile, cloudy eyes like pearls in the darkness. There are no ceiling lights here and no *sispa* this far from the city.

"What are you doing here?" I ask her as I swim close enough to see that her pink tail is almost entirely covered in algae by this point. She sweeps a cloud of pale hair from her face and looks straight at the plastic bag. Although I know she cannot see it, her stare unnerves me. I'm glad to see her, but her position here frightens me. We are at least an hour out still. With the damage she's sustained to her tail, it is dangerous for her to leave the boundaries of Amarana.

"The queen is anticipating your arrival with much pomp and circumstance," she says as she holds out her hands. I go to her and let her embrace me, happy to be held in a pair of loving arms. Yanori will help me in whatever happens next; there is no doubt in my mind as to her loyalty. "I suggest you deposit your things here and I will show you how to get back to this spot later." I look around, seeing nothing but a large, white boulder to mark this place. It is hardly conspicuous which is both good and bad. If Yanori cannot remember how to get here, then my items will be lost forever. Like Seth though, Yanori is good at guessing what I am thinking. "I will not forget. Hurry now before we're spotted. Aleria has guards swimming the perimeter looking for you."

"Why?" I ask her as she releases me and we both drift gently to the ocean floor. "Does she suspect me of something?" Yanori tilts her head to the side and then smiles.

"Why might she come to a conclusion like that, Natalie?" she says in her most playful voice. Yanori knows. She knows everything and I have only just seen her. Something in my silence encourages her to keep speaking. "Do not worry. Aleria is merely interested in touting your success to the city. She sees you as a reflection of herself, didn't you know that?" I didn't, but I don't say anything; I am too relieved. "Nobody will know but me," she whispers, taking my face between her hands. I don't ask how she knows. Yanori always seems to be one step ahead of the rest of us.

"I want to change the world," I tell her instead. She nods. She already knew this, too, of course. She has been saying much the same thing for years. I bury the bag in the sand without another word, trusting in my sister the way I always have. Yanori has yet to steer me wrong.

"I will help you," she says to me as I rise to my feet. I have gotten awfully used to standing; it will be a chore to remember that I am supposed to avoid it at all costs. "But we must be patient. There are already changes in the sea, Natalie. Whispers that come from the darkness, that speak to me. You will be surprised where you might find allies in this war."

"War?" I glance up at her sharply. I had not said anything about a war. I had not even entertained the thought. "I don't want a war," I say quietly as I push off the bottom and begin to swim. Yanori joins me, tail sweeping to the left in an effort to keep her swimming straight. She says nothing which worries me. It means that she does not know what to say; that doesn't happen often.

We travel together in silence for awhile, pausing only when Yanori lays a hand on my arm.

"A Huntswoman is coming this way. I should go." She kisses me gently on the cheek and disappears into the blackness, spinning and twisting like an eel. When she doesn't try to compensate for her injury and instead embraces it, she is one of the most beautiful swimmers I have ever seen. Her tricks would win her great prizes if my mother allowed her to participate.

"Natalie!" I turn towards the voice and find Aremia,

The Feed

the golden Huntswoman, teacher of the fifth Trial. How I have changed since that day. I find a smile somehow and let it fill my purple lips. "We are so grateful that you have returned safely," she says, swimming in a circle around me. Her silver breastplate shimmers brilliantly in the light of the *sispa* that she has attached to her chest. In her hand is a massive spear with the head carved from some sort of bone. She looks strong and immovable, set in her ways. My heart thumps painfully in my chest. "The queen is requesting your presence in the throne room with the other Huntswomen." Here she pauses and I can see her next words pain her. "We expect you will be the last to arrive." I don't need to ask many questions. There is one that will tell me all I need to know.

"How many?" Aremia looks up at the surface, lets her gaze fall past mine and drop to the ground. Her daughter was in the Feed this year I know. There is sadness in her eyes but not despair; I can guess that she made it back. Others will not have been so lucky. Still, when her answer finally comes, drawn from tight lips and an unhappy face, I am left in shock.

"Seventeen."

◆ ◆ ◆

I swim back to the city with Aremia in tow. I feel suddenly desperate to see this dismal number with my own eyes. Seventeen. That is less than a fifth of the girls that left with me only seven days ago. I had feared the worst; I had feared that only half would return. Reality has proven worse than my nightmares as I rush through the dragon's bones, ignoring the calls and the cheers of the citizens that float outside the ribcage. I may be wrong, but it seems to me that they are louder than usual, more cheerful than before. I imagine that seeing me must be a relief. On such a horrible year, the year of their heir, I am one of the lucky few to return.

I spot Yuri by the entrance to the palace. They have let him in along with a handful of other males, ones that were favored by some of the missing girls. There are frowns and signs of despair on nearly all their faces; broken hearts float in the water like bubbles, breaking against my skin as I rush past. Yuri does not see me right away, but I grab his hand as I swim, pulling him up from the throng of desperate faces and alongside me.

His eyes register surprise and then he spots me. Even in my hurry, in my anger, in my frustration at the whole situation, I have to stop and look at him. He had not expected me to come back, no one had, if the guards circling the city are any indication.

"Natalie," he says and his voice is barely a whisper. I can practically see his heart falling from his chest. "You came back."

"I did," I say and let him take my face in his hands. He might be crying, but it is hard to say under the sea. I touch my hands to his belly and keep my gaze away from the *merighean* that are watching us from the entrance. They

The Feed

are staring at Yuri as if they might absorb his relief, his happiness. For a brief moment, I have restored hope to them. They believe there is still a chance; it is written across their faces like a curse. I close my eyes and let Yuri kiss me. I can't help but kiss him back. Something in his lips tells me that I mean everything to him.

"Nearly half the day passed before any of the other Huntswomen came home," he tells me as he wraps his arms around me, blonde hair tangling with my black. "We feared it was another Lost Year." I hug him back and am glad that despite the terrible tragedies we have suffered, that it was not a Lost Year. We have had only one in the history of the Feed; one year where none of the Huntswomen came back. "What happened?" he asks me as he releases me and moves back. I shake my head.

"I don't know," I say, thinking of the beach and the rocks and the dead woman pulled apart by a shark. It could've been anything; it could've been a Jenna when there was no Seth. It might've been the storm that first day. I have no answers for Yuri. "Look," I tell him, taking his hands in mine. At first, I think that his are shaking, but then I realize that it is me. I am furious. With myself, my mother, with the girls who ignored me and swam away when I might've saved them. "I am certain that Aleria will cancel the celebration dinner. If not, then I will stay only long enough to appease her. Why don't you wait for me outside my room? I'll let you in the window when I get there." Yuri nods, but I can see that he doesn't want to let me go. I plant another kiss to his lips and release him. The burden of my responsibility with him seems pointless at this moment. Whether I love him or not is irrelevant. He has missed me and needs comfort. Yuri has been my friend for as long as I can remember and I will not abandon him now, no matter what awkwardness it may create between us later.

Yuri swims away in a flash of silver and I turn myself back towards the throne room. This will take great control to overcome. If anything is a test to my strength of will then it will be facing my mother and my instructors. I float to the wall of rock on my right and use it to kick off, bursting into the middle of a silent gathering the likes of which I have not seen. The Huntswomen are always loud and outgoing, always eating and chasing one another. To see them sitting still and silent on the ground is sign enough that we are in trouble.

"Natalie," my mother says. She doesn't sound surprised, but Aremia is already at her side and would have told her I was coming. She seems relieved to see me if not particularly overjoyed. I count the girls below me and find that Aremia was being generous with her number. When she said seventeen, she meant seventeen *including* me. I look desperately for Kiara but do not find her. "Congratulations on your accomplishments." I look up into her purple eyes and search for some sign that she knows this isn't right. I see nothing but boredom and a slight irritation, as if the world has scratched her the wrong way and she will be even. "Now that we are all here," she says, raising her voice so that it carries throughout the room. Her Huntswomen are everywhere, on the walls, in the windows, floating near the ceiling. There are

The Feed

thousands of them and only seventeen of us. It is not a good sign for me. I had been counting on the girls in my Feed to be at my side. As I look around the room, I know for certain that Yanori is wrong. A war would never work; it would only get me killed. "We can begin the feast. Lower the table." She waves her hand dismissively and several *merighean* servants began to unfasten the screws that hold the great table in suspension. Normally, we would eat there, floating instead of sitting, as is the preferred way for most. Today, I can see that my mother has made an exception for the weary bodies that sit before her.

I drift down and join the other girls. Some of them catch my eyes and hold me, telling a story with the pain in their faces. They were close, the other Huntswomen. Most of them were good friends, sisters in every way but blood. Then there are the girls that won't even look at me. I briefly recognize some of these as the ones I saw by the rocks of Muoru. A great shame hangs over their heads and makes me wonder if I should have pushed harder, perhaps ordered them to follow me. What would the number have been then?

When the table finally drops between us, I see bowls of mussels, clams, and oysters. There are stuffed crabs and plates with mounds of roe in every color, like a sea of jewels. Another dolphin has been slaughtered, but this time, the pieces have been cut to a manageable size and are separated amongst a collection of the blackened silver dishes that are used solely for this occasion. The most pathetic part of this feast is that there is far too much food for us to eat.

"Welcome to the clan of the Huntswomen," my mother says as she would after any other Feed. It seems she has chosen not to acknowledge the poor numbers. I am back and that is all that really matters to her. "You are now part of an elite group, a sisterhood of souls, whose only purpose is to restore the power to the ocean. You have traveled ashore, you have seen the unfair wealth that has been bestowed upon the Mother Goddess' people. Our father, Neptune, has given us the power to take that back." My mother drops from her throne and allows herself to sink to the floor beside the table. She is wearing one of her ridiculous dresses again. It is white with lace that floats around her body like foam. The sleeves are long and cumbersome and the train drags through the sand like an anchor. "You have captured some of what is rightfully ours and you have brought it back. Tomorrow, you will enter the Sanctum of Amarana and be tested."

I scoop a handful of orange roe, fish eggs, into my hand and put them to my mouth. They are nice, but I imagine that Seth could do something lovely with them. *Seth*. I push his name from my mind and focus on my mother's words. Ignoring her now might prove fatal. Much as I want to leave, to go to my room, to think, I have to stay. As soon as I get my chance though, I will leave. The seeds of change that were planted in my mind have suddenly blossomed, burst open like an anemone. This tragedy has been like a catalyst for my heart. I will find a way to bring my mother to my side or I will take the throne, there is no other option.

The Feed

"Once you have passed the test, your first orders will be to deliver the next generation of Huntswomen. After you have taken that final step towards womanhood, then you will learn of Neptune's true desires and you will dedicate your life to them." My mother is staring at me now, dark lips twisted into an expression of perverse pleasure. She drops her voice to a more conversational tone and continues. "There are some unorthodox changes on the horizon, my beautiful ladies of the Hunt." I cringe when she says this and her eyes land on me. "But in order to enact these, we must be at our full strength." Aleria stretches this last word out like a serpent, running her tongue along her lower lip. My heart starts to flutter in my chest like it's trapped, but I maintain the queen's gaze. I can't let her see the fear that her words have inspired.

Change? I am the champion for change. Whatever it is that she has planned will be bad for the *merighean*. I know this like Yanori knows about Seth; my intuition tells me that it is so. I crack a mussel and wait for her to say the words that I have been expecting since the number seventeen fell from Aremia's mouth. "Therefore, in order to swell our numbers and keep us a prosperous people, I will call upon the strongest warriors in my arsenal to travel to land, to find eligible, fertile males, and bring them back to the gates of our city. I will call upon the powers of the Hunt."

◆ ◆ ◆

I leave the celebration early, sneaking out when a latent group of girls appears in the entranceway. There are only three of them, but it causes a huge ruckus amongst the gathered Huntswomen. Shouts and cheers and tricks follow their arrival. Spears are raised and sand is thrown in the air in excitement. Still, twenty is not a good number. I am afraid that this small bit of relief will alleviate some of the pain of the Feed, make the girls forget their dreary faces and their disappointment. There is a parade scheduled for this evening that I will be obligated to attend, but right now, I can give myself a moment of peace. The only good part about all of this commotion is that I have not had a chance to think about Seth. As soon as his name pops into my head, I push it away in favor of other thoughts. Thinking of him now, or ever again for that matter, will bring only pain. When it comes time to talk to Yanori, I will do it from a clinical standpoint; I will forget that I lied to him and fled like a coward in the middle of the night.

Yuri is waiting outside of my window like I had asked. I open the shutters right away and allow him in, plucking a *sispa* from the wall as I go and blowing into its shell. When no light emerges, I see that it is dead and push its body out of the window.

"Would you mind grabbing one from the hall?" I ask Yuri and he nods, spinning into my room with a rush of water and disappearing out the door just as quickly. I close the shutters carefully and sit on the floor with my legs crossed, letting the weight of the ocean and the

The Feed

darkness fall over me before putting my face in my hands. I have so much to think about and now, so little time to do it. The Hunt will ruin everything. If I let that happen, the city will be alive with the twin thrills of sex and violence. The *merighean* are notorious for falling into a mob mentality. Once my mother gets them into the cycle, it will be almost impossible for me to break it.

"Found one," Yuri says, swimming in and closing the door behind him. He looks down at me briefly before blowing in the shell and placing the green and yellow snail on the wall behind him. Once the bright glow of the *sispa* flickers to life, Yuri bolts the door with the sliding lock I found on a shipwrecked captain's door. It is the color of gold and the only one of its kind like it that I have seen in the city.

"Aleria has called for the Hunt," I tell Yuri as I raise my face and watch him settle to the floor on his belly. He rests his head on his hands, arms propped by his elbows, tail waving gently in the water behind him. I'm not sure how much to tell him. He will be an ally, that is for certain, but what trust should I place in him today? How far should I go?

"I had thought as much," he says with a sigh. Bubbles twirl in the space between us and tickle my hand when I hold one out. Talking is so animated in the water; it is one of the things I missed the most. "Are you concerned?" He asks as he scoots forward ever so slightly. I can see that he wants to touch me, which I understand. It could not have been easy wondering if I were going to return alive.

"I am," I say, rising to my feet and stepping over Yuri.

He spins in the water as I pass so that he's floating, face pointing towards my chest of coins. I bend down and push the heavy, wooden container to the side, digging in the sand beneath it for the crown. "Yuri," I begin in the most serious voice I can manage. It doesn't take much effort. I am not in the mood to be silly. "I'm going to show you something and I'm going to tell you something. What you choose to do with that knowledge will be your right and I will not hold any of your decisions against you. Do you understand?" I grab the edge of the crown with my hand, happy to see that it has not been disturbed. There is no doubt in my mind that my mother snooped around my room while I was gone. Since the crown is still here, it means that she did not find it. If she had, I would've been questioned right away, dismal numbers or no. I decide that when Yanori takes me out to retrieve the pictures, that this is where I will hide them. I glance over my shoulder and wait for Yuri's response. His pale eyes are sparkling with interest now.

"I told you that would not forget," he says quietly, moving over to me and settling with his shoulder against the wall and his tail curled gently beneath him. I stare at him for a moment. Yuri leans down and presses his hands to the sides of my head, kissing me gently on the scalp. "You did not forget who you are," he explains. I move away from him and look into his eyes. He is right. I had feared that when I left for the Feed, that I would forget myself. I came to find that I did not even know myself at all.

"I got stronger," I say instead and he nods.

The Feed

"I knew that was true the moment I saw you," he tells me with a smile. "Now show me something, tell me something. You know that I would never betray you. I love you, Natalie. You are my oldest friend and the only person in the sea that I believe in." I try to take a breath, a new habit I have developed on the shore and end up swallowing an exorbitant amount of water. I lift the crown from the sand and pass it to him. Yuri's eyes are instantly on fire and he's spinning across the room, holding the object as close to the *sispa's* light as he dares get. He turns it around in his hands several times and brushes the abalone shell on the front with his thumbs. "This is the front piece for one of the ancient headdresses," Yuri says almost immediately. "It would've had a comb here," he points to a spot on the back that I had not noticed where the metal is a bit jagged, a bit rough.

I rise to my feet and approach him, trying to gauge his reaction. There is nothing there but curious excitement. I breathe a sigh of relief. Yuri pauses his examination and looks up at me. I can see that it hurts him that I am being so cautious. My very first memories are of Yuri and I cannot even say when or how I first met him. We have scoured ships together, explored sea caves, looted items from rooms all over the palace. Never once have I ever questioned his loyalty.

"It's not just you," I tell him, trying to be honest. "But what I have planned is liable to drop me straight into Imenea's slippery arms. I will test everyone I trust, even Yanori." Yuri nods his head and I can see that he will drop the subject without a fight. He is more interested in the crown anyway. I smile and step a bit closer. I let my hands drift up and touch the back of his.

"This would've been worn by one of your ancestors," he continues, very much the oral scholar. Yuri knows all kinds of things that I don't. He learns them by spending time with the oldest *merighean* in the city and by communicating with nearly everyone he comes across. I am more likely to swim away than to engage another person in conversation. I see now that this was a mistake; it will certainly complicate things. *Perhaps I should marry Yuri,* I think idly. *As a king, he would be well loved. Unlike my poor father, he would not hide in the shadows and blend with the walls. He would be bright, noticeable, and likeable, someone the people could trust.* I frown briefly but try not to let him see. He can't know what I'm thinking about him or it would break his heart. I'm thinking about love. Yuri loves me, true, but is that enough? I bite my lip and wait for him to speak again. "This would've held the front of the headdress together. From these points," he touches the sides gently. "There would've been strings of beads, shells, jewels, bits of metal. They were grand affairs and worn rarely, as cumbersome as they were. There are also rumors of magic, that the head pieces themselves were made in such a way that they were a conduit of power from the sea."

Yuri pauses and lifts the crown up, setting it gently in my hair.

"Where did you get this?" he asks as he admires me. Before I have a chance to answer, he makes a guess. "Yanori?" I nod and he smiles.

The Feed

"She gave me three objects," I say, thinking of the lost weapon. "A knife that I gave to a failed Huntswoman." Yuri nods and removes the crown for me, drifting back to my hiding place and burying it for me. "And a necklace that I left outside of town. Tonight, I will go with Yanori and retrieve it." I don't ask if he will come; I know that he will. He also doesn't bother to ask why Yanori gave them to me. He knows her as well as I do. It is something we will have to figure out for ourselves.

"I cannot wait to see it," he says instead as he pushes the trunk back into place and drapes his body across it. As I watch him, I realize how much more comfortable it was to talk in Seth's living room. It was designed to keep us happy and relaxed. We don't have enough of that here. "You were wise to leave it," Yuri tells me as I move over and sit in front of him with my legs crossed. "If it is as old as the crown, then it will be something your mother will want." I nod my head and close my eyes. The crown was the easy part, just a test. What I have to say next could very well push Yuri over the edge.

"Yuri," I begin again. I drop my chin to my chest and lose my words.

"Tell me about the Feed," he says as he puts a finger under my chin and lifts my eyes to his. He is curious but also sad, maybe jealous.

"You would've loved the shore," I tell him, thinking of Sarah and the trees, the soups, the video games, the bed. Seth. "There was so much to learn, so much beauty." I lock my eyes with his and force the words through my throat. "I couldn't do it, Yuri," I say to him hoping beyond all reason that he will not feel betrayed. I know that I will need his help to accomplish my goals. "I couldn't kill him." I grab his face and rise to my knees. "I left the human alive."

I wait for surprise, anger, and suspicion to cross his features. I wait for him to pull away from me, to draw back and swim away. Maybe he won't tell my mother out of respect for our friendship, but certainly he will not just sit there and smile.

This is exactly what he does.

"I knew you would," he says to me with another sigh. The bubbles tickle my face as I lay my forehead against his. Yuri lets his body slide off of the chest and curls himself and his tail around me. The warmth of him helps me to keep speaking.

"He was lovely," I say thinking of all the wonderful things Seth and I did together. "He didn't deserve to die." I shake my head and try to decide how to put my overwhelming emotions into words. "I chose not to touch him for the first few days and he resisted the thrall of the Feed and befriended me." I hold my hands out before me and examine my nails. "Before I left, I coupled with him and took a bit of his flesh, just a small piece, not enough to hurt. I very well may not come out of the dark room alive." Yuri's arms slip around me and hold me tightly. "And I can't say if I am carrying his child. I don't know if what I did was enough." I don't bother to tell him about the tattoos, not yet. There's so much more to say, I barely know where to begin. "My mother," I begin and Yuri cuts in gently.

The Feed

"I know," he says and I look up at him. He's smiling a strange smile and brushing blonde hair from his face with one hand. It's gotten tangled with mine again and I raise my hands, trying to help him unknot it. "Yanori and I have been talking about it for awhile."

"I have to stop the Hunt," I say. "And I have to change the Feed. I thought I had time, but now I'm not so sure." After our hair is untangled, I drop my hands and spin to face him. "I need your help."

"It's yours," he says without hesitation. "Whatever it is that you need, I'll do it." In Yuri's pale eyes is love. I don't know if I reciprocate it, but I can see that that doesn't matter to him. However I feel, whatever I may do, his love is mine.

"After the parade, after we get the necklace, we'll talk with Yanori. I have so much more to tell you." I touch my hand to his chest. "The Hunt is immediate and I cannot say what will happen in the Sanctum, but there is something you can do for me now."

"Anything," Yuri says as he waits patiently, eyes sparkling with curiosity and questions.

"If I am not pregnant with the human's child, it will not be long before my mother notices and she will punish me harshly. If, at the very least, I was carrying a *merighean* child, it would buy me time."

"Of course," Yuri says, lifting my face to his and kissing me gently on the lips. I kiss him back, enjoying the sensation of comfort and understanding I get in his arms. In the back of my mind however, is the image of Seth and the feeling that somehow, I will never be able to let it go.

Chapter Eighteen

The parade is ostentatious to the point of being disturbing. My mother gives one of her uplifting speeches wherein she promises things she can't possibly deliver and hints at surprises to come. The people are mollified by the three Huntswomen who showed up late and cheer as if we have not had one of the worst Feeds in almost two decades.

It is only after the first procession of trick swimmers that I notice Kiara amongst the new Huntswomen. I move over to her, convinced that the crowd is currently more focused on the display of weaponry that is being paraded through the dragon's bones like the world's finest arsenal.

"I'm glad to see that you're still alive," I tell her as she smiles at me and her lavender eyes light up with thanks.

"Because of you," she tells me and I tilt my head in confusion. She rushes to explain, whispering quietly enough that the others won't hear her. "The girls that went to the beach," she begins with a quick glance to her left. "They weren't able to get ashore because the beach was nearly overrun with buildings, all of them full of humans. After they left, the storm got progressively worse and they were forced to try an undesirable spot along the coast, just west of there. They lost nearly thirty Huntswomen before they ever set foot on shore." I try to keep my face neutral but several of the other girls look over at us. I'm sure they can feel the waves of frustration rolling off of me. The attitude of the fallen women is just another symbol of carelessness and disrespect for the ocean. "If I hadn't followed you, I'd most likely be dead." I smile and plant a friendly kiss on her forehead, trying to pull back on my emotions. Most likely my mother will want me to give a speech of some sort and I know that if I don't calm down, my emotions will flow in my words. I need to be calm, likeable, and dependent. These are the most important things I could communicate to the *merighean* right now.

"I'm sorry I didn't see you earlier," I tell her with a gentle smile. "All I could think about was getting out of that room." Kiara grins at me and flashes a look at the group of colorful males, like a sea of rainbows, that are floating across the way from us. Yuri is right in front, pale eyes taking in every detail of everything: the expression on each face, the number of weapons, the whispers of the crowd. She understands my statement in a different way than I had intended, but I soon decide that it's preferable anyway. I should try to seem as oblivious to the tension around me as I can; it's what the other Huntswomen are doing and it's what will keep me alive until I know who will have my back.

"Yuri's quite beautiful," she tells me honestly, lavender

eyes moving to a different male, one with turquoise hair that matches my nails and a tail as blue as the sea around him. "I can understand why you would want to be with him so quickly." She shivers and I can see from her expression that she did not enjoy her human the way I enjoyed Seth. "*Merighean* men are a hundred times more beautiful than any human. Mine was brown eyed and brown haired, too stupid to please me, and pale, white even." I don't know how to respond to her statement, wanting suddenly to get my knife and go. I like Kiara, but I can't get into a conversation like this, not now. "He hadn't a splotch of color on him, not anywhere. Dull as a bit of sand." The other girls have heard and are giggling along, adding their own stories to the mix. I ignore them and try to pull Kiara's attention back to me, leaving the rest in an immature frenzy, as they've always been prone to do. I don't know when these girls will turn into the quiet, brooding warriors that sit at my mother's side, but I hope it is soon or I will not stand a chance.

"Do you have the knife?" I ask her with a kind smile. I don't want her or anyone else to see my irritation. She nods and reaches to the belt of kelp around her waist. She cuts it with her nails and slides the sheath off, passing it and the knife to me.

"I want to thank you for this," Kiara says and her eyes become serious. "I used it to kill my human and carve him. The beauty of the knife gave me the strength to fulfill my duty." A shiver crawls down my spine, but I don't let her see it; I don't let anyone see it. "You will make a great queen one day," she says suddenly and I can finally give her a genuine smile.

"Thank you," I say, letting as much strength into my voice as I can. I want her to believe her own words so that when the time comes, she might stand by me. "Now," I say as I look around and catch my mother fawning over my father's hair. "I think I will go and see Yuri." I add a wink to this to make Kiara, and the eavesdroppers around her, think that what I have in mind is coupling. It is their favorite conclusion to come to after all. They laugh as I scoot away, edging Kua's bones and trying to find a way to cross that will not draw Aleria's attention. I have to find a way to get the knife to him before I am called to the skull to give my speech. If the queen sees how desperate I was to get it back in my possession, she will have questions that I will not want to answer. When I left for the Feed, she did not notice that it was anything other than an ordinary knife; I can't afford to take that chance again.

"I could hold onto that for you, perhaps," says a voice from below and behind me. I turn and find Yanori alone, leaning against a coral statue for support. This one is of my mother, pink and exaggerated with bigger hips, bigger breasts, and a brighter smile than Aleria has every possessed in real life. I drift down to her and don't ask how she knows what I was doing. Yanori has incredible hearing, a byproduct of her blindness, and I do not doubt that she has heard every word.

"Where are we meeting tonight?" I ask her as I swim down beside her and tuck the knife into the pouch at her waist.

"At Yuri's house," she says, turning her blank gaze to

Kua's head. "Aleria has never been fond of my dabbling in ancient arts, but lately, she has become almost violently suspicious. She had my house searched and I often feel hostile eyes at my back. If you were to come there, she would know." I shake my head and know that Yanori will sense the gesture in the disturbance of the water around her.

"She can't possibly know anything, can she?" I ask. I haven't even spoken my thoughts aloud.

"Not in the sense that you are imagining, but Aleria is a predator. She senses the feelings of those around her and acts upon them. This is all that she is doing." I try not to sigh, but I am already tired and the revolution has barely begun. The stress may very well kill me.

"I want to tell you everything," I say and Yanori smiles.

"And you will," she says, moving behind the statue. "But first you will address the people." I turn around and find my mother's gaze swinging to me. She has not seen me with Yanori, which is good, but when she holds out her hand and gestures at me with a single, wicked finger, I know that I'd be wise to choose my words carefully.

I use the base of the statue to kick off and spin through the water as fast as I can, adding a loop and a twist to my route. This sort of behavior is exciting to the *merighean* although I can't say why. *I must be likeable and relatable,* I remind myself as I near the skull and pause, perching on the area behind Kua's empty eyes.

My father smiles warmly at me, yellow tail waving softly in greeting.

The Feed

"I missed you, daughter," he says as he kisses the backs of my hands and looks up at me through his tangle of sandy hair. "But I knew you had the strength to overcome your trials. If any girl is worthy of being heir, it is you." I grin at him and give him a gentle hug, aware that my mother's eyes are on my back, boring into my flesh and searing me. When I turn around, the rest of the crowd is waiting in silence, looking up at us with eyes hungry for promises of strength and safety. I step forward and push my chest out, as if I have taken the biggest, most cleansing breath.

"Make me proud, Natalie," Aleria says, voice full of false cheer. I survey the *merighean*, enjoying the brightness of their tails and the shimmer of their eyes. We are truly a beautiful people, at least on the outside. Inside, we are damaged and hurting. I went to the Feed afraid for myself, afraid of what I would have to do, desperate to save a single life. Now, I am afraid for them; I *must* protect them from themselves. And their queen. I glance over at Aleria's dark eyes and steady myself. *I hope Yanori does not mind if I steal her words,* I think and let the humor of that show in my face. If Seth has taught me anything, it is that a joke can help break the ice in an otherwise serious conversation. I must remember that.

"When I left for the Feed," I say, wanting to remain as honest as I can without giving myself away. "I was afraid. I was afraid of change, of the unknown, and of myself. I was stubborn, set in my ways. I have never been social, always quiet. I have spent the majority of my life on the outskirts of the city I am supposed to embrace. It's not that

I wanted this, it's just that I didn't know how to change it.

"What I did not know at the time was that to change the minds of others, a test of courage must be passed. This was true, even for myself. So I did what I had to do. I followed the path that was revealed to me and I proved myself. I earned my own respect and changed my life." I pause here and look out at the crowd, wanting to judge their reactions from their faces. Yuri is smiling gently, face beaming with love. I know then that I am on the right track.

"Protection, power, and understanding are the cornerstones of the changes we need to make to stay great. Here," I touch my chest with my hand. "We are one with the sea and the earth. It is only once we realize this that our cities can be whole again. So this is my promise to you: I will pass whatever tests this life may throw at me and I will prove myself to you." I glance over at Aleria and see that she is not happy. I hope my next words will please her. She doesn't have to know that I am talking about myself. "Your queen will lead you through great changes that will build our cities to new heights, bring prosperity like we have never seen, and restore the magic that once belonged to all of us." My next words are drowned out, not by shouts or mindless cheers, but by a beautiful silence that builds into a crescendo of hope. Somehow, I have reached out to them and they have seen it. I look around me and see the Huntswomen, and my mother, watching me with interest. Now all I must do is live long enough to make good on my words.

The Feed

◆ ◆ ◆

Yuri and I do not hesitate after my speech ends. We use the frenzy and the excitement to disappear into the throngs of people and edge the kelp forest until we reach his house. It's like the home of any other unmarried *merighean*: a short, squat bit of stone that's been hollowed out at the center. The roof is a weaving of kelp for privacy and all around, holes have been drilled as windows, large enough for us to pass through as we approach.

It is once we are inside that I can see the difference. Hanging from the roof are bits of rope, twine, thread, fabric, anything really that Yuri can use to tie things in. He wraps stones and jewelry, dishes and driftwood, shells and bones, into them and lets them dangle around us like the branches of a drooping tree. I drop to the floor immediately and am in shock to see that his collection has nearly doubled in size since I was last here.

"You've been busy," I tell him as he strings up a hammock for me to sit in. It takes up nearly the entire room, floating like a white cloud in the gentle currents that pass through.

"I was trying to keep my mind off of you," he replies with a smile. I lie in the hammock without hesitation, hoping that the gentle rock of the sea will help me relax. I feel like my nerves are stretched taught, strung between my heart and my brain, and that they may snap at anytime. "Your speech was wonderful, very inspiring," he says. "I could hear the males behind me whispering their praises of you."

"I hope I was not too frank," I say, thinking of Aleria's curious face. Yanori's words about her being a predator are all too true. If she sees me as a threat, she will look for any excuse to get rid of me or lock me up. Yuri lifts a container from a small table that sits against the wall. He swims over to me and presents me with a jar of tiny starfish. I'm not hungry, but I take one anyway, glad that the desperate hunger I've been feeling for human flesh is gone. I don't know if it's because I took a piece of Seth or because I'm back in the sea, but I'm happy to be rid of it. It was an unpleasant desire to entertain. Seth's face pops into my head again and I find I have to close my eyes and concentrate to be rid of it. Maybe later, after I have retrieved my items and explained my plans to Yuri and Yanori, I can think about him. Right now, there are more pressing matters.

"I don't think you have anything to worry about," Yuri says in latent response to my statement. His eyes are thoughtful again and I can see that he's got a plethora of questions to ask me. I decide that I will wait for Yanori to get here before I say anything. My words are treasonous enough to get me locked up or killed and I want only to say them once. "Would you like me to stay in your room tonight?" Yuri asks me as neutrally as I think he's able. He's trying to be polite, trying to maintain the cool distance that most Huntswomen prefer from their males.

The Feed

Still, in his voice is a quiver, a slight tremble, that tells me that he's afraid. I have yet to ask for his hand and I have yet to return his vows of love. I decide that he needs a bit of reassurance, something to hold him over until I make my decisions.

"I would love that," I reply and hold out my arms for him. He sets the jar of starfish back on the table and swims over to me, curling himself around my body and settling into the curve of the hammock. I play with his hair for awhile, knowing that Yanori will come as soon as she's able. There may very well be Huntswomen who have their eyes on her and if she has to persuade them that she isn't up to something, she'll spend hours making sure they're convinced. "How is Ira?" I ask, realizing that I haven't seen him since I've been back. Yuri is silent for a moment.

"He was in love with a failed Huntswoman." Yuri pauses and I can feel his body tense slightly. He is empathizing with his friend and I am glad that I'm still here to press a gentle kiss to his forehead. How selfish it was for me to even consider staying on land. I would've harmed Yanori, Yuri, and my father – the people I care about most. *Foolish.* "One of the first Huntswomen back told him how she perished at the hands of a shark." I feel my chest constrict. The girl that Ira was infatuated with, a woman named Ilia, was the one I saw splayed out like a feast, filled with crabs and nibbled at by fish. I shiver and decide to say nothing. At least now though, I know her name. It makes me feel just the slightest bit better.

We say nothing more to one another, just lie together in

warmth and enjoy the pleasure of one another's company. I try keep my mind blank, try to use this moment to catch up with myself. Changes are happening quickly enough and I know that this is just the beginning. My revolution has not even started yet and already my mother is up to several somethings that need handling. The Hunt for one, fueled by Imenea's dark magics, will launch twenty Huntswomen in groups of four to the shore where they will find men and drag them back to the sea. Five men will be tied down and taken by every available Huntswoman of age until they are all certain that they are pregnant. And then they will eat them. They will carve their bodies and share their flesh amongst themselves. It's a desperate tactic, a last ditch effort to swell our ranks. And it's the first thing I must put a stop to. The second I can't be sure about. My mother says changes are afloat, but I can do nothing until I know what they are. I must focus on passing the tests in the Sanctum and staying alive long enough to find out.

I close my eyes and enjoy the weight of the water against my skin. Just as I'm drifting off to sleep, I hear the strange gurgling sounds of Yanori's tail.

"Hurry," she whispers from the doorway, rousing both Yuri and myself. "The city's alive and running. I don't know what the people sense, but the queen's mood and the Huntswomen's actions are exciting them. We need to get out and back before the frenzy reaches a crescendo."

Yanori waits for us, head tilted to one side as she listens for the sounds of swimming, lets the water brush her skin and allows the currents to warn her. When I swim

The Feed

close enough to her, she hands me a silver belt, made from large links of chain. It is clean and shimmers like the bracelet Seth gave me. There are no black deposits on it, making me quite curious as to its origin. The knife's sheath is already connected to it, looped on one of the links where the belt connects. I put it around my waist and look up at my sister's face.

"I will tell you when there's time," she says as if it isn't important. I put my questions aside and follow her north, towards the edge of the city's boundaries where the undersea mountains begin, shielding us from the worst of the ocean's rage. Yuri and Yanori are much faster and more agile than I am, making me remember how easy it is to envy the mers' swimming skills. Still, I have something that they don't; I have legs. Legs that carried me ashore and showed me Seth and allowed me to meet Sarah and walked across grass. I keep this in my head as I lag behind, pausing to kick off the edges of houses and propel myself along the rocks we pass by. They don't relax their pace until we are passing over the kelp forest and I am nearly desperate for breath. Had I been on land, I would've been heaving, chest scrambling for the sweet touch of air. Down here, all I can do is slow myself and hope that they notice. They do, circling back to me and falling in line on either side.

"I'm sorry," Yanori says, but I know that she only pushed me as far as I could go. I say nothing at first, trying to let my blood replenish itself with oxygen so that I do not pass out. Once I recover, we pick up our pace and I start to talk. Yanori, although she is blind, has a better sense of direction than anyone I have ever met and although none of the landmarks around me seem familiar, I trust her judgment.

"I did not kill the human," I begin, knowing that they're both aware of this fact but needing to say it anyway. "His name was Seth and he was special." I tell Yuri and Yanori about the tattoos, about the dreams, the necklace. I tell them how he easily he resisted the pull of the Feed in the beginning and how, miraculously, even as we were coupling, he had the strength to find himself outside of it in the end. I say everything that pops into my head, no matter how pointless it may seem. Yanori and Yuri both are the type of people that can take a meaningless thought and expand it into an enlightening hypothesis. So I tell them about Sarah, about the basil, the video games, the car, the Chinese food, the shower; I relate Seth's stories about his neighbors, his relationship with Jenna, his brother. And then I tell them my feelings – all of them. The ones about my mother seem to be no surprise, about uprooting our people, changing the Feed, bringing harmony to sea and earth. I even admit to my brief thoughts about wanting to stay on land, to stay with Seth.

"Do you love him?" Yuri asks me, not judging, not accusing, just curious. I think long and hard about my answer. Finally, I'm forced to admit the truth.

"I don't know," I say and that is it. Neither of them question me and soon I am on my knees in the sand, digging up the plastic bag. It is undisturbed, still intact. The items inside are still dry for now. I hold it up and pass it to Yuri first. "We could go to the library to open it," I

The Feed

suggest, not wanting to ruin the book. Yuri's enthusiasm is palpable now.

"A new book," he says and I can see that he is just as excited as I was to have something new to read. I smile and am infinitely glad that during the last few years, I have been teaching him English. It's frowned upon but not forbidden. Even if it was, I would've done it anyway. Yuri flips the bag around and stares at the picture that is pressed against the plastic on that side. It is the only one visible, but it shows Seth's image quite clearly. He is leaning against the tree, dark hair blowing in a gentle breeze. His brown eyes are wide and sparkling and his tattoos burst from the image like a school of bright fish. Yuri smiles gently and hands the bag to Yanori. She may not be able to see it, but she uses her fingers to judge the contents, taking in information that even I have missed.

"What is this?" Yanori asks, pressing her fingers against the lump of the bracelet. I look up at her and rise to my feet, taking the bag in my hands.

"This is a bracelet made of silver that Seth gave to me," I say, examining the inscription. "It says *Sailor* in English." Yanori does not speak the language as far as I'm aware so I relate it to her in *Tersallee*. She nods but doesn't comment.

"Hide it where you will," she says. "But be cautious. If the queen finds this, you may not live to see another day." I nod my head and tuck the bag under my arm. "I want you to go home and sleep, relax yourself and prepare for the Sanctum. Once it is over, meet me at the library and we will study these items further." From Yanori's voice, I can surmise that she either knows something or has already come to her own conclusions. "I will remain here as I have some things to look into. Take a different route back to the city, one that is more direct." I look around but see no reason why she would want to stay out here alone.

"It's dangerous," I say, not wanting to patronize her. She did, after all, come out here by herself and return by herself earlier this same day. Or perhaps it was the day before. The time on land was so strict that now that I am back under the sea, I am finding myself confused.

"I have a friend waiting for me," Yanori replies cryptically, looking over her shoulder as if she can see. "Don't worry about me. Today is not the day I die." I look at Yuri and see that he is as confused as I am. That is the way with my sister, the way it has always been. She may be ten months younger than I am, but she seems years older. With a sigh, I grab her hand and kiss it gently.

"You'd best be telling me the truth," I say and once again use her own words against her. "Because I would miss you quite a lot. Especially in the afterlife."

◆ ◆ ◆

Yuri and I arrive back at my room without incident and I immediately bury my bag in the sand next to the crown, replace the chest of coins, and clean up my tracks. I decide to put Yanori's belt inside the wooden box, buried under a couple of handfuls of blackened silver. It is unlikely that someone would find it there, but if they do, it is just a knife after all, albeit a unique one. Without my mother's jealousy and suspicion to fuel them, I'm sure that most *merighean* would hardly notice it. Once the hype of the Feed has died down, I will begin wearing it regularly.

Yuri says nothing about Seth or the tattoos or even the book. He just curls himself on his side in the sand. I pace the length of the room for awhile, watching as the *sispa* we brought in last night captures a small, blue fish with the tentacles that protrude from its head like antennae. I am glad that it has finally lured its prey; the glimmering orbs that it waves as bait are bright enough to blind.

"Come relax with me," Yuri says. "You must be exhausted. I imagine the swim back was not easy." I raise my arms above my head and feel my muscles protest. They had finally gotten used to life on land and are now adapting back to the sea.

"I am tired," I admit as I walk over to Yuri and lie down beside him. He strokes the side of my face with his fingers and wiggles his body close enough to mine that he can wrap my legs with his muscular tail. "But I don't know if I can sleep. There's so much to think about, I can hardly stand it."

"Then don't," he says as he brushes his lips against mine. "For just this moment, don't think. Yanori and I are here to help and you know that between the three of us, things will get done." I smile and take his advice, certain that by morning, my fears will relax and everything will become clear.

Chapter Nineteen

The Sanctum of Amarana is hidden by a pair of doors carved from stone. They are never left open and require the strength of thirty Huntswomen to part. Normally, as a gesture of our newly elevated status, the Huntswomen who are to be tested would draw open the doors together. Since there are not enough of us, some of our instructors are required to step in and take hold of the ropes that are bolted into the stone with metal screws, fashioned long ago when the *merighean* had the means to do so. This room is one of the few that has escaped the deterioration of the rest of the palace, and although I am scared, I can, at the very least, appreciate the beauty inside. Or so I hope.

I struggle in the water, wishing that my mother had let us all pull from the floor. It would've been so much easier than trying to swim and drag the weight of the doors along with us. Only the instructors have been allowed to stand which I find strange.

She is testing you and tiring you out at the same time, I realize with a jolt of anxiety. The adrenaline coursing

The Feed

through my body makes me that much stronger and I push myself harder, satisfied to see that the stone has slid forward enough to create ample space for us to pass.

"That's enough," Aleria says, swimming forward nimbly and abandoning her entourage of servants. Only Huntswomen who have passed the Feed are allowed in the dark room; the *merighean* are forbidden to even enter this hall without her permission. She moves past us and disappears into the darkness without another word.

"Line up in order of rank," Coreia shouts as she floats up to join the rest of us. "Except for Natalie. Come see me." Confused, I drop my place at the front of the line and swim to the back. I don't ask why she wants to see me; I merely wait for the other girls to organize themselves in front of me. I can't assume there is a problem. That would be the first step to admitting there is anything going on. I must feign ignorance and impassivity.

Tejean spearheads the group with a pair of my mother's favorite Huntswomen at her sides and the girls follow her forward and away, swallowed by the black seawater before them. I don't look at Coreia, merely cross my arms and tread the water gently with my feet. We stay there quite awhile in silence, making me wonder if Coreia is waiting for some sort of signal. Just as my legs are starting to get tired and I'm forced to uncross my arms, she speaks.

"Natalie, your mother has requested that you go last. Normally, an heir would be tested first, but I think she senses the fragility of the girls. If you were to fail ... " She doesn't need to finish. I can see where she is headed with this conversation and nod briskly. What I don't do is tell her what is really going on, as if she doesn't know. My mother doesn't care about the other Huntswomen and I hardly believe that I am close enough with them to affect their outcome in whatever trials await us. She is testing my strength of will, allowing me the most time to sit with my anxiety, trying to find cracks. My speech last night did not put a smile on her face this morning. When I showed up in the throne room, all she did was stare at me with her eyes narrowed and her nails clacking a terrible threnody on the arms of her chair.

"I understand, Instructor," I say, wanting to move forward and discover the Sanctum's secrets. Coreia smiles at me for a moment and leads the way as a group of warriors fan out behind us, blocking the open door from intruders. As if there ever were any. The *merighean* have not had an undersea war in over two hundred years.

I lag behind Coreia just a bit, trying to allow my eyes to adjust to the darkness. I want to see everything in here, no matter how insignificant. But it's too dark. It is the type of dark that is found only in sea caves where the sun's light never penetrates. No matter how large my pupils may dilate, I will not be able to pierce these depths. Disappointed, I continue swimming forward, hoping that I am still behind my mother's most favored Huntswoman. I try to imitate Yanori's actions, letting the water guide me while I use disturbances in the sea around me to try to detect movement.

As I get farther and farther away from the entrance, I become worried that I have gotten lost somehow.

"Coreia?" I say, hoping for a response, a sign that I am on the right track. There is nothing but silence and the sound of bubbles. I feel them against my belly and breasts as I swim faster and faster, hoping to catch up if I've been left behind. "Coreia?"

Silence and darkness are all that greet me as I swim blindly. I keep myself going in a straight line, not wanting to scrape my body along any of the walls. There are sighs and bursts of warm water every now and again making me think that perhaps there are vents below me. If I were to run into them, I could be scalded, perhaps killed. I stop talking, knowing now that it is useless. If Coreia is here, she is not speaking. I am coming to realize perhaps that this is some sort of test. My mother's actions make even more sense. What might've been a team building exercise for the other Huntswomen is now a lone feat that I must accomplish, further proving myself useful to her.

The quiet and the lack of visual interest take my mind on paths it would not have otherwise crossed. This makes me think of Yanori and her seemingly infinite wisdom. Perhaps her blindness has granted her a different perspective of the world, one that makes her seem at times as if she is prophetic. Maybe all of her strange thoughts and whispered advice are products of this silent loneliness that penetrates me now, drags my soul to places it does not want to go.

When I finally see a sliver of light in the distance, I write it off as another vision. I've been having a lot of them: images of Seth and Yuri swim together next to scenes of tragedy where I lie dead at my mother's feet. I see Muoru and Amahna and Kua rise from the sand beneath my feet and take to the waters above me like birds to the sky. None of it makes the slightest bit of sense, so I ignore it, certain that it means nothing or that if it does, I am in no position to analyze it. All I want is to escape this darkness and see a bit of sun, a *sispa*, an electric light, anything.

Then I hear my mother's voice chanting along with a chorus of others. Hauntingly beautiful, the sound draws me forward quickly and the light grows into an archway. I burst through it in a spin, shooting above the heads of a hundred Huntswomen and pausing before the queen. She sits in a different throne, this one carved in bone with a massive ribcage for a back. The bones circle around her like arms, hug her in a macabre embrace.

Aleria stops chanting and smiles at me.

"Congratulations," she says as I look around for the other girls. They are nowhere to be seen. "You will be tested now, Natalie," she continues, enjoying my confusion. "The others have all passed as you've lingered." I turn back to her, my eyes raking the room as I go. There are symbols everywhere, thousands of them across the stone walls and the ceiling and the floor. They are in the same vein as the ones that grace the necklace and Seth's skin. I search for some that I recognize but find none. Still, I file that information away for later, sure that this is yet another piece to my growing puzzle.

"How is that possible?" I ask, meeting Aleria's dark eyes with my own. I was not in the darkness for more than an hour; I am certain of that.

The Feed

"Almost half a day has passed since you entered the Sanctum," she says, nodding her chin at Coreia who sits in the black sand near the base of the throne. Her violet hair is wrapped atop her head, pinned with bits of bone and pearly clips that the queen must have lent her. She wasn't wearing them when she lead me through the doors, but that doesn't prove my mother's words true. I say nothing but remain convinced that I am being played. After all, I do not see Tejean or the other Huntswomen here and I know that I did not pass them on the way. I would've felt their presence the way Yanori always senses mine.

There are no doors in this room that I can see and I am disappointed to discover that the only furniture is the chair in which my mother sits. Either the stories our instructors had whispered about this place are false or all of the beauty and the relics I've been craving to see are buried in that perpetual blackness outside the archway.

"Come here," Aleria says, holding out her hands for mine. I drop my palms against hers and wait in quiet anticipation as Coreia stands and draws a knife from her belt. I would be afraid if I thought it would be useful to me. If my mother desires me dead now, then there is nothing I can do about it. There isn't the faintest chance that I could slip away. I keep myself calm by thinking of the night Yuri and I shared together. It was peaceful and comfortable, nothing at all like the tense anxiety that grips me now.

"State your purpose," Coreia intones in a dreadful voice. She sounds flat and emotionless and not like the woman who has led my combat training for the past ten years. I think carefully about this answer, knowing that to give the same words I supplied to Tejean before leaving for the Feed will not suffice.

"To even out the balance of power," I say, remaining purposely vague. What I mean to say is that I want to bring a bit of the earth to the sea and give a bit of the sea to the earth, just as Yanori had said. I am hoping that my mother believes I mean to bring all of the magic here and give none of it away. She can never know that that is exactly what I did not do.

"State your intent." I smile inwardly; outwardly I keep my face neutral. I have passed.

"Bring the Huntswomen to glory, lead the *merighean* to prosperity and honor the power of the ocean." I am proud that all of my words are true, although misleading. My mother is not smiling now. I do not know what she expected, but whatever it is that I am doing, this is not it.

"State your punishment."

"Punishment for failure is an eternity in the waterlogged hells of Imenea's kingdom where the sea runs black and the salt is as poison. There is no love, no wonder, and no joy, only the bleak realization that one has failed and that redemption is a thing of the past." Here I quote the words straight from my texts. If I am right, this is exactly what they want to hear.

Coreia bends down and places the silver of her blade against my skin. For a moment, I fear that I have not passed. Then I realize that we have just moved onto the next portion of this strange ritual.

"In your journeys, did you find a human male?" she

asks, tongue sliding over her red lips. I look her straight in the face and answer.

"I did."

"And did you couple with him?"

"I did."

"And did you taste his flesh, pull his magic into you for the good of the sea?"

"I did."

Coreia slices my wrist sharply and without warning. Crimson blood spirals in the water before me, twisting like a column of red smoke. My mother moves a silver cup over it, with the stem held in her fist and the opening pointing downward. The blood moves up and curls in the bowl, resting there as if it's been drawn. Aleria turns the goblet over as Coreia steps back and puts it to her purple lips. I watch, disturbed, as she opens her mouth and draws in the seawater like a breath. My blood follows, rising from the cup and snaking over her tongue like lightning. The queen snaps her mouth closed along with her eyes and begins to hum. The other Huntswomen behind her join in and soon, I'm forced to put my hands over my ears. It's so loud, I can barely think. I drop to my knees and fight back a scream.

And then as suddenly as it started, it stops. I look up at my mother and find her eyes wide and her mouth agape. A glowing ball of green escapes from her lips and drops into the cup with a splash. All around it, the silver is dry, as if the light of the thing repels the water around it. I stare at this in wonder, finding myself on my feet without even realizing how I've gotten there.

C.M. Stunich

Aleria looks up at me, surprise etched across her sharp features.

"Natalie," she says as she hands me the cup and I know without knowing how that I'm supposed to raise it to my lips and drink. "Congratulations, you have passed." I sip the power down my throat and watch my mother struggle to control her emotions. She seems both pleased and irritated at the same time. "You have come back with the magic of a man in your breast and bestowed a great gift upon the people you serve." She pauses and I can only guess that her next words are a deviation from the ritual of tradition. "And somehow, you bring back to me a power I have never seen."

◆ ◆ ◆

Coreia guides me back through the blackness with a small *sispa* clutched in her hands. It isn't enough light to illuminate anything, but it does help me follow her back to the stone doors and the guards that watch me pass by with interest. As I'd suspected, the swim takes just about an hour. I don't know if my mother thinks me a fool or if she believes the darkness will trick my mind into believing her; I don't ask. I have passed the tests in the Sanctum of Amarana and will live to see another day. All is going well. As I had suspected, just a bit of Seth's flesh was enough to pass. As far as my mother's parting words, I am not sure what to make of them, but I guess a long talk with

The Feed

Yuri and Yanori will go a long way.

"Congratulations again, Natalie," Coreia says as she leaves me in the throne room with a gentle pat on the shoulder and a parting smile. "May Neptune carry you on his loving shoulders." I nod in acknowledgment of her words and watch as she swims away, moving like a dark cloud through the brightness of the palace. Once she is out of sight, I head immediately to my room, unable to sit still for even a moment. The power of Seth's magic is burning in my body; I feel as if it is the fuel and I am the flame. I use this excitement to speed through the hallways in twists and spins that rocket me past my door and force me to double back. Still, the feeling is a good one and I cling to it as I open the door, desperate to share this information with someone.

Unfortunately, Yuri is nowhere to be seen, and I guess that he is still on gathering duty. All of the males must participate in the chores around the city. In fact, most of them spend their entire days devoted to keeping Amarana running. Yuri is lucky that for years now, he has been seen as a favorite of mine. *Merighean* males that spend the most time with the Huntswomen are given less duties as a result. It isn't a spoken rule, but it is acknowledged by all without complaint. If I were to marry him, his duties would disappear completely and he would have no other obligation than to please me. I consider this for awhile before deciding to retrieve the bag. As soon as Yuri comes back, we will head to the library and meet Yanori. It is there that I suspect we will come to at least a few of the answers to my many questions. With one last flip in the water, I let myself drift to the floor.

I drag the chest away and begin to dig. It is only when I reach the rocky bottom that I start to panic. *Perhaps I'm not in the right spot,* I tell myself although I am almost certain that I am. I move over and start shoveling handful after handful of sand out of my way. My excitement is fading fast and is being replaced with a cold knot of dread that sits at the bottom of my belly like an anchor. When, once again, I find nothing. I open the chest and dig through the coins for the knife. It is still there, but I can tell that it's been disturbed. I was right; whoever searched my room did not think it of any importance. I slam the lid closed and start in on a new spot, knowing that it's futile but needing to be sure. A knock at the shutters pulls me out of my frantic search. I kick off the floor and swim to the window as fast as I'm able, ushering Yuri in along with a bit of fading hope that I have not just made a terribly costly mistake.

"I'm sorry," Yuri begins before he sees my face, spinning in the water to look at me. "I was collecting oysters and … " He stops talking and stares at me with his pale eyes.

"Did you take it?" I ask, hoping beyond hope that he did. *I should've asked him to; I should've known.* "Do you have the bag and the crown?" Yuri's face drops and I can see from his expression that already, he fears for me.

"No," he says and my stomach rises to my throat. I sit down on the floor hard and try to think. In my desperation to keep the items close, I've just slit my own throat. If they aren't here, then there is only one explanation for it.

The Feed

My mother had someone search my room. If she doesn't have my items in hand now, then she will soon enough.

"More's the pity," I say, my voice nothing more than a gentle current in the room. Yuri moves back to the shutters and closes them quietly, glancing over his shoulder at me. My mind is turning frantically, spinning as fast as the trick dancers in the parade. I have to decide how severe a punishment this will be. I analyze the lost items quickly in my mind. The bracelet is nothing; many of the Huntswomen steal jewelry during the Feed. The fact that I did not offer it to her is just a slight irritation. The necklace as well; it is beautiful, obviously a piece of our history and the symbols on it do match the Sanctum's walls, but it is not a crime for me to have it. Certainly, she will punish me for trying to hide it from her. The fact that I chose not to wear it and instead, bury it away will infuriate her. But not as much as the crown. This is one of her strictest rules. It is tantamount to treason for me to have it. Hopefully, she will not recognize its history as Yuri does or it will triple her anger. Perhaps though, as heir, I may be able to come up with an argument that no other could think to pull off. If any Huntswoman besides her deserves to have a crown, then it should be her daughter, should it not? The book is of little consequence; certainly the queen will look at it, but as soon as she finds it is nothing of importance, she will toss it aside. I will never recover it, of course, but if she pays it a second thought, I would be surprised. That leaves only … "The pictures," I moan aloud, grabbing my hair and pulling it around my face. Yuri drops to the floor and tries to pry my hands away.

"And they mean what?" he asks, head tilted to the side, his blonde hair wrapping around my face like kelp. "They mean nothing. They are only photographs. The tattoos," here Yuri sighs and I look up at him. "The tattoos are certainly curious, but that is all." I look at him and realize that he is right. The pictures will tell my mother only that Seth was unique, that he possessed knowledge he shouldn't have. With a few carefully placed lies, perhaps I can get out of this with little damage. Nothing in that bag will alert her to anything that I have planned, any of the treasonous thoughts that are buried in my mind. "We should go to the library as planned and tell Yanori what has happened. When your mother calls for you, you will be ready." I nod my head and release my hair, breathing out a mouthful of bubbles in a sigh.

"You are right," I say as I allow him to pull me to my feet. I put the belt around my waist, wanting to take it with me. When I see Yanori, I will give back the knife. It isn't safe with me. "This is bad, but it is not catastrophic."

"Yes," Yuri says as he kisses my cheeks one after the other. "You will get through this and rise to the top like sea foam." I realize that this is Yuri's attempt at a joke and laugh, enjoying the soothing touch of his skin and the humor in his eyes. The pulsing flame of Seth's magic has diminished, but somehow I know that it is still there. I wonder briefly if Yuri's might be able to burn alongside it.

The Feed

◆ ◆ ◆

I squeeze through the narrow passage ahead of Yuri and am relieved beyond words to see Yanori's pink and green tail in the water above me. I burst through to the air filled chamber and find her with a soggy book in her hands. I recognize it as the same book I tried to study before I left. The one with the symbols. I gasp in surprise and Yanori looks up at me with a sad smile on her face. Yuri joins us shortly after, sliding along my skin as he tries to put his head above the water. The room is so small that our bodies are pressed together as tightly as if we were coupling.

"The symbols," I say, realizing how blind I've been. The ones in the book were in the same style as the ones on the necklace, on Seth's arm, in the bizarre chamber that I have not had even a quiet second to think about. I put my hands along the edge of the rock and try to peer over at the pages. Yanori tilts the book down for my inspection and I find that the ink that was so clear before, is now runny and fading. The book has finally given in to the dampness that permeates the air here. I drop back to the water with a sigh. Yuri and Yanori are already blinking furiously, trying to wet their eyes. They are not meant to operate outside of the sea. I consider suggesting we head back into the water but realize that we don't have many options as far as places to meet. As soon as my mother has my items in hand, there will be Huntswomen looking for me.

"Tell me what happened," Yanori says, setting the book aside. I start with the Sanctum and the strange blackness, moving to the oddity of my mother's ritual and her strange words. I try to be as thorough as possible, once again wanting to give my friends every possible detail. If I choose to leave something out, it could very well be the key to all of my problems. I refuse to make that mistake. The one thing that I do discover however, is that my mother was telling the truth. I was lost in the blackness for half a day even though the swim took only an hour on the way back. I guess that this is because of my visions and tell Yanori this. She doesn't respond, just nods her head and gestures for me to continue.

"One of the Huntswomen searched my room," I continue as calmly as I'm able. "They found the bag. It's gone – the crown, the necklace, the pictures." Yanori is already nodding, but her face is thoughtful, not grave.

"And the knife?" she asks. I attempt to reach down to my waist but find that I cannot get to the belt. There isn't enough room in the tiny chamber.

"I have it," I say. "But I'd like to give it back." Already Yanori is nodding her head.

"I suppose," she says with a smile and reaches down for a handful of the seawater that fills the tiny area between Yuri's and my chest. She splashes it on her face and lets it run down her lips and off the tip of her nose. "In light of today's events, I can hold onto it for awhile, but soon I must give it back." I don't ask her to clarify;

The Feed

she won't. It's just the way that Yanori is. I reach my arms up to the stone and try to lift myself enough that I can take off the knife. Yuri sees what I'm doing and grabs me under the arms, pushing me up and out of the water just enough so that Yanori, in the precise way that always seems to surprise me, can reach out and undo the links of chain. Once it is in her hands, I slide back into the water.

"What about the crown and the necklace?" I ask her, certain that she gave me the pieces for a reason. If ever there was a time to tell me why, it would be now. Yanori puts the belt around her own waist and smiles gently.

"The necklace has served its purpose," she tells me cryptically. "The crown we will have to get back, but it will not hurt for Aleria to hang onto it for a short while." Yuri and I exchange a glance and I can't resist splashing his face with water. His pearl pink eyes are dry as bones. I watch as his chest rises and falls with strange, quivering shudders. When I look back at Yanori, I see that she is doing the same. I can only guess that they are not used to breathing dry air. Although the *merighean* have lungs, they rarely use them. I imagine that it must be a strange sensation.

"Do you think you could get into my room tonight?" I ask. Yanori normally does not go near the palace; Aleria cannot stand her for even a moment and is always suspicious when she sees her. If her warning bells have already been rung, then finding my sister in my room would further convince her that something is going on. But I can already guess what is going to happen in my upcoming confrontation. "I may need the both of you there," I say, trying to keep my voice even. I am not looking forward to a poisoning from my mother's Spindled Blade or even worse, from her nails, but I know that at least one of these two things awaits me tonight. At least it is a punishment that I am familiar with. This is nothing that has not happened before. The thought is oddly comforting.

"Of course," my sister says, as unselfish as always. I imagine briefly where I would be without her and do not like what I see.

"Thank you," I say to them both, wanting them to understand how much their assistance means to me. If the queen were ever to find out the things the three of us have been doing together, what we've been talking about, or even worse, what we have planned, she would not hesitate to torture and kill them. I start to speak again and pause when bubbles break the surface around me.

Without a doubt, I know that we have a visitor. Yuri knows it, too, and his arms tighten around me comfortingly. I sigh briefly, letting out the last of my fear and trepidation. Whatever happens now, I must remain in complete control. The extent of Aleria's rage will hinge on the words that I say.

"Stay safe," I tell them, knowing that I must get out of there before whoever is coming sees the two *merighean* with me. I slip suddenly from Yuri's grasp, sliding along the smooth, silver scales that line his muscular tail until there is only rock around me. I use my hands and feet to propel myself downward, heels first.

When I run into the Huntswoman below me, she is

The Feed

forced to stop and back up so that we both emerge from the tunnel around the same time. I don't recognize the woman before me, but I smile anyway. I don't know what she has been told, or how loyal she is to my mother, but if I let on for even a moment that I knew this was coming, I will be in even worse trouble.

"I'm sorry," I say, voice smooth, without even the slightest hint of a quiver. "The library is occupied." The Huntswoman before me smiles back and inclines her head.

"Yes, Your Majesty," she says with great humility. *She knows nothing,* I realize with relief. My mother has not told them why she wants to see me. This is a good sign. "Thank you for that information, but I have been sent by your mother. She would like to see you in her room as soon as possible." I nod as if this is just a normal day, one where I haven't the slightest clue why the queen wants to see me.

Chapter Twenty

The Huntswoman does not accompany me to the palace;

instead she spins away from the library's tunnel and disappears behind the rows of houses that line this part of the city. Most likely she is off to tell the others that she has delivered the queen's message. This is another positive sign for me. I know now that I will make it out of my mother's room alive. If she were planning on killing me, she would have sent a specific messenger, someone like Coreia, who would have been as secretive as possible and who would've escorted me personally back to her chambers.

I decide to swim there immediately but not to rush. I will go as I did the day she called me there to discuss my lack of care in arranging my hair. I don't look behind me to see if Yuri and Yanori have emerged from the tunnel; I know that they will wait a while before leaving. The small chamber is not a popular spot for anyone to go and their chances of being discovered there now that I am gone are slim.

I spot the girls from my Feed in the throne room and count them quickly, glad to see that all nineteen are present and accounted for. Kiara waves at me and I wave back.

"Come join us," she says as she swims up to meet me. "We are going to celebrate our victory over the Sanctum." Normally, this is the type of activity that I would avoid at all costs. Now I know that this type of bonding is important if I want to make these girls loyal to me. Unfortunately, my mother's summons cannot be ignored.

"I must attend to the queen," I say apologetically but with a smile. "Next time though, I would love to go. I could show you where the best pearls are found." Kiara grins and bows her body respectfully. If anything will win over the girls in my absence, it is this. In order to propose to a *merighean* male, a Huntswoman must present him with a pearl. Oftentimes, these are borrowed from friends or relatives, but to have one that does not need to be returned, that they themselves have found, is a temptation that I doubt any of them will pass up.

"Yes," Kiara says and her lavender eyes glitter brightly. "Yes, that would be lovely, Natalie." I wave again at the other girls before swimming down the series of winding hallways that will take me to my mother's room. I pause just outside her door and listen briefly. She is having a rather snippy conversation with my father whose replies are so quiet, I can barely hear them.

I kick my legs loudly against the wall, using the power to propel myself forward and announce that I am here at the same time. Coreia is standing just inside the doorway which is not a good sign, but she doesn't even look at me when I come in. Her gaze is fixed on my mother is who is sitting at her dressing table, turquoise hair piled atop her head and stuffed with pearls, shells, and bits of bone. It's as if Coreia, whose hair is now down and floats freely around her face, has merely transferred her previous style to the queen's head. Nobody acknowledges me.

"Mistakes don't involve consent, Katsu," my mother says. She's bent over the table top, examining her makeup and the bowls and shells that are filled to overflowing with jewelry. It is on the top of one of these that I see the *Sailor* bracelet. Aleria has tossed it there is if it means nothing. This is good for my case, but it also infuriates me. I want it back so badly it hurts. I drift to the floor, confident that if my mother is sitting and Coreia is standing, that nobody will mind that I am not swimming. "Mistakes are made when something outside of your control occurs." I listen to her words, sure that she is talking about me. When she continues, I realize that she is not. "Was this out of your control, Katsu?"

My gaze swings over to my father who is lounging on the bed, tail hanging listlessly off the side.

"I was overwhelmed with love, my darling," he tells her as his eyes find mine and he smiles gently. Whatever is going on between them has nothing to do with me, and I can see from his expression that my father also has no idea why I'm here. "If you don't want the child, you might take a bit of – "

Aleria smashes her fist on the table, crushing a shell in the process. Little bits of pink drift in the water around her like leaves. I hold very still, not wanting to get in the middle of another argument. I feel for my father, but I know that, unlike me, my mother loves him very much. Whatever it is that he has done, she will forgive him. This is not true for me. I remain silent and watch a school of blue fish swim through the doorway and pick at the algae that grows along the edge of the curtains.

"No," she says in her fiercest voice and the fish scatter as quickly as they came, disappearing out the window and fading into the sea. "At this stage in my pregnancy, it would just be easier to birth the damned thing." My mother picks up a pink shell from the edge of the table

The Feed

with her right hand, moving it in front of her so that I cannot see what she is doing. "But this does complicate things," she continues, smearing pink pearl dust along her right cheek. "I have already begun the necessary preparations for the Hunt and it would be a shame to put it off now." Aleria sighs as if this idea is completely off-putting. "Now, I will have to keep our visitors alive until I am ready to conceive again." I hold back a sigh of relief as I realize what is going on. My mother is carrying my father's *merighean* child which means she cannot get pregnant with another Huntswoman if the Hunt successfully brings back a human. If I can't put a stop to it, which I may be hard pressed to do if I am lying comatose in my room, then things are best this way. I have no illusions that my mother cares about me in any way. My only saving grace thus far has been that I am the only siren daughter she has. If she gets pregnant with another Huntswoman, I could very well find my claim to the throne compromised.

"Darling," she coos and my father rises from the bed in a burst of color, twisting across the room and coming to rest at her left side. I love him more than anything, but if ever there was a *merighean* male who took their duties of plaything seriously than it is my poor father. My mother turns away from her table to face him and kisses him fiercely on the lips. "I will forgive you this time because I am a generous and kindhearted woman, but next time I may get angry." My father nods and does not argue; he knows better. I watch as he sweeps a bow and moves towards the door, planting a gentle kiss on my forehead on his way out. He does not need to be told that his presence is no longer required.

"Coreia," Aleria says and now her voice holds venom. I assume that it is for me and not her faithful right hand, but Coreia rushes to her side anyway and helps her to remove the cumbersome shawl she has tied around her neck. The queen adores anything gaudy or ostentatious, especially when it comes to fabric. I have never found the long pieces of silk anything but cumbersome, but she favors them greatly. I watch without interest, not understanding the slow, almost sensual way that Coreia removes the fabric until I see the necklace.

I swallow a bit of seawater but maintain a calm expression. It is no surprise that she is wearing it; it is exactly the type of thing that she adores. I close my eyes and reopen them in a slow blink.

"Natalie, my darling daughter," Aleria says without turning around. Her face is still down turned, eyes still glued to the dressing table. "You are so very precious to me," she says, false love dripping from her every word like poison. I say nothing and remain still, watching Coreia out of the corner of my eye as she moves back and waits behind my mother with her arms at her side. "Do you know why that is?" I remain silent, aware that she truly does not want to hear me speak yet.

"It is because you're my only heir, the princess of Amarana, a full blooded Huntswoman." She lifts a string of pearls in her hand and squeezes them until they bleed white glitter across her flesh. This she massages into the scales at her wrists until they shimmer like stars. I know all of what she says is true, of course. I know that she doesn't love me as a person, doesn't even care for me as her child. I am an extension of her, a reflection only. I mean nothing in and of myself. I bow my body forward in the water as a symbol of respect.

"Thank you, Great Mother," I intone. I don't bother to say anything else in response. My heart is pounding a steady rhythm in my chest and I can hardly think above the din. Aleria finishes rubbing the pearl dust on her arms. She then reaches for a jar of sea spiders. I have never cared for the spindly things, but my mother loves to put them in her hair. I watch as she drags the jar towards her and reaches down to twist off the top, once again blocking my view with her body.

"And I would assume," Aleria pauses and I watch as she places one of the creatures above her ear. It tries to swim away, but she clips its leg in place with a metal barrette. It struggles, but it is thoroughly pinned down and cannot move. Aleria repeats herself. "I would assume that you felt the same way about me. I am your mother, after all, the woman who braved the treacherous shores of man to conceive you."

"Of course, Your Majesty," I respond, unsure of where she is going with this. Until I find out what she is most angry about, I cannot combat it. I must know her angle before I say anything further.

Without another word, Aleria spins around to face me, revealing the fact that she is wearing my crown atop her head. Again, this does not surprise. In fact, I should hope that she will dwell on this and leave the pictures well enough alone.

I watch quietly, still unmoving, as she twists the lid back on the jar of sea spiders and holds them in front of her belly. It is already smeared with pearl dust and glitters like a chest full of jewels. "Interesting then that you would not think to share your bounties with me." Aleria turns back to the table carefully and sets the jar down. She waves her hand dismissively at Coreia who moves to the wardrobe on the far side of the room. She opens it and extracts a pale, green dress sewn from a gauzy fabric that floats like a cloud. It is decorated with as many odds and ends as my mother's hair. Aleria waits for Coreia to approach her and allows her Huntswoman to pull the garment over her head while she continues speaking. "I shared with you, did I not? I gave you my precious armor, my heirloom, my treasure, and you did not return with it. Then, against my most fervent wishes, you chose to hide a *crown* and a stash of lovely gems away from me, as if I would steal them from you like a common thief."

"I was saving them," I say, trying to smile. What I am about to say is a blatant lie and she may very well know that, but I can at least try. It will not make things any worse, at the very least. "I was going to present them to you as a birthing gift." It's common practice for the Huntswomen to exchange gifts after the birth of a child, either theirs or someone else's, so my lie is plausible enough.

Aleria does not answer me as Coreia buttons up the back of the dress. After she is finished, my instructor moves away and bows her head respectfully. The queen ignores her and swims back to her dressing table. I watch as she opens the drawer on the front and pauses. From it, she withdraws the boney hilt of the Spindled Blade. The needled point coruscates with poison. I can see that she has replaced it recently, stolen it from the back of an *iral,* a spiny, green fish whose venom is not normally powerful enough to kill a Huntswoman. It will make me nauseous certainly, and it will hurt, but my life will remain mine, especially with Yuri and Yanori by my side. Strangely enough, I am happy to see it. It means she has chosen to punish me with the blade and not her nails. The *iral's* poison is a much more pleasant alternative.

"You're such a clever girl, Natalie. Always so smart, always so learned." Aleria spins around to face me and in her left hand are the pictures of Seth. This is what has angered her most, put points of pain in her eyes and the Spindled Blade in her hand. "So what, my dear, does your scholarly mind make of these?"

"I wanted memories of my conquest," I say, hating the words but knowing that I need to say them. "I found those when I rummaged through the human's house to look for jewelry." Aleria smiles and it is not a nice smile. Her purple lips remind me of a pair of sea snakes as they twitch with anger.

"I see," she says as she turns the pictures around to look at them again. "Humans encase their photographs in plastic nowadays?"

"I had the human do it after I found them," I supply, hoping that's enough. But the plastic covering is not really what my mother cares about.

"Did you ever happen to notice that this human has the mark of Muoru on his chest, the mark of Neptune on his belly and your sister's likeness scrawled across his hip like a curse?" I decide not to respond to that. The more she says now, the better. Then I can decide on the words that are most likely to soothe her rage.

Aleria floats to the sandy floor and walks towards me slowly, deliberately. Each movement of her body is sinuous and full of violence. When she's close enough to touch me, she reaches around my body and places the photographs on the bed. I stay still, well aware that if I move, I could very well make things worse.

"Do you want to know what the strangest part of all of this is?" Aleria asks, gently brushing the needled point of her blade across my shoulder. I swallow another mouthful of seawater but say nothing. "That this human has your name written on his hands." She grins like a great white shark, all teeth and no mouth. "Isn't that odd to you, Natalie? It certainly was a surprise to me."

"He was like that when I found him," I say, not knowing what else to do. "He said he dreamed of me."

"Did he now?" Aleria asks, eyes locked onto mine. In her gaze is a hatred that I have never understood. Why does she dislike me so much? What have I ever done to her? I have always been the enemy in her eyes and so perhaps that is why I have chosen to take up that roll. She has forced me into it.

"When I enthralled him, I asked of it, but that is all he could say. He knew nothing more and has taken his secrets to the grave." Aleria is nodding, turning away from me and swimming across the room with purpose.

"When I tested you in the Sanctum, Natalie, I knew there was something odd going on. Never have I seen power as great as that. It was like the earth itself was growing in my belly, swallowing me whole from the inside. Honestly," she says, tossing a look over her shoulder, dark eyes glittering as brightly as the pearl dust on her face. "I was a bit jealous of you, my dear. The man you chose was obviously quite powerful. I thought, what a shame that he was wasted on just one woman." My mother clicks her teeth together in disappointment. My mind scrambles for words. Now is the time to interject, and if there is anything that my mother understands, it is arrogance and self-pride.

"I thought that he was meant to be mine," I say and watch as Coreia's brows raise. She thinks I am being foolish; I know I am being smart. "I thought that, as heir, I was destined to have this power, that I was guided by Neptune to find it. I did not think to share it with you because I thought it belonged solely to me." Aleria spins in the water to face me, kicks off the floor and rockets towards me. I have blinded her with her own rage and so, even as the point of the Spindled Blade buries itself into the flesh of my arm, I do not scream. As I drop to the floor, she hits me again, and again, and again, but I know in my heart that somehow, I have saved myself and Seth both.

◆ ◆ ◆

I have fevered dreams that I do not remember; I think that I mumble things, treasonous things that will undo everything I have started. Cool hands touch my face and part my lips. I eat although I cannot say what it is that passes down my throat. There are voices around me, familiar voices, and after a time that could be hours, days, or even weeks, my eyes flutter open and I find myself in a white hammock, curled on my side and shaking with heavy tremors that rock me to my bones.

"*Pannae,*" I mumble, hoping that someone will hear me. If I can get some of that vile flesh down my throat then I will feel much better. Yuri responds immediately, handing me an *iral* wrapped in kelp leaves. He's already removed the spines and the head as well as deboned the poor creature. It is now known as a delicacy called *pannae* that I have never had the palette for, but that will cure many of the aches and pains that are plaguing my body. It can only be eaten while awake however, because the pungent flesh produces such a strong gag reflex that it would be easy enough to choke on.

Without allowing myself too much time to think, I bite down into the spongy flesh and swallow the piece whole, holding my mouth closed with my free hand.

"I'm glad you're awake," Yuri says, laying his head on my stomach. "Each time this has happened, I've been gripped with the cold fear that you will never wake up." I eat another bite, fighting through the nausea with a smile. My mother does not know the true extent of my treachery and I know that after one of her punishments, the matter is generally dropped. The queen does not like to dwell on things she finds offensive.

"But I did," I say, glancing at the door and the shutters. They are closed, but that does not mean that there is not someone outside, waiting for me to wake up. It has happened before. My mother loves to know the agony I suffer. "I did," I say again, much more quietly. Yuri raises his head and inclines his chin slightly. Yes then, there is indeed someone listening. With a small sigh, I stuff the last of the *pannae* down my throat and nearly choke, swallowing mouthful after mouthful of seawater to keep it down. "Tell me, how does Yanori fair?" I ask, wondering where my sister has gone. It could be that she has left to retrieve another *iral,* for the fish's potency lasts only a few hours after it is killed. I know that the one I ate is most likely only one of many that Yuri and Yanori have been preparing in preparation for my return.

The door opens before Yuri can respond and I raise my head to find a Huntswoman that I do not recognize bowing her head respectfully.

"Your Majesty," she says, greeting me as if I have not just awoken from a near coma. "Your mother requests your presence as soon as you are able bodied." I nod in response and clear my throat so that my words are clear and confident, just enough to convince her that my authority matters.

"I understand. Please tell the queen that I will arrive shortly." Without complaint, the Huntswoman closes the door and I listen for the sounds of swimming in the hallway. Shortly after, Yuri checks the hall and the water outside my window, and confirms that, at least for now, we are alone. "Yanori?" I ask again, suddenly worried. Yuri has not responded to my question.

"Natalie," he begins and I sit up, letting my legs fall from the hammock to the floor. If my sister is dead, then I will not forgive myself.

"Tell me, Yuri," I say and I think something about the fear he hears in my voice convinces him to speak quickly. He pulls his blonde hair away from his face and drifts to the floor, crossing his arms over my knees and laying his chin atop them. He locks my green eyes with his pearl ones and sighs gently.

"Yanori is safe," he begins and I cannot help but feel a surge of relief. I feel a coldness against my hips and look down to see that my sister has returned the knife. Its sheath hangs off the links in the silver belt and brushes against my outer thigh. "But she has gone to check the progress of the Hunt. They are due back at any time today." I drop my head and remain silent. I had wanted to stop it, perhaps even needed to, but there was no room for that. I had to make choices based on the situations given me. I comfort myself by believing that I did the best I could. The men will not be killed right away; my mother's pregnancy will see to that. I cannot stop them from being violated, but perhaps I can find a way to send them off with their lives intact.

The Feed

Yuri's information also tells me about how long I have been out. The Hunt lasts three strict days: two for travel and one to search for a good specimen. The Huntswomen who have been sent will be my mother's best, her strongest, which is why it makes this such a risky venture. While they are gone, our single city is that much more vulnerable. This, and the sorry fact that out of the five groups sent, usually only two or less return. I remember Seth's expression, *a pretty piss poor return,* and smile sadly.

"Natalie," Yuri begins again and I can see that this is not the whole of his bad news. Before he can speak again, there is a gentle knock across the shutters and my lover's silver tail flashes brightly in his rush to open them. Yanori enters quickly and the porthole is closed up behind her.

"A single group has returned," she begins and turns her cloudy eyes straight towards me. It is obvious from her slight smile that she knows that I am awake. She pauses for a moment and holds up a hand. "Huntswomen approach in the hallway." The three of us wait in silence until my sister inclines her head and continues speaking. "It is a group fronted by a Huntswoman from last year's Feed. Her name is Avier and she returns with her group intact and a small man who remains enthralled." I frown but say nothing. "They are displaying them in cages hung from Kua's empty belly. In the queen's infinite arrogance, they have already strung up five of them." My sister touches a hand to her bare chest and draws a small circle in honor of Neptune. It's an old gesture of protection that I have seen only Tejean do. Neither Yuri nor I ask how she has obtained this information without her sight; we trust that what she tells us is the truth. "I cannot be certain, but I do not believe that it is him. You can confirm this for me when you report to the queen."

"I have not told her," Yuri says quietly and Yanori nods her head. I stand up and look across the hammock at the two *merighean*.

"Tell me," I say, feeling my chest constrict as if I am drowning. I want air so desperately in that moment; my lungs feel as if they have caved in on themselves. "Whatever it is, I am prepared to hear it."

"Aleria gave a speech before the Hunt departed. She spoke highly of the power you brought back, of how it would aide greatly in our rise to greatness and the changes that she promises lie just on the horizon. She recalled the brave and fortuitous route you marked from the rocks of Muoru to the roundness of the lake where she claims men of great power and importance reside. It is there that she has sent the Hunt." There are several moments after Yanori finishes her words where none of us speak or even move.

"Who did she send?" I ask, wanting names. Yuri responds for me.

"She announced only the leaders of the five groups and unfortunately, I did not recognize the faces of the others."

"List them," I say, desperate to hear. I cannot be sure who my mother shared Seth's image with, but there is one name that I know cannot be listed or I could very well be finding myself reunited with the man that I risked my life to save.

The Feed

"Avier, Midori, Timis, Aremia, and," Yuri pauses and my heart drops as we both know what he is about to say. "Coreia."

Chapter Twenty-One

Yuri, Yanori, and I play a waiting game.

Yuri stays carefully camouflaged in the colorful sea of males that hover just below and to the right of the honored Huntswomen who float at my mother's back. As a reward for our safe return from the Feed, the nineteen surviving girls and I are included. Yanori does what she does best and disappears into the shadows, so that I haven't the slightest guess where she might've gone. The fact that I know she is there does provide me with some sense of strength however.

My mother did not acknowledge me when I swam out of the palace and followed the other Huntswomen's instructions to join her entourage. The other girls were tired but happy to see me. It seems as if they've been waiting hours. This is understandable considering that, like the Feed, the Hunt's arrival times are not specific. All I can do now is wait with them, treading water, and staring at the queen's back as she surveys the sea to her right with dark eyes. She is standing on Kua's skull, a beacon of brightness on the whiteness of the bones.

I turn to the man in the cage and watch him, relieved that he is not Seth. He is small with haunted eyes and pale skin. Even as I stare at him, he hangs on the bars and cries out for the Huntswomen that retrieved him. They are waiting in a patient circle around him; pride and fatigue both stain their faces as they prepare themselves for the celebratory feast that will soon follow and then after, they will claim their prize. Unless Aleria herself requests a male, the women who have brought him back, starting with their leader, will take their turns first. I fight back a shiver as Aleria's eyes swing to me briefly. A slight smile teases her dark lips and I know that she believes me subdued, at least momentarily.

I ignore her and the crying man who is so desperate for these women that it makes me sick. Even at his worst, Seth was not like that. He never begged for me in a keening wail like this man, making me wonder if he was at least a little bit resistant all along. This one is so weak that at first, I have to wonder why they have chosen him. He is not handsome or strong, but when he turns his attention to a Huntswoman behind him and flashes me his back, I see why.

This man is tattooed. Across his pale skin is a pair of black limned wings that line his shoulder blades and droop down to disappear into his pants. This is the only piece of

The Feed

clothing that he is wearing and it will soon be stripped off, but for now, it floats in the water around him like a second shadow. I stare for a long while and try not to let fear and anxiety sweep down on me. Just because they were looking for men with tattoos does not mean that they will find Seth and if they do, unless Coreia is around, they will not recognize him from the picture. If they do choose him, it will be a one in a thousand coincidence. I have to hold myself together and hope the statistical chances fall in my favor.

"Please," the man continues screaming and it takes great effort for me not to put my hands over my ears. The other Huntswomen are laughing at his pain, recalling memories of the men they took. I do not blame them, do not judge them for it; it is all they have ever been taught after all, but seeing the reactions on the faces around me, I know that I have my work cut out for me. "Take me, please. My skin is on fire!" I block out his words and watch the crowd of *merighean* that are clinging to Kua's ribs and looking up at the cages that swing from his naked spine. The crowd that has shown up today is at least three times the size of the one that greeted us on our return from the Feed. And they are riled up. As I had thought, this excitement has stirred up the violence in their blood and made them hungry for more. What a disaster.

A cheer goes up from the gathered crowd and my gaze swings to the dark ocean to my right. Swimming above the kelp forest is a group of Huntswoman, just barely visible at this distance. The one thing that I can discern however is that there are not five of them; there are six.

Another group has returned and brought with them a man. I raise my chin and uncross my arms, needing the strength in them to help keep me afloat. I let my eyes drop to Yuri and see that he is watching me, not the Hunt. He is closer to the edge of the forest and does not have as good of a view. I think he is waiting for confirmation from me on whether the human is Seth or not. I don't know so I shake my head gently letting a small frown grace my lips.

"Praise Neptune," my mother shouts, rising into the water for just an instant before she settles back into the spot behind the dragon's eyes. Her own eyes are so dark with hunger that they look as black and empty as those bare sockets. "Praise Imenea," she says, this time in a whisper. I ignore her and finger the links at my waist. Aleria is so preoccupied that she took no notice of the knife. I was leery of wearing it, but Yanori convinced me otherwise telling me that I would soon have use for it. I cannot argue with the sea's wisest woman, so I adjust the belt and make sure that I have easy access to the blade, just in case. It is not truly that I think I will have need or use for it, but it gives me something to focus on to pass the time. It's so difficult to wait here like this. If it had been at all feasible, I would've swam out and intercepted the Hunt, just to make sure that Seth was not with them. If they bring him back, I am dead; he is dead; Yanori and Yuri are dead. In turn then, the *merighean* will carry on with their ways and it will not be long before they, too, rejoin the sea's silent embrace.

"It is Timis' group," one of the girls near me says. I watch and soon am able to make out a woman in the front

The Feed

whose hair is as bright as Ira's, crimson as blood. She leads the group with the human behind her. There is a Huntswoman on either side, holding his arms but not restraining him. They don't need to waste the effort; he is enthralled enough that he would follow them anywhere, even under the sea. All they are doing now is helping him swim. The final Huntswoman takes up the rear, but there is blood leaking in a thin line from her side. As soon as her injuries are visible to my mother, she gestures for some of the idle Huntswomen on her left to move forward and tend to the wounds. I ignore all of this and squint my eyes, trying to take in the details of this man. It is obvious right away that he is not Seth, but something about him seems familiar to me. He is young and attractive, with brown hair and brown eyes.

It is the man with the satchel, the one in the gray pants and jacket that I whistled at to test my attraction to Seth. When I saw him, I felt my body respond, but not in the same way. Now, I feel nothing but pity and guilt. It is partially my fault that he has been brought here. Because of my carelessness, my mother had gotten it into her mind to follow my path to the shore. This man will suffer because of me, but I will be damned if he will die.

I swallow some seawater and try to maintain my calm. This man lived awfully close to Seth which is worrisome, but on the other hand, this is the second group to return. Normally, there would be only the slightest chance that a third group would be successful. But the idea that Coreia is still out there frightens me. She is competent and strong, my mother's favorite and very likely the most powerful Huntswoman of us all. I believe strongly that she will return and if she does, there is the chance that she will come with Seth.

I glance down at Yuri as the group passes by above him and shake my head. *This man is not Seth,* my expression says, *but he could very well be on his way.*

The brown haired man is already nude and is shoved into the cage with lascivious laughter and the sliding of tongues across lips. It is already quite obvious that the crowd of women finds him much more attractive than the first man. I feel so sorry for him that it nearly drags tears to my eyes.

"See the power of Imenea," my mother calls out, lifting her hand to her hair and removing a large, metal clip. The turquoise waves drift around her in a massive cloud that twines over her outstretched arms and curls across her waist like a dress. Her hair is the longest of any of the Huntswomen, nearly as long as a male's, and produces quite the effect as it drapes her naked body. "Praise the Goddess of Failure for allowing us this final chance at redemption." She is referring, of course, to the Goddess' dark magic that Imenea allows my mother to bestow among the ladies of the Hunt. It grants them the power to bless the humans with the ability to survive beneath the sea. I don't trust it for a moment, certain that since this magic is provided by the slimy goddess of the deep, it is a sign that the Hunt is not right. If needed, Imenea will also temporarily grant a burst of strength to the women in order to fight off a certain enemy or hunt down a fugitive. No one has ever managed to escape the Hunt before.

The Feed

I close my eyes for awhile and try to find a quiet place inside of myself to wait. There is so much going on around me that, with the lingering effects of the Spindled Blade, I feel dizzy and exhausted. I have been treading water for several hours now and am finding it increasingly difficult to stay afloat.

I think that somehow I fall into a light sleep because a while later, Kiara is at my side, shaking my arm and pointing.

"Another group has returned," she says, excitedly, her crimson nails pointed once again towards the kelp forest. I open my eyes and follow the faces of the crowd to the approaching party. I don't recognize this leader and assume it must be Midori. Aremia and Coreia have yet to show and while I like Aremia, I have little hope that she will return. Coreia however ... My waiting game is still not over.

The blonde Huntswoman parades her prey before my mother before dumping him in another cage. My luck continues to hold as this is still not Seth. He is tattooed though and I am surprised to see that across his arms swim fish and tidal waves in an array of bright colors that could rival the rainbow of males below me. I give Yuri another shake of my head in confirmation.

"Excellent," my mother says and I can see from the hunger in her eyes that she truly believes this man will hold the same type of power that Seth possesses. She looks down at me then and catches my gaze with a wicked smile. *You see,* her look says. *You cannot outdo me, Natalie. I will always, always, always be one step ahead of you.* I look away first, not caring that the gesture will give her the impression that she has obtained yet another small victory.

◆ ◆ ◆

Hours later, my mother gets tired of waiting and demands that the feast be arranged. The stone tables are brought out and anchored beneath the cages where they hang suspended by chains from Kua's bones. Food is laid out across them in a show of extravagance that gets the *merighean* excited again. The crowd had thinned out for a time as the mers went back to their daily duties, but I see that they are now back or have otherwise been replaced three times over with other *merighean*. This is absolutely the largest gathering I have yet seen in my life.

"Honored people," my mother begins, stepping forward so that she stands as close to the base of the dragon's skull as she can get without swimming. "Today, we have reached a milestone in our history together. My mother passed away, quite tragically, during the year of my Feed. Since then, I have done my best by you to provide a safe and happy life. Thus far, I have succeeded." Raucous cheers follow this blatant exaggeration. The Huntswomen around me spin and dance, happy that their wait is over. But not me. I can tell that the Hunt is not yet finished. Something in my bones tell me that Coreia is coming back. "But that is not enough," she nearly screams, holding her arms out to encompass our crumbling city. "I want more. I want our buildings to tower above us, to break the waves of the surface and reach into the sky. I want the ocean to expand, cross the earth and drown the humans in their own hubris." More cheers. I close my eyes and listen carefully. If my mother is about to reveal her secrets to the city, I must be ready to plan. Wasted seconds could cost me everything. "With the arrival of these men, we can swell our ranks to a number that has not been seen since ... " Aleria pauses and I open my eyes, following her gaze back to the infamous darkness above the kelp forest. There, I spot another group just as the crowd does.

The tension in the city rises to new heights and the water around me thrums with the vibrations of splashing tails and spinning Huntswomen; the males around Yuri explode into frenzied activity, diving and looping, rising up to us and pressing gentle kisses against our cheeks.

I see her before I notice anything else. Coreia is leading the group with her head held high and her violet hair framing her face.

"Coreia," my mother breathes and in her quiet voice, I hear the love she feels for the woman. I had known they were lovers, but I did not know that she actually cared for her. I try to find my father's face but do not see him. I hope that he does not catch Aleria's gentle expression for it could very well break his heart. I wait in horrible, tense anticipation as the group nears. The man they are carrying is asleep, hanging between the two Huntswomen at his sides. His hair is dark and short, like Seth's, and he is fully clothed in a long sleeved shirt and jeans. I move forward, just a bit, and try to catch a glimpse of his hands. The group is still too far away for me to see clearly. I swim back and forth, spin a small flip. Nobody notices; they are all doing more of the same, cheering and leaping and dancing amongst one another. The mob mentality that I had so feared before is in full force now. Any little thing could set chaos upon the city that would be as fierce as the descent of an army.

The noise awakens the man with a start and he looks up, seemingly straight at me. For a moment, I am blinded by his brown eyes and handsome face. My heart screams in my chest and I find myself moving forward, wanting to act but not knowing how. *Smart choices, Natalie,* I warn myself as I drop back and wait. My fears become unfounded as the group approaches the cages. The man is not Seth. He is bigger in the chest and wider in the jaw. My almost certain fear that Coreia would bring back my human lover nearly cost me my mother's increased suspicion, if not my life. With a huge sigh of relief that the wait is over, I shake my head at Yuri with a sad smile. I am glad that Seth is not here, but I still have the fate of these four men on my shoulders. I cannot rest yet.

"Do you see?" my mother cries out, riling the people of Amarana even further. "Do you see the great blessings that have been bestowed upon us? Our years of poverty come to an end today. This is the beginning of a great and glorious age, one that will forever be recorded as the – " Once again, my mother's speech is interrupted. Screams have broken out amongst the people and a forest of fingers

The Feed

is raised in excitement.

It can't be, I think as I stare towards the darkness and make out just the slightest hint of people, like ghosts, that shimmer so far away that they could very well be a trick of the eye. *It can't be; it just can't.* My mother is shouting orders to the women at her sides, telling them to swim ahead and check. I do not think that any one us can stand the anticipation of waiting to see what will happen. *I have the heads of five men on my shoulders*, I think as I cross my arms and watch. I am not glad to see another man brought below the sea, but I am relieved that Aremia is back; she is loyal to the crown, but I am not sure if that is necessarily because of my mother. If I am lucky, I may be able to pull her over to my side. As I try to decide which emotion will win out, the messengers come back whooping and spinning.

"It is indeed, Aremia," one of them says, pausing just long enough to relay this information to my mother. "She has brought back her whole group as well as a man whose beauty outshines the rest." My mother tosses her head back and laughs joyously, enjoying the rush of power around her. This is the sort of thing that she feeds off of. I ignore her and try to stay out of the way of kicking feet and flailing arms as the girls dance around me in celebration.

As the group comes closer, some of the Huntswomen break off and swim towards them. My mother allows this, enjoying their excitement as they dive and spin, circling the incoming Hunt like a school of fish. I watch carefully, waiting to see this newest victim. He is not being carried by the Huntswomen like the rest of the men and is instead swimming on his own between them. I keep my eyes focused on them as they come closer and closer; their progress slowed by the fatigue of the journey they have just undertaken. It is just after Aremia's brightness becomes clear that I am able to make out anything regarding the human.

That I am able to make out that it is Seth.

For a moment, I am frozen, convinced that this is yet another close call. I still myself by touching the knife at my side and letting my breath burst out between my lips in a rush of foamy bubbles. As the group swims closer, I start to see details on the shirtless man's skin: the mark of Muoru, the mark of Neptune, and across his arms, a wash of waves and the symbols of Kua and Amahna. There is no doubt in my mind now; this man is Seth. I glance up at my mother quickly and see it in her eyes: she knows. She knows. She knows.

Dark orbs flash down at me as her purple lips part in surprise. We stare at one another for the longest time before I flick my gaze back towards Seth. I catch his eyes at the same time that he catches mine. *Natalie,* his face says and he smiles, raising his hand in a gentle wave. My heart breaks, explodes, reforms again. This is not the behavior of a man enthralled. Seth is not under the spell of the Hunt; he has come of his own free will.

I have to do something. I know in that second that I cannot see Seth be raped by my mother and the women who I will do anything to save from themselves. This is even assuming that I will live long enough to see that happen. I look back at the queen's face. She is not looking at me; her eyes are glued on Seth, tinted with confusion and surprise. At her side though is Coreia. She has recovered more quickly and I feel my muscles tense as she swings her gaze down to mine. I ready myself to move as I see her press the heels of her feet against the bones beneath her; she is preparing to launch herself at me and I must be ready.

Screams break out behind Coreia and our gazes separate from one another as we both turn towards the confusion. *Merighean* are exploding around us in panicked frenzy, Huntswomen are shouting incoherently, and across the naked, white back of the long dead dragon, a pulsing red heat is growing, crawling down the sides of his ribs and threading between the bars of the cages. Coreia doesn't hesitate, forgetting briefly about me and launching herself into the fray.

"Move the cages!" she is screaming, grabbing Huntswomen by the arms and turning them back to the task at hand. My mother recovers finally and looks down at the head beneath her feet. Pale, silver flesh has already started to grow and is crawling beneath her bare soles in a wash of shimmering scales.

Kua the dragon is coming back to life.

Breath is already escaping from his boney nostrils, releasing massive bubbles that spin up and away, breaking against the bodies of panicked *merighean* who scream and swim crookedly in panic.

"Flee the belly!" my mother calls out, rising slightly in the water so that she is not touching the warm, throbbing flesh that is expanding rapidly beneath her.

I swing my gaze back to Seth. If ever there was a miracle, then this is it. This is my only opportunity to save him. Aremia and her Huntswoman have paused, unsure as to what is going in. Seth is still floating between them, face twisted in horror as he watches any soul unfortunate enough to get caught in the path of growing muscles. Wails of pain join the frenzy as *merighean* and Huntswomen alike are swallowed up by Kua's emerging body. He's so far away; I will have to swim fast if I want to reach him. I throw one quick glance back at my mother and am terrified to find that her gaze is once again on me. I ignore her and start to move forward, finding Yuri's wide, pale eyes locked on mine. Without realizing what I am doing, I nod my head.

"Secure the humans," my mother shouts from behind me. "Detain Natalie."

Yuri explodes from the rainbow of panicked males who are milling around like fish awaiting slaughter. His muscular tail flashes silver as he bursts up behind Aremia and without pausing for breath, wraps his arms around Seth's body. Blonde hair tangles with black as Yuri kicks his tail again and spins like a whirlpool into the darkness of the sea.

Aremia is a good solider, and fast, but she is tired and confused, as are the women around her. They turn together and kick their legs, trying to gain momentum and give chase. But Yuri is a *merighean* and he can out swim a Huntswoman any day, even with Seth clutched in his arms. Already, the two men are fading from my sight, swallowed

The Feed

by the darkness of the sea. Satisfied that, at least for the moment, they are safe, I turn back to Aleria. None of the Huntswomen have come after me, too confused are they by the frenzy and the panic and the dragon; not a soul has responded to my mother's last order. But she is not so easily distracted, not Aleria. Even with the strangeness around her, she will not let me go unpunished.

The queen drops back to Kua's skull for just a brief moment, using that as momentum to launch herself at me. I start to move, afraid that I have reacted too slowly and feel a cool hand on my arm. My body launches upwards into the sea in a spin, turning and twisting in a way that I have never experienced. Yanori.

My blind sister, the girl with the broken tail, the one whom everyone dislikes, but who nobody believes in, is carrying me up and over the top of the kelp forest. I had once thought that if she were to swim in a way that complemented her body, that if she refused to try to mimic the patterns of the other *merighean,* that she would be the most beautiful acrobat in the sea.

I was right.

I turn my body against her, let her wrap her arms around me, and close my eyes as her tail bunches, flashes out and sends us spiraling through the ocean at a speed that none could match. There are still screams behind me, disturbances in the water that say they are coming, but now we are a step ahead. With our speed and the agility of the two *merighean* that none would have expected to stand out from the crowd, we have a chance, however slim. I open my eyes and try not to get dizzy as the sea around me spins like an eddy.

But I know that we can't run away forever because sooner or later, the Hunt will find us.

We must make sure that we're ready.

No one has ever managed to escape the Hunt before.

The Hunt

C.M. STUNICH

About the Author

C.M. Stunich was raised under a cover of fog in the area known simply as Eureka, CA. A mysterious place, this strange, arboreal land nursed Caitlin's (yes, that's her name!) desire to write strange fiction novels about wicked monsters, magical trains, and Nemean Lions (Google it!). She currently enjoys drag queens, having too many cats, and tribal bellydance.

She can be reached at author@cmstunich.com, and loves to hear from her readers. Ms. Stunich also wrote this biography and has no idea why she decided to refer to herself in the third person.

Happy reading and carpe diem!

www.cmstunich.com

Printed in Great Britain
by Amazon.co.uk, Ltd.,
Marston Gate.